# NEVER TOO LATE

SALLY RIGBY

TOP
DRAWER
PRESS
CRIME FICTION BOOKS

*This book is dedicated to my dad*

GET ANOTHER BOOK FOR FREE!

To instantly receive **Nowhere to Hide,** a free novella from the Detective Sebastian Clifford series, featuring DC Lucinda Bird when she first joined CID, sign up for Sally Rigby's free author newsletter at www.sallyrigby.com.

# Prologue

*Twenty-Five Years Ago*

Rob Walker tapped his foot impatiently on the pavement and glanced at the fancy watch his girlfriend Charli had given him for his birthday. Rob had told her that she shouldn't have spent so much money on his birthday present, but she'd just laughed and told him to accept the gift graciously. So he had done. Where was she? The film started in ten minutes. She was often late, but never when it was important to be on time. It wasn't like he'd been the one to choose the film. It had been her choice. *Fools Rush In* which starred her favourite actor. They'd decided to see it when they spoke on the phone on Wednesday night. He could take or leave romantic films, but she loved them.

Maybe he should buy the tickets so they could go straight in. But what if she didn't turn up? That would be a waste of money. If he had a mobile phone, he'd give her a ring. But they were way too expensive for him. Charli had one. Of course. Her family was rich and bought her everything she wanted. Not that he'd want to have her family because they interfered in her life all the time.

1

He sighed and paced up and down outside the cinema. A car horn blasted, making him jump, and a black BMW with tinted windows pulled up a few yards down the road. The driver's door opened, and a man smartly dressed in a grey suit stepped out onto the pavement. He looked in Rob's direction and beckoned to him.

Was he lost? Did he want directions?

Rob walked over to him.

'Yeah?'

'Get in the back.'

Rob stiffened at the man's icy tone. 'What? No way.'

He turned to walk away when his arm was grabbed and twisted up behind his back.

'What the—? What's happening?'

'Do as you're told, Rob, or Charli gets it.' The guy opened the rear door and shoved Rob inside the car and onto the back seat. He landed awkwardly, twisting his leg.

Adrenaline surged through him. He knew his name. He knew Charli's name. Who was he? Rob tugged on the handle, but the door was locked.

He was trapped.

The driver's door opened, and the man slid into his seat. Rob could attack him from behind. That's what he'd do. But what about Charli? What if the driver was telling the truth? He knew who she was. Was she being held prisoner somewhere?

His throat tightened.

'Who are you? How do you know my girlfriend?' Rob demanded, punching the back of the driver's seat.

The man started the engine and pulled out into the traffic. 'Shut up and we won't hurt her. Cause problems …' The driver looked at Rob in the rear-view mirror and grinned menacingly. '… and you won't recognise her face by the time we're done with her.'

Beads of sweat formed on Rob's brow. What should he do? He couldn't risk anything happening to Charli. He loved her. Would do anything to protect her. But why was he being kidnapped? He'd done nothing.

Unless … yeah … Of course.

Why hadn't he twigged straight away?

It was a joke.

Charli had set him up. It would be just like her to do something like this. A couple of weeks ago when they'd been walking through a department store, she'd slipped a leather wallet into his jacket pocket without him realising. It wasn't until they were out of the shop that she'd told him. When he'd got angry, she'd just laughed and told him to be happy that he now had a new wallet for free. She said doing stuff like that relieved the boredom of her life. Though what she'd got to be bored about, he didn't know. She always got what she wanted.

'Okay, I get it. This is all Charli's doing. Isn't it?' He flashed a broad smile in the driver's direction.

The driver lifted his head slightly so Rob could see him in the rear-view mirror again and grinned. 'Yeah. That's right, mate. You've sussed it. But don't tell her you guessed, or I'll be for it.'

Rob relaxed a little. He didn't mind letting Charli think she'd tricked him again. If it made her happy.

'Where are we going?' Rob settled down into the leather seats and gazed out of the window.

'You'll find out soon enough. Sit back and enjoy the ride.'

Outside, the busy city streets gradually became more industrial, but Rob didn't recognise the direction in which they were heading. After ten minutes or so, the driver made a sharp left and drove through a series of warehouses until reaching a dead end. The car came to a standstill, and the driver jumped out. He opened the back door for Rob.

If this was one of Charli's jokes, Rob was missing the punchline. Where were they? Why would she drag him out here? And where was she, anyway? He stood beside the car moving from foot to foot.

'Where's Charli? And what are we doing here?'

'Stop being impatient.' The driver stood beside the car and lit up a cigarette.

Rob clenched and unclenched his fists. Charli's idea of a joke was wearing thin.

The door to the warehouse opened. Finally. Now he'd get some answers. He took a couple of steps towards the open door, but the driver grabbed him by the arm.

'Let go,' Rob snapped, shaking him off and stepping away from him.

'You wait here,' the man growled.

Two scary-looking men, wearing jeans and leather bomber jackets, came out of the warehouse and headed towards Rob. Behind them, he could just make out someone else. Was it Charli? The person came into sight.

Rob's eyes widened. What was he doing there?

Nothing made sense.

What the hell was going on?

He stood frozen to the spot while the two burly men marched towards him. As they got closer, his eyes were drawn to a cosh in the hand of the man on the left. This was nothing to do with Charli.

He had to get away.

And fast.

Rob quickly scanned the area, glancing back at the road they'd driven down, and then he checked what the driver was doing. He appeared distracted and certainly wasn't paying attention to him.

He'd make a run for it. There was no other option.

Rob sucked in a breath, tensed his muscles, and took off. Energy surged through him. He was fast and on the school's athletics team. Once he made it to the main road, he'd flag down a car and escape. He was a sprinter, and it didn't take long to get his speed up.

'Hey, get your arse back here,' a voice from behind bellowed.

He didn't turn around to check because that would have slowed him down. He kept on running. One foot in front of the other, pounding the pavement. His heart was thumping in his chest so hard he thought it might burst. He had to get out of there.

Where *there* was, he had no idea. He tried to remember the exact way they'd driven, but it was all a blur. One road leading into another. He took a right turn, but that led him to a dead end. He then ran back the way he'd come, only this time taking a left. Surely that was the way back to the main street.

He sprinted down the road and had almost reached the end. He could hear road noise. Not much further and he'd be away from them.

A screech of tyres echoed from behind him. Crap. He turned to see the BMW driving towards him and blocking the way.

The two men from the warehouse jumped out of the vehicle's back doors.

'You little shit. Get here,' one of them yelled.

They both came towards him. There was a gap to the right of them and Rob pivoted, aiming to get past. He darted from side to side, keeping them at bay. He skirted around the men, his escape route in sight. Two or three more steps and he'd be away from them. By the time they'd run back to the car he'd be far enough ahead to stop them from catching him.

Rob tensed his muscles, preparing for a burst of speed, when an arm swung across his neck, pulling him backwards. He was forced around, spinning until face to face with both men. He opened his mouth to scream, but nothing came out.

As if in slow motion, one of the men lifted the cosh he was holding until it was high in the air.

He brought it down with a loud smash onto Rob's head.

# Chapter 1

*Present Day*

Private Investigator Sebastian Clifford ducked his head as he walked into the pub in Market Harborough where he'd arranged to meet Detective Constable Lucinda Bird, aka Birdie, who he'd worked with on two cases in the past. He'd offered her the opportunity to leave the police force and join his new company, Clifford Investigation Services, but so far, she hadn't committed. When she'd called and asked him out for a drink, he immediately hoped that it was to tell him yes. His business was in its infancy, but he already had a contract with the Met, thanks to an ex-colleague of his. It brought in some money, but given the choice, it wasn't the type of work he'd want to do on a long-term basis. With Birdie on board, they'd be able to advertise their services and take on more interesting cases, rather than the run-of-the-mill surveillance of cheating spouses or tracing people for probate purposes.

He headed towards the bar, intending to order a drink, and, out of habit, scanned the room. His jaw dropped. At a table in the corner was the officer. She gave him a little wave. He detoured and went straight over to her.

'You do realise that we'd arranged to meet at seven, and it's only six fifty-eight?' He looked at his watch to double-check that he wasn't mistaken.

'Yes. I know,' she said, smirking.

She jumped up from her chair, flung her arms around his chest, as that was as high as she could reach being over a foot shorter than he was, and gave a tight squeeze. He momentarily froze and then responded with a hug. He'd forgotten how demonstrative Birdie was. Very different from most other people he knew.

'It's great to see you. I bought you a pint of stout, I hope that's okay,' she said, when she'd finally released him from her hold and they'd sat down. She pushed back her red curls from her face and tucked them behind her ears, then picked up her glass and took a drink.

'That was a rather extreme welcome, considering it's only been a few weeks since we last saw each other.'

'Only in your eyes. I hug all my friends when I see them. If you'd rather, call it a thank you for helping with Lacey's case.'

Lacey was a little girl who'd been fostered by Birdie's aunt, after being left abandoned on the streets of Market Harborough twelve months previously, identity unknown. Birdie had reopened the case a month ago, and the investigation had put both Seb and Birdie in danger, but eventually, they had discovered Lacey's real name and parentage. Despite the positive result, Birdie had been reprimanded because her sergeant had specifically forbidden her to look at the case again. She'd been advised that her behaviour would be investigated and appropriate disciplinary measures taken. Until then, she'd been confined to desk duty.

'I wasn't expecting you for at least another fifteen minutes, if that.' Seb picked up his beer and took a large swallow.

'I wanted to prove that I can be on time when I put my mind to it. In fact, I've been here for twenty minutes, already.'

Ah. Now he was getting to the bottom of it. There was no way that Birdie would intentionally arrive twenty minutes early. There was most definitely a reason.

'Why now, suddenly, do you have this urge to prove you can be on time, especially as I know you can't?' He arched an eyebrow.

She shrugged. 'I just did.'

'I don't believe you.'

She gave a loud sigh. 'Okay. I finished work early because I had a meeting with one of the human resources managers, and there wasn't time to go home after we'd finished, so I came straight here. Your face when you spotted me was hilarious. It's almost worth me being early again. Except we know that's not going to happen. Plus, it wouldn't have the same effect. I should have taken a photo.'

'Was your meeting with HR to do with your disciplinary?'

'Of course. What else would it be? I've been given a written warning, which will remain on my file.'

'Only to be expected.' He nodded.

'I know. To be honest, I was expecting far worse, like being fired.'

'But you knew that wasn't going to happen because Sergeant Weston had told you that.'

'He said, *not if he had anything to do with it*. That didn't mean the bosses would listen to him. Although it does appear that this time they did. Thank goodness.' Her face softened.

'I'm pleased for you.' Seb clinked his glass against hers. 'Congratulations.'

'Now it's over, it means I'm no longer on desk duty. Sarge said I can go back out and work on cases. Thank God. Being stuck inside was driving me batshit crazy.'

Seb laughed at the serious expression on Birdie's face. 'You're talking as though it's been going on for months and months. It's only been three weeks.'

'That's still long enough. I'm just glad things will get back to normal.'

His heart sank. Did *normal* mean staying where she was?

'Should I assume that you've made the decision not to leave the force and come to work with me?' he prompted.

Birdie nursed the glass in her hand, staring directly at him. 'Look, I haven't decided. I've thought about it a lot. In fact, I've thought of little else. Hardly surprising since all I've had to do at work is answer the phone and explain that it isn't our job to go around to their house and fix their telly.'

'Really?'

'You might think I'm joking, but I'm not. This week alone, I've had three calls from separate people, complaining that their TVs have stopped picking up all the channels and could we send someone round to help.'

'Were they elderly?'

'I think so, but that's beside the point. I suppose we should be thankful that they hadn't called emergency services. Although they do get their fair share of those calls.'

'Yes, I'm aware that's a problem.'

'The thing is, I want to get back out on the streets.

Even if I do decide to go with you, I'm still going to have a notice period. Let's leave it for now, and we'll talk about it again another time. There's too much going on for me to think it through properly. Is that all right?'

She didn't decline him outright, which could be viewed as encouraging. He certainly didn't want to force her hand. The decision had to be hers.

'I understand. Remember, the offer's always on the table any time you'd like to join me.'

'Until you find someone else to work with you?'

'I'm not looking for anyone else. And if I change my mind, you'll be the first to—' Seb's phone rang, and he glanced at the screen. A landline, but he didn't recognise the area code. Curious. It was probably a cold call or something—

Birdie waved him away. 'Oh, just answer the thing. I'll get us some more drinks.' She got up and headed for the bar.

'Clifford,' he answered the call.

'Sebastian, it's Whitney Walker from Lenchester CID.'

He hadn't been expecting a call from her. He'd worked with the DCI on a case the previous year but hadn't been in contact since.

'Hello, Whitney, how are you?'

'Fine, thanks. I've phoned for a favour. Well, not a favour exactly. I'd like to employ you as a consultant to investigate a cold case we have on our books.'

He leant back in his chair. Lenchester was a large force, why would they need outside help?

'I wasn't intending to act as a consultant for the police.'

'But you're working for the Met?'

True. Except Whitney wasn't to know that he didn't intend to continue with working for the police. Not least because of the way his unit had been disbanded when he was a DI.

'That's different. It's for an ex-colleague.'

More than that. DI Rob Lawson was also a friend going back years, from when they undertook their training together.

'That's what I am. Look, it's only for two weeks, and there's no one else I want to ask.'

'What is the case?'

'I'd rather explain in person. Can we meet up on Sunday for lunch? My treat.'

'Okay, but I'm not promising anything. I'll drive over to you.'

It was the least he could do, considering he doubted very much that he'd accept the offer.

'That's fantastic. Meet me at one o'clock at Bistro in Little Hampton. I'll book us a table. Even if you say no, we can still have a catch-up.'

'Looking forward to it.'

'Me, too.'

He ended the call, placed the phone on the table and stared ahead, pondering Whitney's request.

'What was that all about?' Birdie asked, interrupting his thoughts as she returned to the table and placed down another round of drinks.

'DCI Walker, Lenchester CID, remember? She wants to employ me to work with her on a case.'

'Why has she asked you? It's not like they should be short of officers.'

'That was my thought, too. Especially as this isn't ongoing like the contract I have with the Met. This is for two weeks only, to investigate a cold case.' He picked up his glass, absent-mindedly taking a mouthful of beer and swallowing while mulling over Whitney's request.

'Are you going to take it?' Birdie asked.

He shrugged. 'I'll discuss it with her first and then decide. But it's unlikely. I hadn't planned on doing any more work for the police.'

'Have you any other cases now, other than working for the Met?'

'No. I've yet to start marketing.'

'Financially, it could be worth it, then.'

Birdie was correct. It made sound business sense not to turn down a case, at least initially while he was trying to get the company off the ground.

'Perhaps. I've arranged to meet Whitney for lunch on Sunday. I'd have asked you to come but after all the trouble we got on Lacey's case, it might be an idea to not ruffle any feathers for a while if you're staying on the force.'

Birdie's shoulders slumped. 'You're right, I suppose. I'm not free on Sunday, anyway. But you can't complain. It's work and you're going to be paid for it. You're just starting out, so you can't afford to be too choosy. Though I suppose in your case, money's not the issue. What with you being a viscount.' She paused for a few seconds. 'Oops, sorry, *son* of a viscount.' She smirked.

'I don't know why you insist on saying these things. Especially as you know perfectly well my family situation,' he said, feigning annoyance.

'Because it's funny, and I enjoy watching the expression on your face. But you do know I'm only teasing, don't you?' A worried expression crossed her face.

'I should do by now. You still haven't told me why you wanted to meet up today.'

Although they'd worked two cases together and had established a good working relationship, there had always been a reason for the times they'd socialised. Birdie had her own set of friends, who were much closer in age to her than he was, and who she went out with on a regular basis.

'To be honest, it was so we could discuss Sunday. Remember, I told you I'm meeting Marie Davis. It's already been postponed twice because of her health. Fingers crossed this Sunday she can make it.'

Of course. Seb remembered that Birdie had arranged to visit an old neighbour of her birth mother, Kim Bakirtzis, in the hope of finding out more about her.

'My head's about to explode from worry,' Birdie continued, 'and you're the only person I can talk to because no one else knows how far I've progressed with my search.'

'Are you having second thoughts?'

'No, not at all. It's what I want to do. But because Marie Davis is recovering from the stroke she had, I've got to be clear which questions to ask. It was kind enough of her to suggest I call around, especially after her son has already told me plenty about the Bakirtzis family before they moved to Canada. I don't want to tire her out. That wouldn't be fair.'

'What exactly do you want to know from her that her son hasn't already told you?'

'Where Kim is now, and any details about her that she can remember? I also want to know if Marie knew about her being pregnant.'

'Are you going to tell her who you are?'

'As far as she's concerned, I'm asking for a friend. That's what I told her when we originally spoke on the phone. It's also what I told her son. I should tell her the truth, shouldn't I? It's wrong to lie about it.' A guilty flush crept up her cheeks.

'That's entirely your decision. It's worth considering

that she might not want to tell you anything if she knows who you are, but …'

'It's not fair to deceive her. I know. I've always known. I hated lying to her in the first place.'

'Exactly.' While he understood her desire to obtain as much detail as possible, to be deceitful wasn't the way to go about it.

'What am I to do?'

'If you want my opinion—'

'Yeah … that's why I'm asking.' She rolled her eyes.

'As I was saying. It's my belief that it will become clear when you see her. Assess how it goes, bearing in mind how she is, and then decide. I'm not going to tell you what to do. It's for you to make the decision.'

'Yes, I know all that. I just wanted someone to mull it over with. And you'll have to do.'

He frowned. 'Should I be flattered by that?'

'What do you think?' she said, a broad smile breaking out on her face.

'Are you going to ask if she knows anything about your father?'

'That's another thing, isn't it? Because I'm not sure about that, either. So much for you helping me. I don't seem to be any clearer. And you're just adding to my worries.'

He shook his head, fearing he'd now made things worse for Birdie.

'It's not an easy situation to advise you on. It's impossible to pre-empt what's going to happen.'

'I suppose you're right.' She stared at him. 'And stop with that smug expression. You're not right all the time.'

'I wasn't aware there was any such expression on my face.' He relaxed his mouth to appear normal.

'Whatever. Changing the subject, how's your brother getting along?'

His older brother, Hubert, had been suffering from depression and had withdrawn from some of his familial duties. Seb had stepped in for him a couple of times, and he hadn't enjoyed it one bit.

'Funnily enough, he phoned me yesterday, and he seems to be improving. He's having counselling and is on medication, which is helping. Obviously, he's not totally back to normal, but he's doing okay. Thanks for asking.'

'Does that mean that you've still got to go to all those fancy events with your dad?'

'Maybe. I believe Hubert is going to attend some, but we'll see.'

'I've just had a thought. If you're meeting the DCI for lunch on Sunday and my meeting is in the afternoon, why don't I come over to yours in the evening for a debrief?'

'That's an excellent idea.'

'And I can also see Elsa,' she said, referring to his dog.

'She would love to see you, too.'

# Chapter 2

Bistro in Little Hampton was situated in a large, thatched cottage that, according to the website Seb had read before leaving home earlier, dated back to the sixteenth century and had once been lived in by the illegitimate offspring of Henry VIII. The restaurant was crowded, with every table filled. At the rear was a beautiful walled garden where food was served in the summer months, although Seb and Whitney had been seated inside.

He'd become acquainted with the officer the previous year when her team was investigating the murder of international snooker player Ryan Armstrong, and their investigation had crossed paths with a case of his. They'd ended up working together, although initially their relationship had been fraught, mainly because he'd refused to release the information she'd asked for. This had displeased her, especially because she was the senior officer. Eventually, their bosses insisted that they join forces. It had worked out well, and he'd enjoyed his time at Lenchester. They'd kept in contact, and Whitney had helped him out on a case he'd worked on with Birdie.

'This restaurant is delightful,' Seb said after they'd given their order to the waiter.

'Yes, and wait until you taste the food. We've never yet had a bad meal here. I also chose the place because it's far enough away from Lenchester to make sure our meeting is private, and we don't bump into anyone from work.'

That intrigued him. Was the investigation to be done in secret?

'Is this to be an undercover role?'

'No. But until I know whether or not you're going to take the job, I don't want anyone else to be aware of it.'

'I see.'

'I'd intended to wait until after we'd eaten before discussing it, but I'd forgotten how direct you are.' She picked up her glass of water and took a sip.

'Of course, if you'd rather wait until then, I can manage that.' He smiled. 'How's Tiffany coping with being a mother?'

'She's taken to it like a duck to water. I remember when I had her, it was great, but honestly, the enormity of it all blew my mind. Being a single mother is never easy, however much help you get. But she's dealing with it. The baby's dad is back in Australia, so it's just us. I can't believe how well she's doing.' Whitney twirled one of her curls around her finger. 'Actually, I can. You've met Tiffany, she's a dynamo. I'm so proud of her.'

'She's obviously had a good role model.'

'Thank you, but it doesn't feel like it sometimes. Half the time, I have so much on, what with work and private life, that I don't know if I'm coming or going. And I haven't been to a Rock Choir rehearsal in weeks. We've got a concert coming up soon, and I don't even know which songs we'll be singing. Anyway, you don't need to know all this. Tell me what's going on with you?'

'Nothing's changed since we last spoke apart from I'm officially open for business as a private investigator.'

'That's great. And are you excited by the prospect?'

'Not exactly, but it does seem the right thing to do under the circumstances. Although it might take a while to get off the ground, as most businesses do.'

'But for someone in your position, that's not really an issue, is it?'

He bit back a frustrated sigh. 'You're not the only one to think that because of my *situation*, I don't need the money.'

'Sorry, it was a stupid thing for me to say. I should've known better than to make such an idiotic assumption.'

'Apology accepted. I apologise, too. I should be used to it by now.'

'Let's forget it. I imagine your photographic memory will help you a lot in your work. Although … that's not what it is, come to think of it. Remind me what you have.'

'It's highly superior autobiographical memory, known as HSAM. It's like having a search engine in your head.' Having a memory like his could be an advantage; that he couldn't deny. But it was also a curse. At times, he longed to be normal.

'Ah, yes. Now I remember. You do know I'm jealous. It would be amazing to have that skill.'

'And as I've often said, be careful what you wish for.'

'So, tell me more about your business then.'

'I'm working with my ex-colleague at the Met, which is ongoing, and I've already had one or two other enquiries which I'll follow up. I've asked DC Bird, from the Market Harborough station to join me. We've already worked on two cases together, and we make a good team. I'm waiting for her reply. It's a big decision for her to make, especially leaving the force, because she's a good officer, although a little wayward.'

'There's nothing wrong with that. I've managed to progress up the ladder, and you could hardly call me a conformist.'

'You did, but things have changed now, regarding the acceptance of rule breaking, even in the short time since you've been in the force.'

'You say short time, but it's been over twenty years, although I do agree. I would never have fallen out with Dickhead Douglas nowadays because he wouldn't have been able to make unwanted advances and get away with it. So, in that instance, things have certainly changed for the better.'

'I'd forgotten about your nemesis,' he said with a wry smile.

Chief Superintendent Grant Douglas and Whitney had a long and turbulent history. It was being promoted to Chief Super which had brought him back to Lenchester.

'Lucky you, because I can't forget. He's always there breathing down my neck, waiting for me to trip up. Anyway, let's not talk about him. I think Birdie would make a very good partner in the business. You'll have to make sure she sees it as a real career option, not a sidekick role, though.'

'I do realise that.'

'But even if Birdie remains in the force, she could always help you.'

'I wouldn't ask because it's too risky. She's already helped me out a couple of times, and it didn't end well for her. I wouldn't put her in that position again. The offer's there for her to join me, but if she doesn't, we'll remain friends.'

They were interrupted by the food being delivered.

Both had ordered *the catch of the day with fries and salad.* Whitney had been correct; it was delicious. And they sat in companiable silence while eating.

'Let's talk about the case, now,' Whitney said after their plates had been cleared away.

Seb focused his attention on her, his fingers steepled. 'I'm listening.'

'Have I ever mentioned Rob, my older brother?'

'Yes, you've spoken of him in the past.'

'When he was a teenager, twenty-five years ago, he was attacked. The assault left him with irreversible brain damage.'

'You said. Such a tragedy.'

'I wasn't sure if I had. Well, I'm reopening the case and would like you to be the one to lead it.'

He certainly hadn't been expecting that.

'What's happened after all this time for you to want the case reopened?' he asked cautiously, wanting to hear more before he made any decision.

'It might not seem much but, for me, it was huge. When we were together the other day, he blurted out something about keeping a secret and got quite agitated when I questioned him further. Which is strange for him because he's usually such a happy person. Even when his routine changes, which does bother him, he withdraws and doesn't get angry at all. He's never mentioned anything about a secret before. Not ever. It made me think that something must have triggered his memory. I asked him to tell me what it was, and he point-blank refused. All he'd say was that he had to keep it quiet because, if he didn't, all our family would be harmed. After that, he totally clammed up and refused to talk until I'd changed the subject. If you knew him, you'd understand how important this is because it's such unusual behaviour. I'm telling you, it can't be ignored.' Whitney's hands were clasped tightly in front of her, resting on the table. Her knuckles white.

'It must have been a shock to hear that from him. Are you sure that he's never said anything about this secret before?'

'A hundred per cent. At least, not to me. I can't speak for my mum, but she'd have told me if he had because it's so out of character. Although with her dementia getting worse, it might have slipped her mind.'

'Okay, let's assume this is something new. What do you think prompted him to mention it? What were you doing?'

'We were visiting Mum in the care home, and he became upset because of her illness. I told him that he needs to be strong and not let her know how her condition makes us feel. It was then that he said he knew how to be strong and not tell because he'd done it before. I tried to pry it out of him, but all he said was that he'd promised not to tell anyone. I probed a bit more and asked if it was to do with the attack, and he said he wasn't allowed to say. It was obvious from his facial expression that it was. But that was all I got out of him.'

'How has he been since he mentioned this secret?'

'Honestly, since that day, the same as usual. It's as if he doesn't even remember saying it. I wish now that I'd pushed him a little harder, but then he still might not have divulged anything else, and it could have affected him badly.'

'You were right not to go too deep. There are alternative ways of discovering the truth.'

'I know, which is why I got permission from my super to reopen the case. We discussed how it wasn't appropriate for me to be leading the investigation and, after I'd suggested it, she agreed I could ask you to be a consultant.'

'Goodness, considering budgetary restraints these days,

I'm impressed that you were able to get Superintendent Clyde's consent.'

'I had to because no way was any other team at Lenchester going to investigate my family. For a start, they'd try to exclude me, and I know you won't. Plus, can you imagine the gossip? My whole life wide open for everyone in the force to see.'

Seb smiled to himself at Whitney's typical emotional reaction. 'I don't believe it would be as bad as you imagine.'

'I can't believe you've already forgotten what it's like in the force. It hasn't been that long since you left. Anyway, the super trusts my judgement and wouldn't have agreed if she didn't. But having said that, we've only got two weeks' funding. It has helped that there's a big push nationally on cold cases now.'

'Yes, that certainly would have gone in your favour. What background can you give me on the case?' He held up his hand. 'Not that I've decided yet. I need more information, first.'

'I get it. There's not a lot to tell you, other than, at the time, I didn't believe the police investigated it properly. But I was only fourteen and not fully aware of the facts. Now I've been in the job, I'm of the opinion that maybe there wasn't anything else they could've done. I'll leave that for this new investigation to ascertain.'

'This will be hard, but what can you tell me about the attack?'

She visibly stiffened. 'We didn't find out straight away. Rob was found in a park the following day by someone who was walking their dog, and they called the police and the ambulance. He was barely conscious. The park was in a run-down area, where gangs used to hang out. I went with my parents to visit Rob at the hospital. The image of his face still haunts me to this day. It … it was such a mess.' The hurt shone from her eyes.

'Did he recognise you?' he asked softly.

'Sort of. But I could tell immediately that there was something wrong. It was the vacant expression in his eyes. We were all worried that he wasn't going to survive. It was touch-and-go for a few weeks. If he'd have died …'

'Was Rob questioned about the attack?'

'I assume the doctors asked him to explain what had happened. And I know my mum and dad spoke to him about it and, of course, the police. Because I was so young at the time, they tried to keep me out of it. I do remember that he couldn't tell them anything. Couldn't, or *wouldn't* as it now transpires.'

'When he came home from the hospital, did you talk to him about the attack?'

'I tried to …' Her voice cracked. 'B-but he just blanked me. In fact, he hardly spoke for a long time afterwards. It was so bad … so bad.' Tears filled her eyes, and she brushed them away. 'Sorry.'

'Don't be. It's not easy having to relive such an awful time.'

Whitney sniffed and gave a watery smile. 'You're right. But I can't break down every time we discuss it. Rob was in that state for a few years, but now, he's a lovely man.'

'Do you have any idea whether it was a random attack or whether he was targeted?'

'No. We know nothing.' She shook her head.

'Was he out alone when it happened?'

'We don't know that, either. He'd gone out, and none of us knew where or who with. It sounds ridiculous, but hardly anyone had mobile phones then, and it was impossible to track someone.'

'Did he go out often?'

'He was sixteen and a typical teenage boy. He was rarely in. You must remember those days.'

He chuckled to himself. 'I was at an all-boys' boarding school in the middle of the countryside, and we weren't allowed out.'

'Well, we can't all be posh like you.' She chewed on her bottom lip. 'Sorry, no offence.'

'None taken. Do you have the police file? I'd like to see who was questioned.'

'I'll see if I can access it. I'd planned to look for it before today, but I've been inundated with meetings and admin. Mind you, we're talking twenty-five years ago, and you know what records can be like. So, there might not be much.'

'Something is better than nothing. Is it possible for me to speak with your brother?'

'I'm not sure, yet. But if we do, we'll have to be very careful how we approach him.'

'Of course, I understand. And what about your mother?'

'We can certainly visit her at the care home. If she's having one of her good days, she might be able to tell us something.' She paused and stared directly at him. 'Does this mean that you're going to take the case?'

How could he not?

'Yes, because it's you. I hadn't intended on undertaking any additional police consultancy other than the Met work, but this is different.'

She flashed a smile. 'Thank you. I really appreciate it. To be honest, you're the best person I can think of, besides me, to undertake it. I don't know what I'd have done if you'd said no.'

'I'll take that as a compliment. How's Dr Cavendish, by the way?'

'She's fine. You know what George is like, busy trying to combine her university work with working for us. Added to that is that she's buying a house with her partner Ross. They're selling their own houses and moving in together. Life's full on for her at the moment.'

'Send her my best wishes next time you see her.'

'I will do. And what about you? Are you enjoying living in Market Harborough?'

'I am. For now. Obviously, when my cousin Sarah returns from her overseas travels and wants her house back, I'll have to rethink my situation.'

'Well, at least you're not too far away from us here, which will make undertaking this job easier.'

'Exactly. If I'm only working for two weeks, I'll start tomorrow. Monday. And perhaps you can arrange a time for us to visit your mother. I'll spend tomorrow preparing. If you can find me the old case file as soon as possible, that would be a great help.'

'I'm on it. We have to find out what happened to him, Seb. We have to.'

# Chapter 3

Seb poured himself a coffee and settled down in the large study of his cousin's seventeenth-century home, Rendall Hall. It was a perfect place for him to work, and Elsa enjoyed sleeping by the large French doors which overlooked the beautiful garden. Birdie had changed her mind about visiting Seb the previous night, instead having an evening out with her friends. Her meeting with Marie Davis had been rearranged again, this time to Wednesday because the woman hadn't been up to visitors. Seb had opted for an early night and had woken before six. He'd taken Elsa out early for a long walk in the fields adjacent to the house. She loved being able to race around and not have to stay on the lead. It had rained during the night, and the air had been fresh and invigorating.

Although all this fresh air and greenery was perhaps more of a distraction than inspiration. He had to get down to business. But he'd certainly miss working there when Sarah came back from her travels. Not that she had any plans to come back soon.

The latest he'd heard was that she'd left South America

and was heading for India to embark on a pilgrimage. He planned to give her twins, Benedict and Caspian, a call later to catch up with them. They'd kept in regular contact since their mother had left, although they were both busy with their university studies and enjoying themselves, in typical student fashion. He was relieved they had each other, especially after the tragic death of their father and the scandal surrounding it.

Putting his coffee aside, Seb sat upright at the desk and opened his laptop. He began typing his plan of action for undertaking Whitney's case. First, he wanted to look at the police file as soon as possible because that was all he initially had to go on. In particular, he was interested in ascertaining who had been interviewed, and how the investigation had been conducted. Were there any glaring omissions? Had anything not been followed up which should have been? Had there been any witnesses and, if so, were they still around to interview? Was there any CCTV footage? Also, he'd like some background on Rob from before the attack.

He was also mindful of the need to manage Whitney's expectations. Twenty-five years was a long time, and whether he'd be able to shed any light on the attack in such a short space of time remained to be seen. He sincerely hoped he'd be successful. Whitney needed the closure. Her whole family did.

His phone rang, and he glanced at the screen. It was the officer.

'Good morning, Whitney, I was contemplating getting in touch myself.'

'I must have sensed it and pre-empted you. I've managed to get hold of the police file, which is a miracle in itself. So many files have been misplaced since we moved into our new station last year. It's currently being scanned in. I'll email it to you. I also thought we could visit my mum later today if that fits in with your plans.'

'Yes, that's an excellent idea.'

'It will have to be after five, though, because it's the earliest I can get away.'

'Yes, of course. Shall I pick you up from the station?' Whitney was well known for always wanting to be driven by whoever she was working with. According to her, she hated her old car and much preferred to be comfortable.

'No need. Meet me outside the home because it's closer to where you're coming from. I'll email the address details when I send the file over. Is there anything else you need from me before I go?'

'Yes. Do you remember who Rob's friends were at the time of the attack?'

She sighed. 'Sorry, no. I wish I did, but it's such a long time ago, and being younger than him, we didn't go to the same places. Mum might be able to help us, providing she's having a good day.'

'I understand. What about the place where the attack took place? I intend contacting people who were living close by at the time. They might remember something. I'll check with the file for names of those who were interviewed.'

'We don't know where the actual incident took place, only the park where Rob was found. There were no CCTV cameras around there, then. There also weren't many houses that you'd consider close all those years ago. It's more developed now, though.'

He deleted the CCTV note he'd made on his list. He hadn't considered the lack of cameras, which he should have, bearing in mind how long ago the event took place.

'In that case, I'll visit where he was found. I'm going to stay at a hotel or pub in Lenchester for a couple of nights.'

'Why don't you stay with me? We have room.'

'You have Tiffany and the baby to consider, and I don't wish to get in the way. I may be working into the early hours of the morning, so it's best if I'm on my own. Thank you for the offer, though.'

'If you're sure. You can change your mind at any time. Don't forget to charge your accommodation to expenses.'

'I won't.'

He ended the call and went online to find a place to stay. There was a pub on the outskirts of Lenchester that appeared suitable, and he booked himself in for two nights. He glanced at his inbox, but the police file hadn't yet appeared.

Having Whitney's input would be useful, even though she wasn't meant to be getting involved. Thankfully, because she ran the department, she was unlikely to find herself disciplined over giving assistance, unlike when Birdie had helped him.

Elsa came up and nudged his leg.

'Do you want to go outside, girl?' He opened the French doors to let her out when a thought struck him. He hadn't asked anyone to look after her. In London, he'd always had his neighbour, but up here he didn't have anyone to ask on a regular basis. Apart from Birdie, but she had her work. Then again … Elsa and Birdie did have a great relationship, and it wasn't going to be for too long.

He picked up his phone and gave her a call.

'Birdie speaking.'

'It's me, Seb. I wondered if I could trouble you for a favour?'

'Um … sure. What is it?'

'I'm going up to Lenchester for a few days and— –'

'You need someone to look after Elsa,' Birdie interrupted, finishing his sentence.

She sounded relieved. What had she thought he was phoning for?

'Yes. I'm going to Lenchester and wondered if you'd come and stay here for a few days. You've looked after her before, and she loves being with you.'

'Of course, I'd love to. But I need a key.'

Good point. He could take it to her.

'What are you doing at present?'

'I'm at work, but I can pop out to meet you.'

'Who are you talking to?' Seb heard Birdie's colleague, DC Branch, aka Twiggy, ask in the background.

'I'm going to look after Seb's dog for a few days, and I need the key.'

'You can't go before the morning briefing, or Sarge will go apeshit.'

'Shut up, Twiggy. Of course I'm not going to do that. Seb, are you still there?'

'Yes. Phone me when you're free, and I'll meet you outside the station. Thanks for agreeing.'

'It's my pleasure. You know how much I adore her.'

Birdie had once worked at some kennels, and she loved dogs. Every time Elsa saw her, she forgot all about Seb and wouldn't leave Birdie's side.

'I'll wait to hear from you.' He ended the call and headed upstairs to pack a bag. He'd head to Lenchester immediately after seeing Birdie. The police file still hadn't arrived. Hopefully, he'd have it by the time he reached his accommodation. With only two weeks on the clock, he didn't want to waste any more time.

# Chapter 4

'Birdie. Twiggy. My office now,' Sergeant Jack Weston called out from the entrance to Market Harborough CID. He turned and headed back down the corridor before they'd even got up from their seats.

'What's that all about?' Birdie said, glancing up from her phone after texting Seb to arrange for him to bring her the key. 'We've only just finished the briefing.'

'I've no idea. Strange as it may seem, the man doesn't confide in me.' Twiggy pushed back his chair until he could get out from behind his desk.

'Are we in trouble?' Birdie was paranoid about having to return to desk duty. Though she definitely hadn't done anything to warrant it. But Sarge could be very unpredictable as far as she was concerned.

'Why would we be? Just because we get called into his office doesn't mean we've done anything wrong. You of all people should know that,' Twiggy said, walking beside her as they made their way to the door.

'Yeah, well, you know what it's like for me. I've only

just got back on ordinary duties. I can't risk anything else happening.'

'Have you done anything you shouldn't have?' He turned and scrutinised her face. 'Because if you have—'

'No, not that I know of. I was even on time this morning. Give or take a few seconds.' Sarge expected them to be sitting at their desks at least thirty minutes before their morning briefing. Sometimes he'd stick his head in to check. It wasn't easy, however hard she tried.

'I noticed. Everything should be fine. Stop worrying, or you'll get me started.'

Sarge was already seated behind his desk when they arrived at his office. There were folders everywhere apart from the one chair that was always kept clear.

'Right. Who's going to sit down?' she asked Twiggy, who'd already got his hand on the back of it.

'Come on, you two. Let's get started. Use that chair over there, Birdie.' Sarge nodded to one in the corner with piles of files on it. 'Drop the stuff on the floor.'

'Yes, Sarge,' Birdie said.

She moved the precarious paper tower from the chair to the floor before placing her newfound seat next to Twiggy.

'Right, I've got a special assignment for you both. This has come via Inspector Curtis,' he said, referring to his boss who split his time between their station and Wigston.

Birdie exchanged a look with Twiggy. Were they being offered a juicy case?

'What is it?' she asked, leaning forward but trying to contain her excitement.

'You're both joining a special operation being run by the Wigston force. They've received information regarding Victor Rawlings, and if this turns out to be true, it could be big.' Sarge paused and stared at them.

Twiggy nodded knowingly before asking, 'Victor Rawlings? What sort of information?'

'You'll find out soon enough when you get to Wigston.'

'Am I meant to know who he is?' Birdie frowned. She'd never heard the name before.

'You should do,' Twiggy said. 'He owns VR Machinery.'

'And? I need a bit more than that.'

'They import and export farm machinery.'

'I don't know any farmers. I'm a townie. You too, so how come you know him?'

'Because he's high profile, lives locally, and is well known for all his charity work. He's always in the media for something. I can't believe you haven't heard of him,' Twiggy said.

'He can't be that high profile if I don't know him. Then again, I don't read the local newspaper, if that's where you've seen him. And just because he's in there doesn't make him someone special. It's not like Market Harborough is some mega hotspot—'

'It doesn't matter whether you know of him or not,' Sarge said, cutting in. 'Rawlings *is* a big fish and is also friends with the chief constable. So that should be enough.'

'In other words, we have to tread carefully,' Twiggy said.

'You've got it in one.'

'Did Inspector Curtis specifically ask for me and Twiggy?'

'No, he asked for two officers. I was the person to choose you two, so don't make me regret it. You're to go to Wigston now for a briefing. Your roles in the operation will be explained once you get there. Don't let me down.'

'We won't. Thanks, Sarge.'

'Don't thank me. It's your job. I want you to leave

immediately. The briefing will begin when you get there. So, I expect you to go straight there and no stopping for snacks, Twiggy.'

'I—'

'Don't bother trying to deny it, Twig. Sarge knows exactly what you're like. I'll make sure we avoid any detours, Sarge.'

Twiggy stared daggers at her. He no doubt already had a snack spot planned. If he didn't take too long, she supposed they could stop somewhere. Sarge would be none the wiser.

'Good, I'm glad we've got that straight. Off you go. Report to me on your return.'

Sarge nodded at the door. Their cue to leave.

'I wonder what this Rawlings guy has done. It won't be the first time a supposed pillar of the community has dirty dealings on the side,' she said, once they'd left the sergeant's office.

'At least wait until the DI has briefed us before maligning the man.'

'What's got into you? Since when do you care about people like him?'

'I met him once at a charity event for the hospital. It was when my nephew was being treated for leukaemia. I have a lot of time for him, that's all.'

'Just because he does work for charity doesn't mean he gets a free pass to doing something illegal. Whatever it is.'

'Yeah. But it will be sad if he's involved in something shady.'

'Don't tell me you're going soft in your old age, Twiggy. You must be objective. This is an investigation.'

'Maybe it is. Maybe it isn't. I'm going to reserve judgement. Oh, and by the way, you didn't really mean it about not stopping for something to eat on the way, did you?'

'What would Evie say about it?' she teased, referring to Twiggy's wife, who was hell-bent on him losing weight. Although Birdie reckoned she should give it up as a bad job. He could never stick to any diet plan.

'You know what she'd say.'

'If you're quick, we'll stop, but before we leave, I'm going to quickly google Victor Rawlings to see what I've been missing.' She sat at her computer and keyed in his name. Thousands of hits. 'Bloody hell. You're right, he's a total do-gooder. One charity event after another. A good front for illegal activity, that's for sure.'

'Only you could say that.'

'Stop being so naïve, Twig. It's not like you at all. Oh, and here's a photo of him with the chief constable. This is getting more interesting by the minute. I can't wait to hear about the investigation. Who's going to drive?'

'I will. Every time I squeeze into your Mini, I end up having trouble with my back,' Twiggy said, giving it a rub.

'You should exercise more.'

'When do I have the time? Between work, the kids, and keeping on top of jobs at home, my days are full. Unfortunately. It's okay for you, being single. You get to enjoy yourself all the time.'

It wasn't like him to be so negative about his life. If there was a couple destined to be in it for the long haul, it was Twiggy and Evie. They had their arguments, but what couple didn't. And he loved his kids, always spoke proudly of them. Perhaps he was having a bad day. It happened to everyone.

'True. I can't deny it. Come on, Seb's going to be waiting outside with his key, so let's go. And we might still have time to stop at a bakery on the way.'

# Chapter 5

'You're very quiet this morning,' Twiggy said, glancing over to Birdie, who'd been staring out of the window during their journey and hardly engaging in any conversation after their initial chat in the office. It was most unlike her.

'Am I? I hadn't realised.'

'Yes, you are. Is everything okay?'

'Yeah, it's all fine.'

He'd known her long enough to work out that something was on her mind. Whether she'd tell him or not was a different matter. He hoped she would because the two of them chatting meant he could take his mind off his own worries.

'You know, you can tell me anything. You must be really pleased now you're not doing desk duty?'

'I am,' Birdie said, turning to him.

'What is it then?'

'Nothing. You're imagining it.'

'I don't believe you.' He tightened his grip on the steering wheel. 'You just don't want to confide in me any more now that you're hanging out with the bloody viscount.'

'Seb isn't a viscount. How many times do I have to tell you it's his father? And that's ridiculous, thinking that I'm only talking to him.'

'Well, you say that, but ever since he's been around, things have been different.'

'You're mad. We're fine, so stop being so stupid. And there's nothing wrong. Stop blaming Seb for something that's in your head. I don't know what it is you have against him, anyway.'

'No, you wouldn't, because you're blind to it.'

'Is it because he's so posh and you don't like it?'

'No.'

'We've worked a couple of cases together, that's all. You know, he's a good guy. Look how much he helped with Lacey.'

'I suppose you're right. But I'm glad that he's not around now. What's he doing anyway?'

'Still in Market Harborough. He's doing some work for the Met as he gets the PI business started. And Lenchester CID, actually.' She paused. 'Though you didn't hear that last bit from me.'

'Why not?'

'Because it's not public knowledge. Forget I mentioned it. We're nearly at Wigston, and I don't want to talk about it anymore.'

Surely not more secrets between the two of them?

'Whatever,' he grunted. Twiggy was too tired to fall out with Birdie, but he was curious about what Clifford would be doing in Lenchester. Then again, if he was working there, it would keep him away from Birdie; and that had to be a good thing. At least, from his perspective.

Wigston Station was housed in a typical 1960s building

with small windows that were difficult to see through. It was much the same size as theirs at Market Harborough. They entered through the automatic glass doors at the front and headed to the reception desk, behind which a uniformed officer was stationed.

'We're here to see DI Curtis. He's expecting us,' Twiggy said, holding out his ID.

'They're in briefing room three. Go through the double doors and it's the second on the right.'

They walked into the room and were faced with DI Curtis sitting at the head of the table with four other officers, none of whom Twiggy recognised.

'Come in, DC Bird and DC Branch.' He introduced them to the other officers, two from Wigston and two from Braunstone. 'Now everyone is here, I'm going to explain about the operation and then allocate duties. Victor Rawlings is a well-known and very well-connected philanthropist from these parts. However, we've been given information alleging his involvement in several illegal activities.'

'What sort of activities?' DS Len Mattas from Braunstone asked.

'Importation and exportation of firearms, using his company, VR Machinery, as cover. We have someone on the inside who's prepared to assist.'

'A whistle-blower?' Mattas asked.

'Not exactly. She's the mother of a young man we arrested for aggravated burglary. Lee Clarke. He told us about Rawlings because his mother had mentioned her concerns regarding what was going on at the company. Her name is Margaret. She lives in Kilby and works in the head office.'

'And she's agreed to help us?' Mattas frowned.

'She has no choice if she wants to save her son from going down for a long stretch.'

'How do we know Clarke is telling the truth?' Mattas asked.

'Rawlings has been on our radar for a long time, but we've never been able to pin anything on him. This is the first time we've had some serious intel, and we're going to follow up on it. Needless to say, because of his connections, everything must be done by the book, and nothing leaves this office without running it past me first.'

'Even to Sergeant Weston?' Twiggy asked.

'I will be updating him on progress, so I give permission for you to discuss anything with him if I'm not available.'

'Thanks, sir.'

'Right. We're going to mount twenty-four-hour surveillance on Rawlings, Monday to Friday for the foreseeable future. You can work eight-hour shifts. DCs Branch and Bird, you can do seven in the morning until three in the afternoon, as you're already close to where he lives. Wigston team, you take three to eleven, and Braunstone, the night shift, eleven to seven.' Mattas expelled a loud groan. 'Is there an issue, Len?'

'No, sir,' Mattas answered, sighing.

'Good. In the meantime, Branch and Bird, you're to visit Margaret Clarke at home in Kilby and interview her. She's expecting you. Any questions?'

'Are we to report back here after we've been to see the woman?' Birdie asked.

'Yes.'

'And after our surveillance each day are we to come over here, too?' Twiggy asked. He and Evie had planned to take the kids bowling on Thursday after school. He'd been hoping to nip off early. They'd be disappointed if he couldn't make it. He'd be gutted.

'No. I'll let you know if you're needed here. But keep in touch each day.'

'Okay, sir.'

The inspector ended the meeting, dismissing the various teams.

'We're going to grab something to eat from the café around the corner if you'd like to join us?' DS Mattas said.

Twiggy perked up. He was wondering when he'd get another chance to eat. 'Definitely, it—'

'Sorry, sir, we'd better not. We have to see Margaret Clarke, but thanks, anyway,' Birdie said, a glint in her eye as she interrupted him.

Birdie knocked twice on the door of the double-fronted red-brick terraced cottage, using the highly polished brass knocker, and a woman in her early fifties with grey hair cut into a short bob answered.

'Margaret Clarke?' Twiggy asked.

'Yes. Are you the police?' she said in a soft voice, an anxious expression on her face as she glanced to either side of them.

'Yes, may we come in?' Birdie held out her warrant card.

'I was expecting you.' The woman stepped to the side while they entered and then hurriedly closed the door behind them. 'We'll go through into the lounge.'

'Thank you.'

The room was very neat and tidy, with a dark green leather three-piece suite and a small television on a stand in the corner. There was a feature fireplace with a tiled surround in the centre of the opposite wall.

'Mrs Clarke, does anyone else live here?' Birdie asked.

'It's only me. My husband died five years ago.'

'I'm sorry to hear that. What about the rest of your family?'

'I have a son, Lee, who … Well, you know about him. I'm so relieved that his father didn't witness the way he's turned out. We always tried our best with him, but he got in with the wrong crowd and …' She paused for a moment. 'Can I get you anything? Tea, coffee, something to eat?'

'We're fine, thanks,' Birdie said.

'Are you sure? I've just made some scones?'

'Oh, well, if you insist, that would be lovely, with a cup of tea,' Twiggy said, smiling.

Birdie looked over and rolled her eyes, sure that he knew what she was thinking.

'Okay, I won't be a moment.'

'Come on, Twiggy, we're here to talk about Rawlings, not stuff your stomach, especially as we already stopped for something on the way here,' Birdie said after Margaret Clarke had left the room.

'Look, I take anything that's offered. You don't understand what it's like for me. Evie's been into juicing these last few weeks, and today I had some sort of green concoction for my breakfast. It was disgusting, and I don't know how I managed to keep it down. I couldn't tip it in the sink because she stood there, watching me drink every bit. So I'm going to eat what I can during the day. And no one is going to stop me.'

A couple of minutes later, Mrs Clarke returned, holding a tray with a teapot, cups, and saucers, and a plate of scones bursting with cream and jam.

Even Birdie's stomach rumbled at the sight.

'Here you are,' she said, smiling.

'Thank you, that's much appreciated. I didn't have time for a proper breakfast,' Twiggy said, snatching one off the plate.

'It's not a problem. I love baking, and it's nice to have someone who'll enjoy them. My son Lee doesn't have a sweet tooth.'

The woman's attitude was perplexing. Why was she being so nice to them when she was being forced to turn on her boss?

'You're not at work today, then?' Birdie said, reaching into her pocket and pulling out her notebook and pen.

'No, I called in sick because I knew that you were coming to see me. I thought that would be better than saying I've got a doctor's or dentist's appointment because I didn't know the exact time you'd be arriving.'

'That was a good idea. What's your position at VR Machinery?'

'I'm a management accountant, which basically means that I'm a number cruncher. I advise management on spending and budgeting within the company. Not that they always follow my advice. But that's the nature of the work. Mr Rawlings does tend to do things his way. But sometimes he listens. I've been in this position for a little over two years.'

'And you suspect that your boss is involved in illegal activities?' Birdie asked, glancing up from scribbling down some notes.

The woman nodded. 'Yes, I'm sorry to say.'

'Yet you remain working there?'

'Jobs aren't easy to find at my age. I was out of work for months before being offered this position and I didn't wish to rock the boat. I can't afford to be unemployed.'

'If that's the case, how do you feel about Lee informing on Victor Rawlings to save his own skin? And also getting you involved?' Birdie asked.

'Do you have children?' Mrs Clarke asked.

'No, I don't,' Birdie said.

'I do,' Twiggy said.

Mrs Clarke's face softened as she turned to Twiggy. 'Then you'll understand why I agreed to it. It doesn't matter about my feelings. I must protect my son. If he goes to prison, he'll never get his life back on track. It would destroy him. This is the only way. We've been promised witness protection, which means we can leave the area and start afresh. Not many people get that chance.' She sounded like a puppet, spilling out what she'd been told by the authorities. But the expression on her face told a different story; the woman was concerned about the future.

'Please could you give us some background on Mr Rawlings and the company, and explain what Lee knows about it?' Birdie asked.

'VR Machinery imports and exports farm machinery and has been in existence for around thirty years. It's one of the largest privately owned businesses in its field and has a good reputation. I have access to all the legitimate accounts, and the farm-machinery arm makes a healthy profit. But …' The woman leant forward and lowered her voice. 'It's my belief that it's all a front for the movement of firearms.' She glanced from side to side like she was expecting someone to burst into the room and accuse her of lying.

It was all very cloak and dagger. Was she doing it for effect?

'And how have you come to this conclusion?'

'There have been several instances that alerted me to something being amiss. The first was when I had to pop back to Victor's office one evening because I'd left something behind after our weekly meeting. The meeting been at the end of the day, so most people had left for home straight after, so the office floor was silent. As I approached the door, I overheard Victor talking on the phone. Rather than disturb him, I decided to wait, out of sight, until he'd finished his call. But then I heard him discuss payment for weapons and a delivery date.'

'How did you know it was for weapons?' Birdie asked.

'Because he specifically mentioned "handguns".'

'What did you do then?'

'I bolted to my office before he realised I was there.'

'You mentioned there were several instances that alerted you to some wrongdoing. Is there more? A one-sided phone conversation isn't exactly strong evidence. Certainly not enough for your son to be let off and you both be put into witness protection,' Birdie said.

'S-so it's not definite then? But I was led to believe that it was. What if Victor finds out what I've done?' She gripped both arms of the chair.

'We can't comment on the deal made, but in most cases, it's contingent on the quality of information passed to the police. Everything you tell us is confidential and kept within the boundaries of our investigation.'

'Oh. Okay. I understand. Sorry. It's just this whole thing has been giving me sleepless nights. Maybe this will help. Victor keeps a locked filing cabinet in his office, for which no one other than him has a key. I once asked his PA what he kept in there and she said she had no idea. She did say that when she started at the company, she'd been warned that going in there was a sacking offence. I could tell from her tone that even telling me had unnerved her.'

'Doesn't he keep everything electronically?' Birdie asked.

'Victor's old-school. He hates computers.'

'Okay. So you've heard the mention of weapons and he keeps a locked filing cabinet, is that it?'

If this was the sum total of evidence against Victor Rawlings, then Birdie couldn't see their investigation going far.

'I've seen him with some pretty rough-looking people in the past. One evening, I was coming home after attending the theatre in Leicester, and I drove past our offices and saw him outside with two men who I'd never seen before. They looked like they belonged to a gang.'

'Could you be more specific? What about them appeared gang-like?'

'Well, you know. Wearing those leather jackets and had tattoos. I didn't see them too closely. It was just an impression I got.'

'Did you tell Victor that you'd seen him?' Twiggy asked.

'Of course not. We don't have that sort of relationship. I usually only speak to him once a week during the weekly meeting.'

'Where is the farm machinery stored?'

'It's kept in a storage facility a couple of miles from the offices. Although about twelve months ago he talked about buying an additional place on the outskirts of Leicester, which he said was to be for overspill. But, to be honest, that seemed strange because he doesn't hold a lot of stock at any one time.'

'How much of this does Lee know?'

'Everything. I probably shouldn't have told him, but he overheard me talking to my husband about it.'

'I thought he died several years ago?' Birdie said, frowning.

'He did. But I still speak to him when I want advice. It

helps.' She shrugged, an embarrassed expression on her face.

'I understand. I still talk to my granddad,' Birdie said, wanting to put the woman at ease. And it was the truth, anyway. 'Does Rawlings come into the office every day?'

'He has a set routine. His driver picks him up at eight every morning and then he will either come into the office or he might go out for an appointment, after which he will be here until at least five in the evening, if not later, and then he's picked up and taken home.'

'When you say appointments, do you know exactly where he goes and for what purpose?'

'No. Only his PA would know that … I think.'

'We need you to find out as much as you can regarding his movements during the day and report it back to us. Here's my card.' Birdie pulled a card from her pocket and passed it to her.

'Okay, I'll try. What else should I be doing?'

'Go to work and carry on as normal. Don't do anything that will arouse suspicion. Someone will be in touch with you again soon.'

# Chapter 6

When Seb arrived at the care home, Whitney was waiting for him by the front entrance. He hurried over, annoyed with himself that he was late for their appointment, despite having left with plenty of time to spare.

'Sorry, I got caught in traffic,' he said when he reached her. 'The lights aren't working at the junction off the main road, leading in this direction.'

'Don't worry about it. I know exactly where you mean. There are always hold-ups around that part of the city. It's the worst place to drive through, especially during rush hour.'

'This looks a charming place.' He nodded at the entrance to the large Edwardian building, which had white double doors with brass handles.

'It's not in the best state of repair inside, as you'll see, but the place is clean, and the staff are excellent. Most of them have worked at the home for a long time, and the quality of care they provide is faultless. So what if the furniture is a bit worn and the place could do with a lick of paint? What's most important is how comfortable my mother is, and she's happy. I have no complaints.'

'I'm pleased to hear it. It must alleviate some of the worry of having her here.'

'Yes, that's exactly it.'

'How many residents are there?'

'Only twenty, which means each one is more than just a number. The staff think of them all as being part of one large family. Each person has their own bedroom with an en suite. If we have time after we've seen Mum, I'll show you around.'

'Does your mother know we're visiting her today?'

'I decided against telling her in advance in case our plans changed. Although she probably wouldn't have remembered, anyway. Let's keep our fingers crossed that she's with it and can tell us something that will help. This bloody dementia. She seems to be having more bad days than good recently.' Whitney's eyes filled with tears, and Seb rested a hand on her arm to comfort her.

'I'm sorry. It must be very hard for you.'

She sniffed and pulled away from him, marching towards the front door with purpose. He followed her into a large vestibule and up to the reception desk where a member of staff was seated.

'Hello, Angela. We've come to visit Mum. I take it she's in the day room watching telly?' Whitney asked, a bright smile on her face. Except it didn't quite reach her eyes, which remained a little glassy.

'Yes, she went straight in there after dinner.'

'What sort of day has she had?' Whitney completed the visitors' book and then passed it over to Seb.

'So-so. She tends to be more with it in the mornings but, hopefully, she'll be okay. She does always perk up a bit when you visit.'

Seb hoped Angela was right, or it would be difficult to learn anything from the elderly woman.

When they reached the day room, he glanced around. There were around ten people in there, mainly women, all seated at one end on individual chairs.

'Is that your mother over there?' he asked, spotting a petite grey-haired woman sitting at the back of the room, looking towards the large TV on the wall.

'Yes. How do you know?' Whitney asked, her brows furrowed.

'I could tell straight away, by her build and the shape of her face. It's similar to yours. Also, the way she's seated, leaning over slightly to the left. You have the identical mannerism.'

'Oh.' Whitney laughed. 'I've always thought I was more like my dad.' She sighed. 'He's been dead for a long time now.'

'I'm sorry.'

'It's okay. I still miss him, though. We all do.'

They headed over, and Seb made sure to keep one step behind. He didn't want to alarm the woman with his presence. His size was often intimidating to people who didn't know him.

'Hi, Mum, how are you today?' Whitney leant in and kissed her on the cheek.

'Hello, Whitney.'

The woman appeared alert, which he assumed was a good sign.

'Mum, this is my friend, Seb.' Whitney indicated towards him, and he stepped to the side so he could be seen.

'Hello, Mrs Walker.'

'Goodness, you're tall.' She stared at Seb, her eyes

wide, looking him up and down. 'I've never seen anyone that big in my life.'

'Mum, stop. You'll embarrass him.'

'It's perfectly fine. I'm used to people talking about my height. Good to meet you.' He leant forward and held out his hand. Mrs Walker took it in both of hers and looked up at him.

'And are you and Whitney … you know?' She smiled at Seb and winked.

'No, Mum, he's a friend. There's nothing going on between us.' Whitney laughed and glanced at him.

'We're definitely just good friends,' he added, grinning.

'That's a shame. You're a very handsome boy. Are you married?'

'No.'

'So there's still a chance for you and my Whitney, then?'

'Mum, there's nothing between me and Seb, and there isn't going to be. We're friends.' Whitney rolled her eyes.

'Okay, dear. But he still looks like a good catch to me.'

'Let's go and sit on the other side of the day room where it's less crowded and we can talk,' Whitney suggested, turning her head away from her mother and mouthing, 'Sorry,' to Seb.

He shrugged and smiled. It was no problem to him. He was amused by the older woman's outspokenness, although he supposed it might have been the result of the dementia.

'If that's what you want to do, love.'

Her mum eased herself off the chair, and Whitney took her arm, guiding her to where there were three easy chairs placed near a large picture window.

Whitney leant forward and took hold of her mum's hands. 'We'd like to ask you some questions about Rob and when he was attacked. Do you remember when it happened, Mum?'

'Of course, I'll never forget that.' Tears welled in the woman's eyes, and she brushed them away with the back of her hand. 'It was a long time ago. Why do you want to know?'

'I've got some spare time at work and decided to look into it because there wasn't much discovered at the time. Seb has said that he'll help me.'

'Are you a policeman?'

'I used to be.'

'Have you retired? You don't look old enough.' Mrs Walker frowned.

'I'm working for myself now and—'

'We'd like to know more about Rob before the accident. I can't remember much because I was too young,' Whitney interrupted.

He nodded his approval. Whitney had explained that her mother dropped in and out of reality very quickly, so they needed to discover as much as they could while she was lucid.

'I don't know that there's much to tell you. He was a typical teenage boy. Always out. Never at home. Sometimes your dad would ask him to have an evening in with the family, but he always refused. He preferred to be out with his friends.'

'Do you know where they went?'

'He'd never tell us where he was going, and if I asked the next day where he'd been, he would say, "Just around." He was no different from other boys of his age.'

'What do you remember about the day of the accident?' Whitney asked gently.

'Rob went out early and didn't want any tea. The next morning, I noticed his bedroom door was open and his bed still made, so I knew that he hadn't come home. I didn't think anything of it. It's not like he hadn't stayed out all night before.'

'Where would he go when he stayed out all night, Mum?'

'He'd stay at one of his friends' houses and not phone because it was late. If only we'd known …' Her voice drifted.

'Then what happened?'

'A little while after that, the police came to the house to tell us he was in hospital and had been badly assaulted. It was the worst day of my life. My poor boy.' A single tear rolled down her cheek, and Whitney pulled out a tissue from her pocket and wiped her mother's eye.

'I'm sorry to put you through this, Mum,' Whitney said.

'It's okay, love. If it helps you find out who did this.'

'Can you remember who Rob's friends were?' Whitney asked.

'I'm not sure. It was so long ago. Oh … There were two. One especially wasn't nice. I didn't like him, nor did your dad. He showed no respect when he came round to the house. Marching his dirty trainers through the hall, you know. I think he led Rob astray a bit. His family were bad sorts.'

'How did you know all this?' Seb asked.

'I'd hear them talking sometimes in his room. They both went to school with Rob.'

'Do you remember their names, by any chance?'

'Um … I think … Was one called Gary? No. It was Gareth. That's it. Gareth. He was the nasty one. I don't remember the name of the other boy.'

'Were they with Rob on the night he got attacked?'

'I don't know. Nobody said anything at the time.'

'What about girlfriends? Did Rob have one?' Seb asked.

'I think he did, but he didn't bring her home. I could tell when he was going to see her because he'd take more care with his appearance. His hair would be all nice, and I could smell the aftershave on him. I remember one time asking whether he was going to meet a girl. And he told me to mind my own business.'

'Oh, that was rude,' Whitney said.

'You know what teenagers are like. He didn't mean it. You had your moments, too, if I remember. And I bet you were the same, too,' Whitney's mum said, looking at Seb.

'I'm sure you're right, Mrs Walker.' He laughed.

'Mum, can you remember whether Rob had made an effort with his appearance on the night he was attacked? Do think he was meeting her?'

'I don't know, Whitney … I … Why are you asking me these questions? I want to go and watch the telly now. Who are you?' She looked at Seb and scowled.

'This is my friend,' Whitney said.

'What are you doing here? You haven't visited before, have you?'

'No. This is my first time, Mrs Walker. I wanted to say hello.'

'Well, hello and goodbye. My programme has started, and I've got to watch it.' She pointed to the TV screen.

'It's her favourite soap,' Whitney said to him. 'We'll leave you now, Mum.'

'Okay, goodbye.' Mrs Walker got up from the chair and shuffled back to where she'd previously been sitting.

'This is how it is sometimes. She drifts in and out with no warning.'

'I understand. She's given us some useful information. I can find out who this Gareth was from the school records.

It's not particularly a common name around here. And then we might be able to track down Rob's other friend.'

'Thanks. Why don't you come to the station tomorrow morning and work from there? I've got you a visitor pass in my car. I'll give it to you when we leave. Have you had a chance to look through the police file that I emailed? You'll have seen that there's very little in there. No witnesses, other than the person who found him.'

'Yes, I did read it. It's given me a place to start.'

'I've been thinking about you wanting to visit Rob and decided that you should get cracking on the investigation, first, because it's not like he'll be able to tell you anything. If we need to speak to him at a later date, then we will. But if we can avoid distressing him, I'd much prefer that.'

'I agree, that's the sensible way forward. I'd like to visit the place where Rob was found as soon as possible.'

'We'll add that to our list of things to do tomorrow.'

'Does that mean you can take some time out to come with me?'

'I'm the boss. Of course, I can.'

# Chapter 7

Birdie pulled into the Market Harborough police station car park and grabbed her bag from the back seat. She checked her hair in the mirror and was about to pull out her brush when a car horn blasted out across the street.

What the …?

She looked up. Twiggy was leaning heavily on the horn of his car, looking very animated. All right, keep your hair on. She jumped out of her car and ran over to his grey Toyota Corolla.

'Why did you do that?' she asked, sliding into the passenger seat and pulling across the seatbelt, slotting it in place.

'Because we need to get going and I know what you're like. We can't be late to take over the surveillance.'

'Even if you did wake up everybody in the neighbour-hood. For goodness' sake, Twiggy. What on earth's got into you?'

She didn't get it. He wasn't usually so thoughtless.

'It's six-thirty, and most people will be getting ready for work.'

'In whose universe? What about people who work nights or shifts? There was no need to do it, that's all I'm saying.'

'I wanted to make sure you hurried up so we wouldn't be late. You can hardly blame me with your track record.'

'I'm not getting into this now, there's no time. Let's go. I assume Rawlings is still at home if he's sticking to his routine.'

'Yes, he is. I've received a text from O'Malley to say they're still outside. And I've programmed his address into my satnav. It's Oxendon Road, Arthingworth.'

He pulled off without another word and drove to the end of Fairfield Road before heading out of town towards Arthingworth on the A508.

'Did you have a good evening?' Birdie asked, conscious of the silence that hung between them.

'Had dinner. Nagged the kids to do their homework. Watched telly. Went to bed. Same old boring stuff.'

'Don't you ever go out and have some fun? You know, for a drink, or meal, or something?'

'No, because I'm usually too knackered. That's what happens when you've got responsibilities. What did you get up to?'

'I was at Seb's place last night looking after Elsa. We went out for a long walk, and then I chatted with my friend Tori for a while and later listened to some music.'

'I don't get it.' Twiggy tossed a glance in her direction, a frown on his face.

'Get what?'

'Your friendship with that man. You couldn't be more different from each other if you tried, and it's not like you're working together anymore. Or even planning to.'

Oh, not this again. 'We don't have a case at the

moment, no, but that doesn't mean I won't consider joining him in the future.'

Really? Why did she say that? She'd been thinking about the job offer but hadn't planned on sharing it with Twiggy because she knew what his response would be. He'd let his opinion of Seb cloud his judgement. And she needed objectivity.

'Has he asked you to?' he asked, an accusatory expression on his face. 'Why would you want to give up your career as a police officer to work as a PI? You love police work,' he continued.

'Yeah, you're right. Apart from when I'm on desk duty, obviously. Look, I'm not saying that I will join Seb, but I haven't totally discounted it.'

'You'd be crazy to give it all up. I can't see you spending your time following unfaithful spouses, or worse, being some insurance company's lackey.'

'You're so stereotypical, Twiggy. The work isn't all like that.'

'I think you'll find that most PI work is deadly dull.'

Normally, she'd agree, but Seb had said he was only interested in taking on intriguing cases. But would that be possible? If she was working with him, she'd need money to live, so it could turn out that they'd have to take the boring, regular cases. It was fine for him because he could afford to be choosy with his clients – even if he did say he needed the money, she didn't believe him. How could someone in his position be strapped for cash?

'Maybe. Anyway, I don't want to talk about it now. We need to focus on today. We'll wait for Rawlings' driver to pick him up, and we'll follow them to see where he goes. He could be heading straight into work unless he has an appointment.'

'It's going to be a boring day. Did you bring anything to eat?'

Twiggy and his stomach were so predictable. 'No. We can stop and get something, which I'm sure is what you'd already decided.'

'That was the plan, but whether we have time depends on where he goes.'

'If he's at the office, one of us can pop out and get something. I've had breakfast, so won't need to eat yet. What about you?'

'Some people might describe what I had as breakfast. But I don't.'

'Another smoothie?' She tried, unsuccessfully, to suppress a giggle.

'You've got it in one, and it's not funny.'

They'd reached the quaint village of Arthingworth. Victor Rawlings' place wouldn't be far now. Birdie glanced at Twiggy's satnav. 'Take the next road on the left out of the village,' she said.

They continued for a couple of miles until coming to a long driveway. The large house, with extensive outbuildings and paddocks on either side of it, could be seen in the distance, facing south over the rolling countryside.

'Bloody hell, look at the size of that mansion. Some people have all the luck,' Twiggy said, parking behind the car belonging to the officers from Wigston. They immediately started their engine, did a U-turn in the road, and drove away, giving them a wave as they went.

'Boy … Who knew that *farm machinery* was so lucrative?'

'Farm machinery, my arse. If he didn't inherit this pile, then it's thanks to firearms and whatever other pies he has his fingers in.'

'You've changed your tune. I thought Rawlings walked on water for you,' Birdie said.

'I've been thinking about it more since we spoke to Margaret Clarke. As much as it pains me to say it, all this charity work could be a front.'

After they'd been watching the house for ten minutes, a silver Mercedes drove past them and turned onto the drive. From their vantage point, they could see it the entire time as it went up the long, winding drive and reached the top. The car remained stationary outside the front door. Birdie picked up the binoculars.

'There's one man in the driver's seat. The front door has opened, and it looks like Rawlings is coming out. As we expected. He's in the car and they're now heading our way. Get ready to follow him. Keep our distance so they don't spot us.'

# Chapter 8

'Hey, Seb, wait.'

At the sound of his name, he reversed out of the lift at Lenchester station and saw Whitney heading towards him.

'I was on my way to see you.'

'In that case, you can join me in the cafeteria for a coffee. And, if I remember correctly, you also have a penchant for doughnuts, so we'll have those, too. The cafeteria's over there.' She pointed to the left of the reception. 'Which of course, you already know from when you worked with us before.'

'Are you sure you want to spend time in there? We've now less than two weeks to work on the case – shouldn't we hit the ground running?'

'You've clearly forgotten what it's like working with me. You know I need my regular caffeine fix if I'm to have a clear head. Don't worry – we won't stay there long.'

The cafeteria was busy, but they managed to find a table in the far corner where they sat with their coffee and doughnuts. Whitney had been right about his love for them, and these were especially good.

'First, I'm going to find out where Rob's friend Gareth now lives,' Seb said, voicing out loud his list for the day.

'Already done,' Whitney said with a nod. 'I asked Ellie to look into it when she arrived earlier. It didn't take her long. He's called Gareth Collins and is still living locally. She'll give you the address when we go upstairs.'

He nodded his approval. 'That's excellent. He should be able to tell us the name of Rob's other friend. I'll visit him this morning. Unless you want to go to the place Rob was found, first?'

'Change of plans. I can't get away this morning, so why don't you go and see Gareth and then come back for me. We'll go to the park together later. I've got a meeting with Superintendent Clyde, and, unfortunately, you-know-who is probably going to be there.'

'I'm sure it can't be that bad, considering he's not your immediate boss. Doesn't the super cover your back?'

'When she can. Anyway, let's not talk about Douglas. We should go upstairs and get you started.'

The second he stepped inside the CID incident room, he was comforted by the sound of the officers working. They were a good team, and he'd enjoyed working with them in the past.

'Hey, it's the viscount,' Frank, one of the older detective constables, called out as they walked past his desk.

'You can cut that out, straight away, Frank,' Whitney said, glaring at him. 'Sorry about that, Seb, but you know what he's like.'

'Don't worry, I'm used to it. Good to see you, Frank. I see nothing's changed.'

'You know I'm only joking, don't you? How are you, guv?'

'Not *guv* anymore, Frank. Seb will do.'

'Or you can call him Mr Clifford,' Doug, one of the other DCs sitting at the opposite desk, said laughing.

'Who asked you?' Frank said, scowling in his fellow officer's direction.

Their swipes at one another were legendary, but they were very good friends. In Seb's experience, the whole team gelled, and no one pulled rank. It was down to Whitney's excellent leadership that such hard work and loyalty were engendered.

'Get on with your work boys. We don't want to scare off Seb before he's had time to start work. Ellie, can you give Seb the home address for Gareth Collins, please?'

'Yes, guv,' DC Ellie Naylor said.

DC Naylor was Whitney's secret weapon. There was nothing the officer couldn't discover. Seb had never met such a talented researcher. If she couldn't find it, no one could. It fascinated him that she had no idea how good she really was, despite being praised and helping them solve so many of their cases. Thanks to Whitney, he'd been able to enlist her help on one of the cases he'd worked on with Birdie, and she'd come up trumps.

Ellie called out the address, and he keyed it into his phone. He'd need to use his satnav to find out exactly where the place was because he was unfamiliar with much of the city.

'Before you leave, let's go through to my office to tidy up any loose ends,' Whitney said.

He followed her to the door at the end of the incident room and into her office, a square modern room, which Whitney had mentioned on several occasions lacked character. He glanced at the photo of Tiffany holding her baby situated beside the computer screen.

'What a lovely photo.'

'Yes, it's one of my favourites.'

She headed over to one of the black chairs around the low glass coffee table and gestured for him to join her.

'What else do you wish to discuss? I thought it was all sorted.'

'It is. I wanted to remind you that if you're approached by anyone outside of the team, don't mention my involvement in any part of the investigation. If Douglas gets hold of it, there could be trouble. And that's putting it mildly.'

'Whitney, you should know me better than that. As far as anyone else is concerned, I'm a consultant on your team, and all you're going to be doing is signing off on my expenses and receiving my report at the end of the fortnight.'

'I know, but it had to be said or it will be nagging at the back of my mind. You go and see Collins, and then we'll catch up later. Unless there's anything else you'd like to discuss?'

'No, there's nothing. It's good to be back here with the rest of the team. I enjoy their dynamic. Some things never change.'

'You're telling me, right? But I wouldn't have it any other way.'

Seb took the lift down to the front entrance and returned to his car. He had no idea whether Gareth Collins was going to be at home or if he was at work. Ellie had only given him a home address, so possibly he didn't have a job. Or if he did, it was off the records.

Seb drove through the city to a run-down terraced house on Albany Street. A man who looked to be around forty answered the door. He had a shaved head, a slight paunch, and translucent skin, as if he hadn't seen daylight in a while. An old silver scar ran down the side of his left cheek from beneath his eye to just above his lip.

'What do you want?' he growled, giving a raspy smoker's cough.

'I'm looking for Gareth Collins. Is that you?' Seb stared down at the man, using his height and build to intimidate.

'Yeah, what of it?' the man said, an uncertain tone in his voice. He took a step back.

'My name's Sebastian Clifford, and I wish to talk to you about Rob Walker.'

'Who?' Collins paused for a moment. 'Oh … you mean from school?'

'Yes, that's right. I understand that you and Rob were friends until the time he was attacked.'

'It was nothing to do with me,' Collins replied quickly.

*Too* quickly.

'I didn't say it was. I'm looking into the attack and wish to ask you some questions.'

'Are you the police?'

'I'm working for the police as a consultant on this case.' He held out his ID, and Collins gave it a cursory glance.

'Does that mean I have to speak to you?'

'You have the right to refuse, but if what happened to Rob was nothing to do with you, as you stated, then why would you?'

'Because you're a copper and I don't talk to them unless I'm under arrest.'

'How often does that happen?'

'Check the records for yourself. Anyway, no point in asking me questions because it happened twenty-five years ago, and I can't remember that far back.' He folded his arms and leant against the peeling white paint on the door frame.

'Yet you remember how long ago it was.' Seb took a step closer, and Collins stiffened.

'So what?'

'I'd rather not speak on the doorstep. May I come inside, and we can discuss this matter in private?' Seb glanced to the left and could see people heading up the street in their direction.

'I suppose so.' Collins opened the door, and Seb walked into the narrow hall.

An overpowering smell of stale smoke permeated Seb's nostrils, and he was tempted to request the man accompany him to the station instead, but he wasn't convinced he'd agree. The place clearly hadn't been cleaned in a long time; there were dark stains on the worn floral carpet and splatters up the walls. He followed Collins into a sitting room, which was just as dirty and had a faded green corded two-seater sofa on one side and two single chairs on the other. They were all pointing towards a large television mounted on the wall. Beer cans littered the floor and were piled on the oval coffee table in the middle of the room.

'Do you live here alone?' he asked, scanning the room and seeing no signs of anyone else's presence.

'I do now. My wife and I split up six months ago. She ran off with my best mate, but I'm gonna get him back for it.'

'How do you intend to do that?'

'None of your business. It's got nothing to do with Rob. Right, ask your questions.' Collins sat on the sofa, and Seb sat on one of the chairs after moving a pile of magazines onto the floor. He'd rather have remained standing, but that would've made the questioning awkward, and he wanted as much info as he could get.

'How long were you and Rob friends for?' he asked.

'We started junior school together and went right through to secondary school.'

'And were you good friends for all that time?' Seb stared intently, checking for any tells that might demonstrate Collins wasn't being truthful.

'Not really. We became better friends when we got to secondary school, and we started hanging out a lot more together when we were about fourteen.'

'Would you say that you knew him very well?'

'Well enough.' Collins shrugged.

'Were you best friends?'

'Yeah, I suppose we were. Why?'

'I wish to ascertain how close your friendship was because it might help the investigation. When I spoke to Rob's mother, she mentioned your name.'

'That old bag never liked me.'

'That doesn't matter. Please answer my question.'

'All right. We hung out together, you know. He helped me when I had some jobs to do for my older brother, Keith.'

Seb went on alert. Could that have been something to do with why Rob had been attacked?

'What sort of jobs exactly?'

'This and that.'

'Can you be more specific?'

'I don't know. Taking messages. Delivering stuff. Like I said, this and that. It gave us something to do instead of hanging round town. It was a long time ago and nothing to do with why Rob got beat up.'

'How can you be certain of that?'

'Use your head, mate. Because if that was the reason, why was it just him and not me? Rob never did anything for Keith on his own.'

'If that's the case, do you know anyone who might have

targeted Rob? Someone he'd had an altercation with, perhaps.'

'Don't ask me because I haven't the foggiest. Are you recording this conversation because I haven't given my permission?' Gareth sat forward on the edge of the sofa.

'I'm not.'

'Then why aren't you writing notes? I don't want you going off and making stuff up about what I've said. Where's your phone? Prove you're not recording me.'

'I have a retentive memory and have no need for notes.'

'What, one of those photographic ones?'

'Something like that.' Seb pulled his mobile from his pocket. 'You can see that this phone is not on recording mode.'

'Okay. Well, you better not start when you think I'm not looking.' Collins leant back into the sofa.

'What about Rob's other friends, is there anyone else I could speak to? Mrs Walker mentioned that there were three of you who hung out together.'

'You mean Marty McNeil? Yeah, we were all mates.'

'Did he accompany you and Rob when you worked for your brother?'

'Sometimes.'

'Do you still see him?'

'Nah, not for years. He got a girl up the duff and had to marry her. He left school after that and got a job. I haven't seen him since.'

'Was this after the attack on Rob?'

'Yeah, I think so. Not sure how long after. Is that it? Because I'm going out soon.' He drummed his fingers impatiently on his knee.

'Around the time of the attack, did Rob have a girl-friend that you knew of?'

'You mean the posh bitch?'

'I have no idea of her background. Can you tell me her name?'

'I don't know.' Collins stared directly at Seb, unblinking. A sure sign he wasn't telling the truth.

'Try again. You *do* know who I'm talking about. What's her name?' Seb leant forward in his chair and stared directly at Collins.

Collins squirmed and averted his eyes. 'Look, all I know is her first name was Charli, and she had some sort of hold over him. After she came along, we didn't hang out together so much. Don't ask me anything else about her because I don't know.'

The man's reluctance to talk was telling.

'I'm sure there's more you remember about their relationship. For how long were they a couple?'

'How am I expected to remember that?'

'Try,' Seb demanded.

'I don't know. Maybe six months. Could be a bit longer. You'll have to ask her.'

'And you don't know her surname?'

'I just told you I didn't. Get off my case.'

'Did she go to your school?'

'No, she was too posh for us lot. And before you ask. I don't know where she went, and I don't know where she lives. You know everything that I know. Got it?'

He couldn't meet Seb's eyes. He was lying. But why? How much did he really know?

'Where did Rob first meet her?'

'No idea.'

'How old was Charli?'

'Our age. I think.'

'What did she look like?'

'Why does that matter? It's not like she'll look like that now, after all these years?'

'I'd still like to know.'

'Okay. She had dark hair and was pretty. Spoke with a posh voice, and that really is all I know. I'm saying nothing else without a solicitor.'

'Do you believe you need one?'

'No. I haven't done anything. But I know what you lot are like. You'll try to make out I've something to do with what happened to Rob. So why don't you just piss off.' Collins marched out of the living room to the front door and opened it, gesturing for Seb to leave.

'Thank you for your cooperation. Of sorts. I may return to speak to you further.'

# Chapter 9

'Come in,' Whitney called when Seb knocked on her door.

'I've returned from interviewing Collins. Are you free now for a debrief?' he asked.

She stood up from behind her desk and walked around to join him. 'Of course. I'm glad to be distracted from my pile of admin. Have a seat. Was it successful?'

'It was both interesting and informative. He denied all knowledge about the attack, which was to be expected. I asked about the other friend and Collins gave the name Marty McNeil. He said the three of them often worked for his older brother, Keith, but he was vague about what that entailed. I didn't push it, in case he clammed up all together. Do you remember this McNeil?'

'No. That name doesn't ring a bell.'

'I also learnt that Rob had a girlfriend called Charli. She must be who your mother mentioned.'

'Was the relationship serious?'

'Collins didn't say, but from how he talked about her and the hold she had over Rob, I wouldn't be surprised if it was. Especially from his side.'

'That's crazy. And none of us knew anything about this girl. What else did Collins tell you about her?'

'He thought Charli was about the same age as him and Rob, and he described her as being pretty and posh. She didn't go to their school, and he couldn't tell me her surname.'

'This is ridiculous. How come none of this came out at the time of the assault? Still, the main thing is we now know of the girl's existence. I'm taking Rob to see Mum this evening. I'll try to find out more about her then. Mum might remember something. Rob, too, for that matter. Do think this girl—I mean *woman*. We can hardly call her a girl if she's now in her forties. Does this woman know anything about the attack?'

'It's far too early to make any connection, but it certainly can't be dismissed, and it's a good lead.'

'Hmm. What about if another boy was involved, and he was the person to attack Rob? It wouldn't be the first time a jilted boyfriend went on the rampage. Especially at that age, when they're all hormones, muscle, and not a lot else.'

'Again, it's too soon to make that supposition. But it's certainly something to consider. Although, I'd have thought Collins might have said if there'd been a love rival. We should look into Keith Collins to find out exactly what work the three boys did for him.'

'Was it dodgy?'

'I wouldn't be surprised.'

'True. Stupid question. I'll get Ellie onto it.' Whitney walked over to her desk, picked up the handset, and pressed one of the keys. 'Ellie, a few things. I'd like you to find a Marty McNeil who went to school with Rob. Can you also look into Keith Collins, Gareth's brother, and see if you can locate a girl named Charli, who was Rob's girlfriend ... Thanks.' Whitney ended the call and replaced the phone. 'Are you ready to visit the park where Rob was found?'

'Whenever you are. I'm assuming we're going in my car?'

'You assumed right.' She grinned.

'I've parked in the station car park.'

'No doubt in the far corner, so your lovely car isn't damaged. Don't deny it.'

'I had no intention of doing so.'

'Good. Rob was found in—'

'Anderson Park. It was in the file.'

'Of which you know the entire contents already. I keep forgetting about your weird memory thing.'

'It's not weird. Tiresome at times, maybe, but not weird.'

'That's a matter of opinion. What's your feedback on the file now you've committed the entire thing to memory?'

'Very few people were interviewed at the time or came forward voluntarily. Obviously, the person who found Rob was interviewed, and officers questioned Rob, your parents, and you. They also spoke to students at the school in a group, but not individually. In particular, it seems strange that neither Collins nor McNeil were questioned outside of the larger school group. We don't even know *if* they were a part of the group interviewed. Do you know why they weren't singled out?'

'I've no idea, but it does seem strange.'

'It would be worth speaking to the person who found Rob, if she's still alive and living in the vicinity.'

'Sure. Let's go and see Ellie.'

They left her office through the door leading directly into the incident room and headed over to where the officer was seated. 'Another name to add to your list, Ellie.

Please could you check the whereabouts of …' She turned to Seb. 'Do you have the file with you?'

'It's in the car. Why do you need it?'

'For the name and details of the person who found Rob. Except …'

'You don't need the file,' he said, finishing off her sentence. 'Ellie, the person's name is Mabel Dent, and at the time of the attack, she lived at number thirty-five Tanner Street. There was no phone number listed.'

'So impressive,' Ellie murmured, her fingers already tapping the keys on her keyboard.

'Hopefully she'll still be alive,' Whitney said, turning to face the rest of the team. 'Listen up, everyone. Seb and I are going to Anderson Park, which is where my brother was found following the attack. If anyone asks where I am, say you don't know. Especially if it's Chief Superintendent Douglas.'

'I'm surprised you didn't invite him along, guv,' Frank called out.

'Thank you, Frank,' Whitney said, glancing up at the ceiling and giving an eye roll. 'See you all later.'

Anderson Park was on the opposite side of the city to the police station, and it took Seb a while to drive through the congested centre to reach it. Many of the houses in the built-up area backed onto the park.

'It wasn't like this years ago. All this development has sprung up over the last ten years. The price of progress. Rows and rows of identical boxes. I wonder how they'll be viewed in a hundred years' time.' Whitney pointed to the modern terraced houses across the road and shook her head.

'If they last that long. Properties nowadays aren't built to the same standard as in the past.'

'You're right. They'll undoubtably put a bulldozer through the lot of them. Which might not be a bad idea.'

Seb turned his attention to the park. 'According to the file, they ascertained the attack didn't take place here because there was no blood anywhere other than what was on the bench where Rob had been and that which was on his body and clothes. An extensive search of the park was undertaken, and no evidence was discovered. There weren't any bloodstains on the path leading to where he was found; or on any of the paths coming into the park from any direction. Based on that, we can safely assume that Rob didn't walk here. He was most likely carried and dumped.' He glanced across at Whitney. The lines around her eyes were tight, as if she was struggling to keep focused and distance herself from the event. 'Are you okay? I can do this on my own if you'd rather.'

'Don't worry about me. I'm fine. We can say with confidence that Rob would have been brought here in a car, and we know that all those years ago, there were unlikely to be any cameras in the vicinity. Not that we'd be able to access the footage now, even if there was.'

They walked further into the park. 'It's tidy and the play equipment looks new. How does it compare with twenty-five years ago?'

'You wouldn't know it was the same place. In the past, because the park was isolated, it wasn't the place families spent their time in. Dog walkers and older kids hanging out smoking or doing drugs were the main users. There wasn't any play equipment, other than some old rusty swings going back to the fifties, which were situated much further inside and removed years ago. They were nowhere near the bench where Rob was found.'

'Do you happen to know the exact location? There's no map in the file, so I can't pinpoint the precise spot.'

'Yes, because after it happened, I came out on the bus to check where it was. I was sort of hoping to find a clue that the police had missed. My parents didn't know. They'd have tried to stop me if I'd told them, in case it upset me or put me in danger. I remember standing by the bench and staring at the blood. It was months before it stopped being my first thought when I woke up in the morning.' She grimaced.

'That would have been stressful for anyone, let alone a fourteen-year-old girl. When you were there, did you see anything that gave you pause for thought?'

'Not really. I came with one of my friends, and we walked through the park and went directly to the bench. We saw the bloodstains on it but nothing anywhere else. I don't even know if that particular bench is still here. We'll take a look, and you can see for yourself where it was. It's this way.'

He followed her along one of the paths that led away from the centre of the park and closer to the boundary. She stopped by an old wooden bench with several missing slats, which was situated close to a dense laurel hedge.

'Is this it?'

'Yes. It looks the same as it did all those years ago. I …' She paused, her bottom lip trembling.

'Are you okay? Being here after all this time must be difficult for you.'

'I had a flashback to when I visited Rob in hospital. His face … Oh my God, it was just … I can't even describe it. And … he didn't really recognise me, that's what hurt even more. He didn't talk again for ages after. He spent the time staring into space.'

'It would have been difficult for everyone.'

'Nothing was ever the same again. Not for any of us. He …' Her voice cracked. 'Sorry.'

'Don't apologise. Dragging everything up is bound to affect you.'

'I know, but it's not going to help our investigation if I can't hold it together.'

He rested his arm around her shoulder and gave a comforting squeeze. Then he turned his attention back to the place where Rob was found.

'We know he was discovered here by Mabel Dent, and we have no explanation regarding how he got there. It was certainly a good place to leave him because the area was isolated. If he was carried here, it's likely that there was more than one person involved.'

'There had to have been. Rob's always been tall and well built. He takes after my dad. I'm like Mum in build and height. And we know he wasn't dragged along the ground because there were no bloodstains.'

Seb glanced over his shoulder at the way they'd come. 'But even so, if a car was parked along the main road where we came in, it could have been seen by passers-by, and someone might have phoned it in after, especially if they'd seen the media coverage of the attack. Is there another way to get into the park? Somewhere less public.'

'There's the back road, but it would have meant carrying Rob a long way. But if there were two or more of them carrying him, it would be possible.'

'Is it walking distance from here, or do we have to drive?'

'I know a shortcut. It won't take long. Follow me.'

She led him through the park, off the paths, and over some flower beds until they reached a nicer area, where there were some well-tended borders and modern benches. They passed two mothers with babies in pushchairs, their other young children playing with balls. Adjacent to them was an entrance to the park, which took them into a deserted back road.

'This seems a more likely place for the attackers to park,' Seb said.

'Yes, I'm sure you're right, but how is it helping us?'

'It's giving an overall picture of what occurred. Let's go back to the station, and I'll check how Ellie's doing. By the way, is it possible to speak to DS Jacks, the officer in charge of the case at the time? He might have something to offer the investigation.'

'I'll ask Ellie to track him down.'

Whitney was quieter than usual on the journey back, and Seb occasionally glanced in her direction. But each time, she was deep in thought. Being faced with the reality of her brother's attack couldn't have been easy for her.

When they arrived back, they headed straight for Ellie's desk.

'Any news?' Whitney asked.

'I was about to text you, guv. I have good news and bad.'

'I'll have the good first.'

'Mabel Dent still lives in the same house – she's been there since 1980 – and I've tracked down Keith Collins, who lives in New Parks, close to Leicester.'

'Excellent. Does he have a record?' Seb asked.

'Several minor offences. I also have a home and work address for Martin, aka Marty, McNeil. He's still around here.'

'And the bad?'

'I've drawn a blank on Charli, but I'll keep checking. It's not going to beat me.'

'Thanks, Ellie. Text the Dent, Collins, and McNeil addresses to Seb. Also, I'd like contact details for DS Jacks, the officer who worked on the case. I'm assuming he's retired by now.'

'Yes, guv. Leave it with me.'

Whitney and Seb left the incident room and returned to Whitney's office.

'I'm going to see Mabel Dent and then Marty McNeil. From there, I'll head back to my accommodation to work. I want to do some research, and it will be less distracting than working from here. Collins can wait until I return to Market Harborough, which will probably be tomorrow.'

'Okay. Once I've spoken with Rob and Mum later, I'll phone you with any additional information they give me.'

She turned and faced him, her eyes filled with concern. 'Tell me honestly, do you think we're going to find out what happened to my brother?'

Time might be getting away from them, but he was determined to do what he could. Even if it meant no sleep for the next eleven days.

'If we can't solve the case, then nobody can.'

# Chapter 10

Seb drew up outside the Victorian terraced house in Tanner Road, where Mabel Dent lived. The street was in stark contrast to its developed surroundings. It had character and well-established trees lining the sides. He gauged it be a twenty-minute walk from there to Anderson Park.

He rang the bell and took a step back, not wanting to intimidate whoever answered. After about thirty seconds, he heard a shuffling sound, and a man who looked to be in his early seventies answered.

'Yes?'

'Hello. I'm looking for Mrs Dent. Is she in?'

'That's my wife. Who are you?'

Seb smiled politely. 'My name's Clifford, and I work for Lenchester Police. I'd like to ask her some questions regarding an incident she witnessed twenty-five years ago.'

The man's brow furrowed. 'Do you mean the time when she found that poor boy who'd been beaten to a pulp?'

'Yes, that's the case I'm currently investigating.'

'Why now? She told the police everything she knew at

the time. Which wasn't much. All she did was find the boy. She had no idea how he got there or who he'd been with. It was very traumatic for her at the time, and it took ages before she'd walk in the park again, even with me. She never did go back there alone. I hope you're not going to upset her.'

'That's not my intention, Mr Dent. But some evidence has come to light regarding the case, and although we have no idea whether it will lead to anything, it's important enough not to ignore. Please could you get your wife.' He kept his voice low but insistent.

'You'll have to come inside and speak to her because she's not very mobile now. She's in the lounge watching telly. The afternoon quiz shows are her favourite.'

'Here's my identification.' Seb held out the Lenchester Police ID that he'd been given by Whitney.

He'd been surprised that the man had invited him into his home without first checking. Some people were far too trusting for their own good.

Mr Dent stared at the ID and then opened the door fully so Seb could walk into the hallway. 'This way.'

Seb followed him into a small, bright, and airy room, with floral curtains pulled back with ties and cream walls covered in photos. There was an electric fire housed in an old fireplace.

'Who was at the door, love?' The elderly woman was sitting on a chair facing the TV. She didn't turn to look at her husband.

'It's the police.'

'What?' She jerked her head around and stared up at Seb.

'Hello, Mrs Dent. My name's Sebastian Clifford from Lenchester CID.'

'Why? What's happened?' Her bony fingers clutched at the edges of her cardigan.

'It's nothing to worry about. I'd like to ask you a few questions about the time in Anderson Park when you discovered a teenage boy who'd been attacked.'

'Oh, thank goodness. I thought you were here to tell us that someone had died. You gave me such a shock.' She released a loud breath. 'It all happened years ago. Why are you asking me questions now?'

'As I explained to your husband, we're now in possession of certain facts that we weren't at the time of the incident. This won't take long.'

Mrs Dent reached for the remote control and muted the TV. 'Sit down,' she said, gesturing to the chair beside her. 'And please call me Mabel.'

'Thank you.' Seb relaxed back in the chair, wanting to put the woman at her ease.

'I'm not sure there's anything else to add to what I told the police at the time.'

'I'd like to go through the details again, in case anything comes up that you didn't mention to the officers. It's not uncommon for new details to emerge after a substantial period of time.'

'Something in my subconscious, you mean? I watch lots of crime programmes.' A knowing smile broke out across her face.

'Yes, that's exactly it,' Seb agreed, hoping it would encourage the woman to be more cooperative. 'I have read your original interview in the police file, but if you wouldn't mind starting at the beginning, from when you left home that morning, that would be most helpful.'

'Okay, if it's going to help, then I'm happy to.' The woman sucked in a sharp, wheezy breath. 'It was when I was working at the canning factory. I was there for over thirty years as a supervisor. I'd worked the night shift, which went from ten until six, and got home around quarter past. I parked outside the house, as usual, and went inside quietly because I didn't want to wake up Fred and the kids. Seven o'clock was always the time everyone got up in the morning during the week. When I got inside, Benji, our dog at the time, wanted to go out for a walk.'

'Did you always take him out when you came home from work?' Seb interrupted. The woman sounded breathless and perhaps needed a quick break.

'Sometimes I did. Sometimes I didn't. It just depended on Benji. That morning he was very excited, so I grabbed the lead from the hook on the wall and we went out. We had a regular route taking us to the park, where he'd have a quick run, then we'd head back home. The whole thing would only take about forty-five minutes.' She paused, her eyes misty, like she was reliving the experience.

'And the bench where you found the young man, was that part of your regular route?' he asked, bringing her back to the present.

'No, it wasn't. Benji got a scent for something and went charging off through the park, and I ran after him. He wasn't always good at coming back when we called him, so I had to follow or he could disappear for hours. Benji ran through the trees until coming to the bench. He stopped and stared, not moving. When I was about ten yards away, I saw the lad lying there.' She paused and took a loud breath.

'What did you do then?'

'I wasn't sure whether to approach him or not. I didn't know if he was drunk or on something. I called out to Benji, but he ignored me, so I had no choice but to go over. I couldn't leave the dog there. I took a couple of steps closer and saw the boy was sitting back but leaning over slightly. There was blood all over him, and his face was a greyish colour. I realised that he wasn't going to hurt me, so I walked over and spoke to him.'

He'd been right about wanting the woman to go through the events because she'd already given him more than had been recorded in her original statement.

'What did you say?'

'I asked him if he was okay, but he didn't answer. I picked up his arm and felt for a pulse, and I could feel a very weak one. I knew how to do that because I'd had first-aid training at work.'

'Mrs Dent. Mabel. Please will you picture the scene in your mind and scan the area. I'd like to know if there was anything out of place in the vicinity.'

She closed her eyes, frown lines deep in her forehead, and was still for a while. 'No. There was no one there. It was quiet. Very quiet. Even the birds weren't singing.' Her eyes opened. 'Sorry.'

'No need to apologise. It helps to clarify the situation. What did you do after you realised that the boy was still alive?'

'I wasn't sure if he could hear me, but in case he could, I said I was going to get help. I ran to the edge of the park where there was a phone box and called 999. The operator asked me to wait with him until the emergency services arrived. Which I did.'

'She didn't get home for several hours, and I was getting worried,' Mr Dent said. 'It wasn't like now, when everyone has a phone. Some people had them, but not us. We didn't get our first mobile until about ten years ago.'

'Then what happened?' Seb prompted, not wanting to get off-topic.

'I waited for the police and the ambulance to get there,

and they asked me lots of questions, and then they took the boy away in the ambulance.'

'I know we've established that there was no one in the vicinity when you found him, but did you notice anything out of the ordinary while you were waiting for the ambulance and police? Or even when they were there? Were there people staring?'

'I did see some people while I waited, but no one who stuck out. There could have been people staring once the emergency services were there, but I can't remember who. I'm sorry I can't remember anything else.'

'And did the young man say anything to you at all? Did he realise you were there with him?'

'He occasionally let out a low groan like he was in pain. He mostly had his eyes closed, but when he did open them, they were sort of glassy, as if he didn't know what was going on or couldn't really see. I took hold of his hand, and he squeezed my fingers, but that was all. He ended up with brain damage, didn't he? I phoned the police to find out what had happened to him. That poor kid. For something so bad to happen to him at such a young age with his whole life in front of him. It's tragic.'

'Yes, it is.'

'Now you're looking into it again. What evidence do you have?'

'I wish I was able to tell you, but we're not allowed. Police protocols.'

'I understand. I hope you do find whoever did this to him. I wish I could've told you more.'

'You've helped put everything into perspective and given me a picture of what went on at the time. That's very useful. Thank you very much for that. I'll leave you to get back to your TV quiz.' Seb nodded at the television.

'It's my favourite show. I never miss it.' Mabel picked up the remote and pointed it at the screen.

'I'll show you out,' Mr Dent said.

Seb followed him to the front door, the sound of the raucous television show resuming behind them, and bade Mr Dent goodbye. Mabel Dent might have given a more in-depth account of the incident, but it still hadn't given him anything to work with. He hoped to get more from Marty McNeil, his next port of call.

# Chapter 11

Seb headed into the Lenchester supermarket and made his way to the customer service desk. There were several people in front of him in the queue. He usually did his shopping in the evening, and he could see why. The place was teeming with customers. When he finally got to the counter, he pulled out his ID and showed it to the girl behind the desk.

'I'd like to speak to Martin McNeil, if he's working today.'

'Yeah, I think he is. You'll probably find him outside collecting trollies. That's what he's normally doing when we're this busy.'

'Could you call him for me?' Seb asked, as he didn't have a picture of the man and it would have taken him a while to find McNeil in such a large place.

She gave a sigh and pressed the button on the tannoy. 'Marty McNeil, please report to the customer service desk, thank you.' She turned to Seb. 'I don't know how long he'll be. You'll have to wait over there.'

Seb moved out of the way, allowing the woman to deal

with the queue of customers that had built up behind him. He kept an eye on the surrounding area, and within a couple of minutes, a man wearing a supermarket uniform approached the desk. He was around five foot eight, had a shaved head, tattoos on both arms, and a gold stud in one ear.

Seb stepped forward. 'Are you Marty McNeil?'

The man moved awkwardly from foot to foot. 'Um … Yeah. Who wants to know?'

'My name is Seb Clifford from Lenchester CID. Is there somewhere quiet we can talk?'

Panic crossed his face. 'Has something happened to one of the kids?'

'No. As far as I'm aware, your family is fine.'

'What's it about then?' he said, nervously looking to either side of himself.

'It would be easier if we could sit down and talk.'

'I suppose we can go to the staff canteen, but I can't be too long.'

McNeil led him up one of the aisles until they reached the back of the shop. They walked through a set of double doors marked *Private* and took the stairs situated to the left. This led them into a cafeteria area, which had a long counter situated down one side, with glass display units containing food.

'Let's sit down over there,' Seb said, pointing to an empty table by the window.

'Well, what is it?' McNeil asked when they were seated.

'I'm investigating the attack on Robert Walker twenty-five years ago. I understand you were a friend of his.'

'Seriously, you come in here while I'm at work to ask me about that. Couldn't it have waited until the end of my shift?' He glared at Seb, his lips set in a pinched line.

'If you would rather, I can speak to you later when

you're home,' Seb offered, although he was reluctant to do so, because he didn't have time to waste.

'You're here now, so we might as well get on with it. Yes, me and Rob were friends. But I can't tell you anything about what happened to him because I wasn't there.'

The man's blink rate increased. Why had he volunteered that information before being asked? That was certainly a red flag.

'Tell me more about your friendship. I understand you both hung around with Gareth Collins as well.'

'The three of us were mates. We were in the same classes at school. So what? What else do you want to know?'

'According to Gareth Collins, you worked for his older brother, Keith, on occasion.'

'What?' McNeil frowned.

'He informed me that you all did odd jobs for him.'

'Yes, that's right. We'd take messages. Or deliver packages for him.'

'Did you know what was in the packages?'

'Nope. We didn't look.'

'And were the messages verbal or written?'

'I don't remember – it was too long ago. Why do you want to know?'

'How often would the three of you work for Keith Collins?'

'I didn't do as much as Rob and Gareth. But I suppose we would do something every week, or every two weeks.'

'Why did you work less often?'

'Because I had to look after my younger sister when my mum was at work, which meant I couldn't get out as often as they could.'

'And did you get paid every time you helped Keith Collins?'

'Yeah. We wouldn't have done all that running around here, there, and everywhere, for nothing. We weren't stupid.'

'Can you remember the places that you did go to?'

'No – it's too long ago.' The man avoided eye contact with Seb and moved awkwardly in his seat. 'Is that it? Because I've got to go back to work, or I'll be in trouble.'

'Just a few more questions. I understand you left school soon after the attack on Rob?'

'I had to. My girlfriend had a baby on the way. We got married, and I had to go to work. It didn't last, but I still had to pay for the kid until she left home and got a job. I'm married again now and have two more kids.'

'But you were still at school when the assault on Rob happened. Did the police question you?'

'They talked to the whole class at once.'

'Did you indicate to the officers that you were close friends?'

'You must be kidding. If I'd gone up to them, they'd have started questioning me about everything. And knowing them, they'd have tried to pin it on me.'

'Have you been in contact with Rob since the attack?'

'Of course not. He wasn't right in the head after it happened.'

'But he was your friend, why didn't you go to the hospital to visit?'

'I didn't want to get involved, in case someone thought it was me that did it.' He paused. 'And it wasn't. It was nothing to do with me.'

'That doesn't make sense. Why would visiting your friend indicate you were guilty of the attack?'

'I don't know. Look, I was only sixteen. I wasn't thinking straight. That's all. So stop trying to read something into it.'

'Do you have any suspicions for who was responsible?'

'No.'

The man was lying, Seb was convinced of it. 'When did you last have contact with Gareth Collins?'

McNeil shrugged. 'I don't know. We might have bumped into each other sometimes, but we never hung out together after I left school.'

'So he didn't warn you that I might be in touch to ask questions about Rob.'

'No,' McNeil said, avoiding all eye contact with Seb.

'Are you sure about that because your body language is telling me otherwise?'

'He might have texted me. All right? But so what?'

'When did you give him your number?'

'I don't know. When we bumped into each other, maybe. It's not a crime.'

'Do you know why he saw fit to warn you about the investigation?'

'For fuck's sake, stop going on. I don't know anything about Rob. Or why Gareth texted me, okay?'

'Tell me what you know about Charli, Rob's girlfriend.'

'Nothing. I've had enough of these questions. I'm going back to work. I don't want people thinking I'm in trouble with the police, or I might lose my job.'

It wasn't worth Seb questioning the man further. If it proved necessary, he'd arrange for him to be brought into the station for a formal interview.

'Thank you for your time. If you do think of anything, which might help the investigation, please give me a call.' Seb handed him his card.

Seb settled himself down in front of his laptop, which he had on a table beside the window in his accommodation, and keyed in Marty McNeil's name. The man hadn't been telling the truth, in particular about his supposedly non-existent relationship with Gareth Collins.

The first place he checked was the man's social media account. McNeil's friend list was private, so Seb couldn't check, but the posts weren't. Most of them were political memes, although he did see the occasional photo of him with members of his family. Starting with the most recent and working his way backwards, Seb checked who had reacted to the posts. There was a hard core of people with similar viewpoints who would 'like' them, and McNeil did the same to theirs.

'Ah-ha,' Seb said, after chancing upon a particular post from two years ago. Gareth Collins had liked it. He then flicked through to Gareth Collins' page, but it was private and he couldn't see anything. 'Damn.'

He opened another tab and keyed in *Gareth Collins* and *Martin McNeil*, hoping that something would come up. Maybe an image of them together. But all he got was a reference to a school sports day from 1992, listing both of their names. He stared at the screen, pondering what to do next, when his phone rang.

He glanced at the screen. It was Whitney.

'Hi, it's me,' she said once he'd answered. 'I'm still with Mum and Rob but I ducked outside to give you a quick call. I wanted to tell you that I've found out more about Charli.'

'That's excellent news.'

'I know. Rob didn't remember her when I asked but, according to my mum, Dad once saw him out with a girl who was wearing an Oakford School uniform. It's a private girls' school ten miles out of Lenchester. Fingers crossed, the girl he saw was Charli.'

'I'll visit the school tomorrow morning. My interview with Mabel Dent confirmed what we already know. However, speaking to Marty McNeil proved much more interesting.'

'Do you believe he was involved?'

'He certainly lied to me regarding his relationship with Gareth Collins, although it's too early to ascertain whether he was a part of the attack. But he's on my radar. Any joy on finding DS Jacks?'

'Yes, but unfortunately he emigrated to Canada years ago. Ellie's trying to see if we can track him down. I'll keep you updated on that. The other officer who worked with him on the case, DC Mole, died a few years ago.'

'I doubt they can give us any more information than we already have on file and from Mabel Dent, but it's always worth checking all avenues. Now we have a link to the girlfriend, it is looking much more positive.'

'Yes, you're right. Keep me informed of how it goes. Sorry to cut you short, but I have to return to the day room. Mum was fine when I left a few minutes ago, but she can drift off in a matter of seconds, and Rob can't cope when that happens.'

'Of course, I understand.'

'I have a good feeling about this. We're finally making some progress.'

# Chapter 12

'Hey, that's not the way to his office,' Birdie said. Rawlings' driver had been following the same route from Arthingworth to Leicester as he did yesterday, until he abruptly turned left, leaving the A6 before they'd reached the city.

'Shit.'

Twiggy had been so wrapped up in his own thoughts that he hadn't noticed them turning off. He twisted hard on the steering wheel, moving into the left-hand lane, narrowly missing a car coming up on the inside, who sounded his horn loud and long. Twiggy indicated to turn off, making it just in time.

'What the hell, Twig. You almost got us killed.'

'Well, I didn't and we're all okay,' Twiggy said, not prepared to admit that his heart was beating overtime because that had been close. Too close.

'Apart from I nearly brought up my entire breakfast. If it's all the same to you, I'd rather you paid attention to where we are, rather than drifting off into a dream world.'

Keeping his eyes focused on where they were heading,

Twiggy followed until they reached an industrial estate in Mandervell Road.

'I won't stop, or they might spot us,' he said when Rawlings' driver turned off the road and parked on the forecourt of a building with a small storage unit behind it.

'Go over there,' Birdie said, pointing to the car park in front of a gym. 'We can still keep an eye on the place and see when they leave, but we'll be out of the way.'

Twiggy did as she'd suggested and, once stationary, he reached over to the back seat and picked up the binoculars. He held them up to his eyes and stared in the direction of the building. They didn't have high-powered lenses but were strong enough for him to take a good look. 'It seems like Rawlings has gone inside. The driver's still in the car. There's no signage on the front. I wonder if it's the storage place Margaret Clarke mentioned that he was planning to buy? Although it doesn't look big enough to house lots of farm machinery. Then again, it could be for parts.'

'I'll search the address for ownership and see what comes up.' Birdie pulled out her phone from her pocket. 'Hmm. This is interesting. According to this, the property has been vacant for twelve months. I can't find who owns it.'

'It doesn't look empty to me, with those cars outside,' Twiggy said, staring through the binoculars again and counting six parked cars.

'I'll do some more research when we get back to the office to see what I can find out.'

It was a further twenty minutes before Rawlings emerged from the building, talking with another man.

'Here he comes. Quick, Birdie, take a photo of the person he's with.'

Birdie held up her phone at the same time as they shook hands, and then the unknown man returned inside.

'Damn. I only got the back of his head. Sorry, Twig. Is there any CCTV around here?'

Twiggy glanced along the street. 'Yes, but not focused on the forecourt of the building.'

'Typical.'

They followed Rawlings back the way they'd come and then onto the A6 leading into Leicester. There were no more stops until they reached the company offices and the driver dropped him off.

Twiggy glanced at his watch. 'Great. It's not even ten o'clock. That leaves us another five hours before our shift ends, and I'm betting that we've had all the excitement we're going to have for the day. I'm bored already.'

Bored and not feeling right. Nothing he could put his finger on, just weird and sometimes phasing out of what was going on. He'd almost phoned in sick but didn't want to leave Birdie in the lurch. Plus, Evie wasn't working today, and she'd make him eat rabbit food for every meal if he was at home.

'What's up with you, Twig? You know how deadly dull surveillance can be.'

'That doesn't mean I have to like it.'

'I'll tell you what, why don't you go over the road to the bakery and buy us both a coffee and cake. That should cheer you up.'

He didn't need telling twice, and he was out of the car within seconds.

When he reached the shop the queue was coming out the door, and it took him ages to be served.

Finally, he made it back to the car.

'Sorry, it was crazy busy in there,' he said, sliding into the driver seat.

'I almost sent a search party out for you. Anyway, while you've been gone, I've had an awesome idea.'

Twiggy bit back a frustrated sigh. He was well used to Birdie and her ideas. It was bound to involve them doing something they shouldn't. He'd put money on it.

'Go on … But I won't agree if it will involve us getting into trouble.'

'Trust me. Nothing will happen to us. I hope.' She took a bite of the brownie that he'd bought her. 'Mmm. This is to die for.'

'Are you going to tell me what your idea is or what?'

'Okay, okay. After our shift ends, let's go back to Oadby and check out the place Rawlings went to this morning.'

'To do what?'

'We hardly had any time there. I want to walk around the outside, take a peep into the windows, see what's going on.'

'And if there are still cars parked outside?'

'We can still go round the back and take a look. What do you think?'

Saying no wasn't an option because she'd nag him to death until he said yes. He actually wouldn't mind returning there, as it was sort of on the way back to Market Harborough. If they found anything of use, the DI might take them off the surveillance and give them something more interesting to get their teeth into.

'Okay. We'll do it.'

'Park in the gym car park again,' she said to Twiggy as they drove into Mandervell Road. 'There are plenty of other cars in there to hide us.'

When they drove past the building Rawlings had visited earlier, there were no cars outside, which meant they could have a good look around. She glanced at

Twiggy. There was something not right with him. He'd been acting weird all day, and yesterday in fact, but when she'd asked earlier if he was all right, all he did was grunt and blame it on their assignment. But she didn't buy it. She wouldn't push him on it; she'd learnt the hard way that if Twiggy dug his heels in, he could be a pain in the arse for hours. He'd tell her what was wrong when he was ready.

In the meantime, she had her own issue to deal with, her meeting with Marie Davis later in the day. Although she didn't want to build her hopes up, in case it was cancelled again.

'Now where shall we go?' Twiggy asked once they were out of the car.

'I reckon if we walk up there, we can approach the building from the rear. It means we won't be seen.' She pointed ahead of them.

'Okay. Lead the way.'

They hurried past the front of the gym, then crossed over the road in front of a double-glazing factory and carried on walking until there was a gap between two buildings. They nipped through and walked along a path that was overgrown with weeds until they reached the rear of the storage part of the building. The small windows were too high for Birdie to see into. There was a door, and she tried the handle gently, but it was locked.

'Crap. I suppose that was too much to hope for. Let's creep around the side and peer through one of the front windows.'

'We couldn't have gone in without a search warrant, anyway.'

'Who said anything about going inside? I was going to open the door and look from there.'

'I think we should go back. This is too risky, and if the

DI finds out, he's gonna go mad for jeopardising the investigation.'

Twiggy was right. But she couldn't waste this chance.

'We can still walk around the front. If anyone stops us, we'll say we were looking because we thought it was up for sale. Come on.'

She took a couple of steps, but then her attention was diverted by something on the ground. 'Wait. What's that?' She pulled out a disposable glove from her pocket and slipped it on. Then she bent down and picked up a piece of flimsy floral material in a triangular shape, like a scarf that could be tied over the head. 'What's this doing here? Seems a little out of place …' She held it up for Twiggy to see.

'Someone dropped it.'

'Yeah, but who would come round the back here? This is recent. It's in good condition and not ruined by the weather. It might be nothing, but I'm going to bring it with us.' She pulled out an evidence bag and dropped it in.

They continued around to the front of the building, and she peered in through one of the windows. All she could see was a reception desk and a couple of chairs beside the wall. At the back of the small area was a door, which was closed.

'Come on, let's go. There's nothing here for us and we don't want to alert suspicions,' Twiggy said.

When Birdie and Twiggy arrived back at the station, they headed straight to Sarge's office.

'Anything to report on Rawlings?' he asked.

'Not much, but first thing, he went to an industrial unit in Oadby. We went back for another look after our shift finished. We spotted nothing, apart from this scarf that I found around the back.' Birdie held out the evidence bag for him to see. 'Shall I send it for analysis?'

'Forensics are slammed at the moment. Put it in the evidence store for now. Anything else during your shift?'

'Once Rawlings arrived at work, he stayed at the office all day, apart from at lunchtime when he headed to a local café. I stayed in the car and Twiggy followed.'

'Why doesn't that surprise me?' Sarge said, turning a wry smile in Twiggy's direction. 'I take it you bought something to eat while in there?'

'Had to, or it would have looked suspicious if I'd just hung around. I ordered us both a sandwich and stayed in there with a coffee.'

'How long was Rawlings at the café?'

'He stayed for half an hour on his own, eating his lunch, and then he walked back to work,' Twiggy said.

'I'm surprised you didn't tell Sarge exactly what Rawlings had to eat, Twig,' she said, smirking.

'Ha, ha, very funny. Not,' Twiggy said.

'Anything else to report on what's happened so far?' Sarge said.

'Nothing, unless you want to know that Birdie's staying at Clifford's place.'

Birdie's jaw dropped. What the hell did he bring that up for? Was he trying to get her back for teasing him? She'd only been joking.

'It's nothing to do with work. Seb asked me to look after his dog, Elsa, while he was away in Lenchester on a case. Anyway, he's coming back today, so I'm off home after work.' She turned and scowled in Twiggy's direction.

'As long as you're not planning to assist him,' Sarge said.

'I'm not, and he hasn't asked me to. He's working on a case for DCI Walker at Lenchester CID.'

'Chief Inspector *Whitney* Walker?'

'Yes, that's the one. Do you know her?'

'Not personally, but she does have a very good reputation in the force, and I think we were at the same conference some time ago. I doubt she'd remember me.'

So, Sarge was in awe of someone. That was a first.

'Well, he's doing some work for her as a consultant on a short-term contract.'

'How did he get that job? Even with a tightening of budgets, I wouldn't have expected a large force like that to employ a private investigator.'

'I'm not his keeper. I don't know.' Her tone was more sarcastic than she'd intended, and he frowned at her. 'I'm sorry, Sarge. He's worked with her before on another case, that's how they know each other. That's all I can tell you.'

She certainly wasn't prepared to divulge anything about the investigation in case Sarge assumed she was going to be involved.

'Just remember it's not your investigation.'

'I know, Sarge. You don't need to remind me. It's Seb's case and nothing to do with me. Surely, looking after his dog when he's away can't be against the rules.'

In her peripheral vision, she caught Twiggy's eyes boring into her. Had she gone too far?

'I'll have less of your cheek,' Sarge said.

'I'm not being cheeky.'

'You're forgetting I know your history. Now go.' He dismissed them with a wave of his hand, and they left his office.

They headed down the corridor, and after they were out of earshot, she turned to Twiggy. 'What did you do that for?'

'What?'

'You know what. Telling Sarge about me taking care of Seb's dog.'

'Because I'm looking out for you. I don't want you to suddenly get the idea in your head that it's okay to help him with his case.'

'I'm not going to.'

'I know what you're like. And now Sarge knows, you won't risk it because you could end up losing your job. If you want to go and look after his dog, then fine, but that's as far as it goes. You're to have nothing to do with his case for this DCI Walker, whoever she is.'

'You're not my boss, so stop trying to act like you are. And remember, she's a DCI, which makes her a lot higher than both of us. And Sarge.'

'Her rank has nothing to do with it. If you want to stay in the job, then keep well away.'

# Chapter 13

Seb drove up the long, winding drive that dissected the extensive grounds of Oakford School and parked in front of the main building, which, according to their website, had been built as a castle in the 1600s. He cast an eye over his surroundings, and in the distance could see girls on the grass tennis courts.

He walked through the wooden double doors into a large entrance hall with a flagstone floor. On the walls hung large portraits of previous head teachers and other aristocrats from over the centuries. He followed the signs to the school office. It reminded him in some ways of the school that he'd attended. That, too, had once been an aristocratic home until it had been turned into an educational establishment.

He reached the administration office, knocked, and waited.

'Come in,' a female voice boomed out.

He walked into a large office with a high ceiling and a big bay window. There were two desks in there and behind one of them was a woman in her fifties, her blonde hair pulled back from her face by a black headband. The other desk was vacant, although a jacket hung on the back of the chair. There was an open door leading to another office, which appeared empty.

'Good morning. I'm Sebastian Clifford from Lenchester CID. I'm interested in a former pupil and wondered if you could spare me a few minutes.' He held out his ID.

The woman stared at him for a few seconds and frowned. 'I see. Our privacy policy prevents us from giving out any information regarding our pupils.'

If he had to wait for a warrant, that would delay the investigation, and he didn't have the time to spare. He had to hope the woman could be persuaded.

'She's a former pupil, would have left the school over twenty years ago, so I'd have thought that wouldn't be breaching the policy.'

'Yes, I guess you're right. I can't ask the head teacher because she's out, but I'll try the deputy head.' She picked up the handset on her desk and made the call.

From the one-sided conversation, Seb gleaned that permission had been granted.

The woman ended the call and looked up at him. 'I've been given the go-ahead to assist, although it's so far back, I'm not sure how helpful we can be. Which girl do you wish to know about?' She gestured to the seat in front of her desk and Seb sat.

'All I have is the first name Charli. We're anxious to track her down, which is why I'm grateful for your assistance.'

'I've only been here ten years, so she won't be a student I'd have known. What other details do you have?'

'Twenty-five years ago, she would have been sixteen, or around that age. I'm not exactly certain. Charli could have been a nickname. Try the name Charlotte as well,' he said.

Seb waited while the woman keyed in the details and stared at her computer screen.

'No luck with Charli but we did have several Charlottes in the school around that time. One was only in the first year, so would have been eleven, but there were two others who, at the time, were in the fifth form, which would have made them fifteen or sixteen. One of them may be the girl you're looking for. I'll print off their details.' She headed over to the printer on the other side of the office, and once the document came through, she handed it to Seb. He glanced at the sheet, which had their names and addresses, although he doubted they would still be current.

'Is there anyone still working at the school who might remember these girls, by any chance?'

It would save him considerable time if there was.

'Mrs Tintern, our matron, has been here for years, so she might be able to help you. I'll contact her.' She picked up the handset from her desk and made the call. 'It's Suzie here, Matron. Could you spare us a few minutes in my office?' She paused a moment. 'Thank you.' She ended the call and looked over at him. 'Matron's on her way. The sickbay's in one of the boarding houses, so it might take her a few minutes to reach us.'

'Thank you. I'll wait here, if I may.'

'Yes, of course. Why are you interested in these girls, anyway? I hope it's nothing that would bring the school into disrepute.'

'My investigation into a cold case has led me here and to a girl named Charli, but it's early days, and we don't know for certain whether she was involved. I'd appreciate it if you could keep the police interest confidential because we don't wish to alarm anyone unnecessarily.'

SALLY RIGBY

The fewer people who knew, the better. It wouldn't be prudent if possible persons of interest were prewarned of their interest at such an early stage in his enquiries.

'Absolutely. I totally understand. Nothing will leave this office, you have my word on that.'

There was a light tap on the door and a small woman with short grey hair, who looked to be in her early sixties, walked in, a pleasant smile on her face.

'You wanted to see me, Suzie?'

'This is Mr Clifford from Lenchester Police. He has some questions about a former pupil from twenty-five years ago, and I thought you might be able to help.' Suzie nodded in his direction.

'The police?' She frowned.

'There's nothing to worry about, and this may not amount to anything,' Seb said, walking over to her. 'We have the name Charlotte and know she was here around twenty-five years ago and would have been fifteen or sixteen at the time,'

'I've come across two girls who might fit the bill. Charlotte Fenton and Charlotte Higgins. Do you remember either of them?' Suzie asked.

'I remember them both, and they couldn't have been more different.'

'In what way?' Seb asked.

'Charlotte Higgins was a quiet, well-behaved young lady who wouldn't say boo to a goose. She was academic, worked hard, and won most of the prizes for her year at prize-giving. An exemplary student. Charlotte Fenton, who was called Charli by everyone, was likeable, vivacious, and very popular. Academically she was average.'

Excellent. She was definitely the girl he was seeking.

'Thank you for your input. It's been most useful. It was a Charli that I was looking for, so I can assume it would

106

have been her. Can you remember anything else about her time at the school? Anything about her behaviour that might have stood out as being odd or different from the norm?'

He didn't want to mention the attack on Rob, so had to skirt around the issue the best he could.

'Funny you should ask because I do recollect a time when she came to the sanatorium, crying her eyes out. I was surprised that she'd come to see me because she was seldom in the san. She said she wanted to be alone but didn't want to go home. I asked why she was so upset, but she wouldn't tell me. It was quite bizarre really, and most unlike her.'

'Did she eventually tell you what was wrong?'

'No. All she said was it was personal. I tried to encourage her to speak further, but she wouldn't.'

'Do you remember the date this occurred?'

It was a long shot, but certainly worth asking.

'I'm sorry, I have no recollection of the date. It was too long ago.'

'Did she come to see you again after that?'

'No, she didn't. I do remember looking out for her on occasion, but when I did see her, she seemed back to her usual self.'

'I'm surprised you can remember all of this,' Suzie said.

'Me too, considering how poor my memory is these days. I think it's because it was so unusual that it stuck in my mind.'

'Thank you, Matron, you've been most helpful. I'd like to see a photo of her if there's one available?'

'She isn't in the system, I'm afraid,' Suzie said.

'I believe you'll find one on the wall in the main corridor. Charlotte was an excellent tennis player and represented the school. The tennis team won the schools All England Championship in both singles and doubles when she was in it. Come with me and I'll show you,' Matron said.

'Thank you for your help,' Seb said to Suzie as he left the room.

Matron stopped in front of a wall full of sporting photos. 'There she is.' She pointed to a dark-haired girl in tennis whites, holding a racket in her hand. 'Charli won the singles that year. There were huge celebrations, and she was in all the local press and on regional television. It was a big deal, and we had more applicants for sporting scholarships the following year than we'd ever had in the past.'

Seb took out his phone and took a close-up of the photograph hanging on the wall. 'That's marvellous. Thank you very much for your assistance.'

'You didn't say why you wish to trace her.'

'I'm sorry, I'm not at liberty to discuss an ongoing investigation. It's a cold case and we're researching all avenues. It may turn out that Charli isn't, in fact, a person of interest. I'd be grateful for your discretion in this matter and if you could please keep our discussion between ourselves. Thank you for your time.'

By the time he got back outside, it was drizzling, and he jogged over to his car and drove to Lenchester police station.

On his arrival, he headed straight to the incident room and Ellie's desk. She turned her head as he got close.

'Hello, can I help?'

'Yes, please. Charli, the girl we're looking for, is called Charlotte Fenton and a past pupil of Oakford School. I'd like you to find out what you can about her if you have the time and don't mind.'

'No problem. I've almost finished what I'm currently working on. It will be my next job.'

'Thanks. Is the DCI in?'

'She went to the cafeteria for a coffee a couple of minutes ago. She said she wouldn't be long.'

'Was she alone?'

'I think so, but I don't know for definite.'

'I'll go and check.'

When Seb entered the cafeteria, he spotted Whitney straight away, sitting on her own at one of the round tables in the centre.

'Well, what have you got to tell me?' Whitney asked once he'd reached her.

He pulled out the chair opposite and sat. 'I've identified Charli.'

'Fantastic. I'll ask Ellie to do some digging.'

'I've already done that.'

Whitney frowned. 'That should be okay this time, but—'

'Am I not allowed to approach her? I thought because we were working together it would be fine.'

Whitney hadn't informed him of any protocols in place regarding the investigation.

'It is, and it isn't. Yes, you're working in my department on this case for two weeks, but in theory, I shouldn't be allocating additional resources towards the case. You should be working alone. And before you say anything, I know we've already used Ellie. The main thing is I keep on top of what we're doing. I don't want the details of the case to get out because you never know who might try to interfere.'

'I'm sorry. I didn't realise. But what we've done shouldn't become public knowledge.'

'You're right. None of the team are going to blab. I'm

just being supersensitive. It's because the investigation means so much to me.'

'I understand. Next time, I won't engage any member of the team without first running it past you.'

'Thanks. If it wasn't for Douglas being around and the chance that he could come into the incident room and check, I wouldn't be so paranoid. Why don't you grab yourself a coffee while you're waiting for Ellie to work her magic?'

Fifteen minutes later, they returned to the incident room and Seb followed Whitney over to Ellie's desk.

'I've got the information you asked for,' the officer said, a broad smile on her lips. 'Charlotte Fenton, who is now Charlotte Newton, is married to a Mark Newton and they live in Great Bowden, just outside Market Harborough, I'll text you're the details.'

'Market Harborough? You've got to be kidding me. Talk about coincidence,' Whitney said, shaking her head.

'Why coincidence, guv?' Ellie asked.

'Because that's where Seb's living.'

'And where I'm heading back to this afternoon. I'll call in to see her on my way back. I'm also planning on visiting Keith Collins tomorrow morning.'

'What else did you discover about the woman?' Whitney asked.

'She has two teenage children and doesn't work. Her husband's a dentist.'

'That's excellent. Thank you very much, Ellie. I'll leave now and head directly to her house. I'll let you know how it goes, Whitney.'

# Chapter 14

Seb had a good run with no hold-ups on his way to Great Bowden, where Charlotte Newton lived. He drove past a church and the village green, where some villagers seemed to be hanging up bunting for what must be a summer fete. But as he drove to the outskirts, the community feel ebbed away and was replaced by a polished and pruned development, a small close of detached houses that looked barely over twenty years old.

The Newtons' house was at the top, and when he reached it, he turned onto the large, gravelled parking area, stopping in front of the integral double garage and beside a metallic blue Mercedes-AMG GT Roadster. He stared at the car for a few seconds, admiring its smooth lines and commiserating with himself that with his size, he could never even consider owning one, despite wishing to.

He approached the front door and rang the bell. Less than a minute later, it was answered by a woman of around forty, wearing leggings and a T-shirt emblazoned with the name of a gym, and with her dark hair scraped off her face into a ponytail. Her forehead glistened with sweat. Had he interrupted her training?

'Mrs Newton?'

'Yes.'

'My name's Sebastian Clifford, and I work for Lenchester Police.' He held out his identification for her to see, and she stared at it for a few seconds. 'I'd like to talk to you about Robert Walker.'

'I don't know anyone of that name. I'm …' Her voice fell away.

'You went out with him when you were in your mid-teens. It was shortly before he was viciously assaulted and left with irreversible brain damage. I have questions for you relating to the attack.'

The lines around her eyes tightened. 'I don't remember what happened because it was years ago. I'm sure there's nothing I can tell you. Why are you even looking into it after such a long time?' She bit down on her bottom lip and shifted from one foot to the other.

'Some new evidence has come to light, and we have reopened the case. As someone who knew him well, I have several questions to put to you.'

'How do you know about our relationship?'

'One of his friends mentioned a Charli, and our investigation has led us to you.'

She sighed. 'No one calls me Charli anymore. And I wasn't even there when the attack happened. Even though we did go out for a while back then, it wasn't serious between us. It was a casual thing, and there's nothing I can tell you about his attack.'

Her words were at odds with the expression on her face. She was clearly desperate for Seb to leave. That wasn't going to happen.

'I do have further questions. May I come inside rather than stand out here?'

She nodded. 'We'll go in the library.'

The library was a small room lined with bookcases and had two traditional easy chairs situated in the centre. She gestured for him to sit down on one of them and she sat on the other, leaning forward with her arms wrapped around her knees.

'I'd like to take you back to the time of the attack. You mentioned that you weren't there when it occurred, but did you know that it had happened?'

'Of course I did. It was on the TV news and in all the papers. Everyone in the city would have known about it.'

'Yet you didn't inform the police about your relationship with Rob.'

She flushed a pale pink. 'I couldn't tell them anything relating to the incident because I wasn't there, and I didn't want to get involved. I was only sixteen, it's how I was then. I'm not proud of my behaviour, but I can't change it. Not now.'

'Did you go to the hospital to visit Rob after it had happened? Or to his home to see how he was?'

'It was tricky,' she replied, avoiding eye contact with Seb.

'Please could you elaborate?'

'What's the point? Nothing's going to change, not after twenty-five years.'

'That is correct, but you might have information that can help us discover what occurred. I'm curious that you attended Oakford, an exclusive girls' school, and Rob Walker went to the local comprehensive and counted among his friends young men with police records. How did you even get to know one another?'

'I don't know. I was rebelling, I suppose, against my

father. He was very strict. Not that it's anything to do with the attack.'

'Did your father know that you were seeing Rob?'

'He grounded me when he found out about us, but—'

The front door opened, and she stopped talking.

'I'm home,' a male voice called out.

'That's my husband. He can't hear what we're talking about.'

'I'd like to question your father, please could you give me his details?'

Panic flashed across her face. He'd clearly touched a nerve. 'There's no need to involve him. Look, I'll talk to you some more but not here, and not now. Meet me tomorrow, midday, at the Olde Worlde Tea Rooms in Thorpe Langton.'

Now he was getting somewhere.

'Okay, but if you don't turn up to meet me, I will most definitely be back.'

'I understand. Please leave now. I'll tell my husband you were here asking whether I'd seen anyone suspicious lurking around here. There have been several burglaries recently, and he won't be suspicious.'

She hurriedly ushered Seb out of the house, and once he was on his way home, he called Whitney.

'I've just been to see Charlotte Newton.'

'Did you learn anything of use?'

'We're continuing our conversation tomorrow lunchtime because her husband came home, and she didn't want him to overhear. She intended to tell him that I was there to discuss burglaries in the area.'

'Did she seem at all suspicious when you were questioning her? Do you think she knew who attacked Rob? Was she even part of it?'

'I know you're anxious to discover what happened, but

please allow me to follow the process and take it one step at a time. Nothing about my conversation with Charlotte Newton so far has led me to believe that she was instrumental in the attack, but we did only touch the surface.'

'Remember, you're not as good at understanding body language as George. No offence.'

'None taken. But I am used to interviewing and know when people are lying to me. Trust me on this, Whitney. The most important thing is that she's agreed to meet me tomorrow. I'll discover more about her and Rob then. Could you ask Ellie to find contact details for her father? She was definitely twitchy when he came up. I may consider interviewing him, too.'

# Chapter 15

Birdie stood outside Marie Davis's terraced house in Saffron Lane and sucked in a breath. Her heart was thumping so hard it was difficult to breathe. She'd never been so nervous about anything in her whole life. Not even when she'd first joined CID, and that was saying something. She stared at the small, neatly trimmed lawn, which was surrounded by an array of pretty flowers. Who was going to look after the garden now, because she doubted Marie would be able to after her stroke?

She knocked on the door, and through the small glass pane, there was a shadow of someone walking down the hall, headed towards her.

'Hello, I'm Birdie. I've come to see Marie Davis,' she said to the woman who answered, who was wearing a royal blue tunic with white piping around the edges and looked to be in her fifties.

'Yes, I'm Del, her carer. Marie's been expecting you. Please come in.' Del moved to the side and held open the door for Birdie to enter.

'How's Marie doing?' The narrow hallway smelt fresh,

as if it had just been cleaned. Surely that wasn't because of her visit.

'Much better than was originally expected. She's a very determined woman and can do many things for herself.'

'But you're living here with her?'

'Yes. Although she's progressing well, she certainly can't look after herself. I doubt she ever will. Her family have employed me full-time to live in and take care of her.'

'What about on your days off?'

'There are two other carers who work on a part-time basis.'

That can't have been cheap, but her son, Craig, had mentioned that the family had all clubbed together to pay for the care.

'I'm so pleased it's all working out for her.'

Birdie had been devastated when Marie had been taken ill before they were able to meet, but her son had been helpful and given her a photo with her birth mother in it. However, Birdie was still curious to know if there was anything else Marie could tell her.

'Marie's waiting for you in the lounge. I'll take you through and then fetch the tea.'

'Oh, there's no need for that.'

'It's all ready. I've been given my instructions. She's really looking forward to meeting you. Would you like tea or coffee?'

'I'm fine with whatever Marie's having.'

Birdie followed Del into the room, which was small and had a dark brown sofa and a matching easy chair, with a small coffee table in the middle. Along the far wall was an oak sideboard.

Marie was sitting on the chair. She was a frail, tiny woman with short curly white hair. A gold chain hung around her neck with a pair of glasses dangling from it.

'Hello, my dear,' the old woman said, sitting forward and looking as if she was about to stand.

'Please don't get up.' Birdie held up her hand.

Marie relaxed down into her seat. 'It's lovely to finally meet you. I'm sorry I had to cancel your visit on Sunday. Sit next to me.' She gestured to the sofa, and Birdie sat at the end closest to her.

Del left the room, closing the door behind her.

'How are you?' Birdie asked, scrutinising the old woman's face.

'I'm fine, but everyone will keep fussing around me. I can do a lot more than they think.'

'It's for your own good. You really need to do what they say, and then you'll feel even better.'

'I can see you're going to be like the rest of them.' Marie shook her head, but her eyes were twinkling.

Birdie had warmed to the woman straight away when they'd spoken on the phone before she was taken ill. She liked her even more now.

'I am,' Birdie said, smiling.

'When you spoke to Craig, he told you a little about the Bakirtzis family.'

'Yes, your son was very kind and took the trouble to speak to me. In particular, about Kim.'

'May I ask you something?' Marie turned slightly so she was staring directly at Birdie.

'Yes, of course.'

'You told me you were interested in finding out about Kim for a friend. Is that really the case?' Her alert grey eyes stared directly at Birdie.

'What makes you say that?' Birdie asked, playing for time, unsure whether to admit the truth or not.

'When we spoke on the phone, and when Craig told

me how interested you were, it just seemed a little more than *for a friend.*'

She couldn't lie. Not to Marie. Hopefully she'd understand and still tell Birdie what she wanted to know.

'Do you remember Kim being pregnant when she lived here?'

'Yes, I do. The family moved to Canada a few months after the baby was born.' She paused and stared at Birdie, her eyes widening. 'Are you …?'

'Y-yes. Kim's my birth mother.'

'Oh, my goodness.' Marie's hand covered her mouth. 'And you want to contact her?'

'Yes. It's what I've wanted for years. But … my parents … I love them and don't want to hurt them. It's just … I can't get it out of my head. When I found out Kim's name from my birth certificate, I reached out to the Adoption Contact Register, hoping to get in touch with her.' Birdie lowered her head, the pain was still so acute. 'But it turned out that Kim had told them she wasn't to be contacted.'

'Yet you're still trying?'

'I want to know why she didn't want to see me. The people at the agency wouldn't even tell me the date her request came in. It could have been years ago, and she might have changed her mind. I have to know. I just have to.' Birdie blinked away her tears.

'This is hard, but shouldn't you respect Kim's wishes?' Marie asked gently.

'I get it. Really, I do. But that doesn't mean I can't try to find out more about her. Even if I can't meet or contact her in person. I can't let it go. Will *you* tell me more about her?'

Marie stared at her, compassion shining from her eyes.

'Kim was a lovely girl, and you actually look like her.'

'Not my colouring, though.' Birdie held her curls out and waved them about.

'Your red hair and freckles are the same as your father, Todd. He was Kim's boyfriend. She went out with him for quite a while, but they didn't stay together after she became pregnant. He was only sixteen and far too young for such responsibility. They both were. Kim was very upset when he ended their relationship.'

'She confided in you?'

'Yes, she'd often spend time here. Not that she couldn't speak to her mum, but she felt comfortable here.'

'Did the family move to Canada because of Kim being pregnant, or were they always intending to go?'

'After the baby was adopted, they all wanted a fresh start. They'd often talked about moving to Canada because Kim's mum, Sheena, had relations out there.'

Thoughts careered around Birdie's head while she tried to process everything. 'Do you know *why* Kim gave me up for adoption?'

The question that had plagued Birdie her entire life. *Why?*

'I'd love to be able to tell you and help ease your pain, but it's a question for Kim to answer, dear.'

'I get it. It's just when you said Kim confided in you, I was hoping that she'd talked to you about her reasons.' She couldn't hide the disappointment in her voice.

'All I know is that after Kim and Todd split up, she wanted to move on.'

'Without me.' Tears welled in her eyes again, which was ridiculous, considering how happy she was with her family.

Marie leant over and rested her hand on Birdie's. 'It all happened a long time ago. Life has changed since then.'

'Not that much. It wasn't like in the sixties when there

was such a stigma attached to having a baby before marriage. It was acceptable when I was born.'

'All I can tell you is that they were a lovely family, and they decided it would be best for you to be adopted before they moved overseas.'

Birdie didn't get it. However hard she tried.

'I could understand it if it was the result of a sexual assault, but why just give me away?' she pushed, desperate for even a little more information.

'I know this is hard, and I'm sorry, but there's nothing more I can tell you.'

Birdie got that she'd come to a dead end regarding the pregnancy, but she couldn't leave it. There was more she needed to know if Marie was prepared to tell her.

'You said that you kept in touch with the family on a regular basis.'

'Yes, I always have a Christmas card.'

'So you have the family address in Canada? Will you let me have it?'

'It's in my address book, but I'm not sure it will help you because Kim doesn't live with them.'

'What do you know about her now?'

Birdie could contact her family, although what were the chances of them telling her where Kim was living?

'I believe she's married and has a family.'

What? Birdie had real siblings.

She sucked in a breath. 'How many children does she have, and are they boys or girls?'

'I believe she has two, but I can't remember whether they're boys or girls.'

'Is Kim still living in Canada?'

'Um … I'm not sure where she lives.' Marie hesitated and averted her eyes.

'Are you sure?'

'Um, dear … I think she may have returned to the UK with her family.'

Birdie's heart did a triple flip. Her mum could be in the country.

'Do you know her married name?'

'No, I don't.'

Was that true? Even if it wasn't, Birdie couldn't push the woman anymore.

'Do you know anything about my father, other than his name?'

'No, I've no idea where he is. Are you going to contact him?'

'I hadn't planned to. Do you know his surname?'

'I don't. All I can tell you is they went to school together and were in the same class. That should help if you decide to go looking for him.'

'Thank you, Marie. I really appreciate you telling me all this. There's one more thing …' Her voice fell away.

'What is it, dear?'

'My mum and dad adopted me when I was six months old, so Kim must have looked after me for a while. I don't understand how she could have given me up after all that time.'

'That's odd because you weren't with the family for long. Maybe only a few weeks. I've no idea what happened to you after that time.'

Birdie frowned. Where had she been placed for all those months?

'Do you think it was Kim who wanted to give me up, or were her mum and dad not prepared to have a baby around?'

Would that make it easier, if Kim had wanted to keep her but her parents had said no?

'I'm sorry, Birdie. I wish I knew more and could help

you. All I can tell you is they were a lovely family and they must have had their reasons, however hard it seems for you now.'

'I understand. Thank you for seeing me and for all your help. I really appreciate it.'

Birdie left the house and sat in her car for ages staring out of the front window, replaying everything that Marie had told her. Myriad thoughts coursed through her mind, all of them competing for her attention. What should she do about the search for her birth mother? Leave it? Pursue it?

She threw up her hands in despair. Not knowing which way to turn.

# Chapter 16

Birdie stole a glance at Twiggy, who was staring straight ahead out of the car window. They'd been parked on the opposite side of the road to Victor Rawlings' house since seven-fifteen, and he'd hardly said more than two words to her. It was most unlike him.

Usually, especially after a night out, she'd be sitting there, willing him to take a breath and shut up for a while. But today she could've done with his chatter. After meeting with Marie Davis, she'd gone out with friends to try and stop from dwelling on everything. It hadn't worked. She'd ended up getting plastered, throwing up in the pub toilets, and having a sleepless night, plagued with thoughts of her birth family.

'Are you going to be like this all day?' she asked.

'Like what?'

'You know full well what I mean. Quiet and not saying anything. Tell me what's wrong? And don't say, "Nothing," because it's obvious there is.'

'You're imagining things. I'm fine,' he said, waving his hand dismissively.

'I don't think you are. Is there something wrong at home?'

Twiggy glared at her. 'Look, there's nothing wrong with me, or at home, or anywhere. So get off my case. Okay?' He turned to face his window. 'Here he comes,' he added, pointing over at Rawlings' car as it was driven down the drive.

Birdie stared, open-mouthed, in her partner's direction. Never in all the time they'd been working together had he spoken to her like that. What was he hiding? Twiggy had always been an open book. What should she do? They didn't have time to talk it through now. And the way he behaved, there was no way he'd speak to her, anyway. She had no choice but to leave it. If it happened again, she wouldn't give in so easily.

Twiggy started the engine and waited until Rawlings' car reached the end of the drive. The driver indicated left, rather than right towards Leicester.

'Where's he going?'

'Your guess is as good as mine. I'll have to do a U-turn.' Twiggy pulled out onto the road and turned sharply.

'Fingers crossed he goes somewhere interesting that will help us nail him. If we can get something, it will put us in Curtis' good books. Sarge's, too, for that matter. And any time I can manage that has got to be a plus, knowing my history.' She grinned at Twiggy, but he ignored her, keeping his eyes focused on the road ahead.

Keeping well back, they followed Rawlings while he was being driven along the A508 and through the outskirts of Northampton. When they reached the M1 turn-off, the driver took the southbound entry point.

'I hope he's not going to London because there might not be enough petrol in the tank,' Twiggy moaned.

'Why didn't you fill up last night if you were running low?'

'I thought I had sufficient. It's not like we've been driving miles when watching him. I'd planned to go to the garage at the weekend because my tyre pressures need checking, too.'

'Well, if we do run out of fuel, I'll be leaving you to explain that away to the DI and Sarge. And good luck with that,' she joked.

That actually raised a smile from her partner. But afterwards, he resumed the silent treatment. Well, if he wasn't going to entertain her, Birdie would have to think of something else, so she used the time to ponder on her friend Tori's request last night that she accompany her on a visit to a local medium on Saturday evening. Birdie had never seen one before and was sceptical, but Tori had been insistent because she wanted to know about her current boyfriend. It wasn't like Birdie had to believe anything the woman told her. It might be fun, and they'd planned to go out after.

'They're pulling in, so I'll be okay for petrol,' Twiggy said when they turned off into the Watford Gap service station.

'More by luck than judgement, though. Park over the other side so they can't see us, but make sure we can still see their car.'

After a couple of minutes, Rawlings headed towards the entrance, holding his phone to his ear.

'Shall we follow him inside together, or should one of us stay in the car?' Twiggy asked.

'Rawlings is the one we're keeping an eye on, so I think we should both go and see what he's up to.'

'Okay.'

The noise hit her as they walked through the double-height entryway. The place was heaving, and it took several scans of the place to spot Rawlings. 'There he is,' she said, nodding towards the rear of a café where he was sitting with two men. 'You get us something to drink, and I'll find a table fairly close by so I can get a good view of who he's with and take photos of them.'

Birdie skirted around the edge of the seating area and found a table behind Rawlings, ensuring that he couldn't see her. She positioned herself in such a way to make it look like she was on her phone and then took several photos of the men he was with.

The men were wearing jeans and sweatshirts and not dressed for business, unlike Rawlings, who was wearing his usual suit and tie. They could be the men who Margaret Clarke had mentioned seeing him with.

When Twiggy arrived, they sat in relative silence, and she kept her eye on Rawlings, who was in deep conversation.

'Shame we can't hear what they're talking about,' Twiggy said, wiping his mouth with a serviette after demolishing a cream cake.

'We're not going to in a place like this – probably why they chose it, so they can't be overheard. We might if we could plant a mic on him, but there is no way we'll get permission for that.'

'Surely he can't be staying too much longer, or the driver wouldn't have waited in the car. He'd have come in and got himself something.'

'Not everyone has to eat every five minutes,' she said, raising an eyebrow.

'Very funny,' Twiggy muttered, scowling in her direction.

'I was thinking, shall we use my car tomorrow, to make sure we're not spotted? We could alternate each day between yours and mind,' Birdie suggested, wanting to change the subject.

'No way am I going to spend a whole day in your car. Not with the havoc it plays on my back. We'll use mine, and I'll make sure to be careful.'

After a further twenty minutes, Rawlings stood, shook hands with both men, and headed out of the café. Thankfully, he didn't look in the officers' direction.

'Okay, let's go,' Birdie said.

They gave him a head start, so they didn't look too conspicuous, and made it back to the car in time to see the driver leave and take a sharp left, which would enable him to double back and head onto the motorway in the direction they'd come.

'My bet is he's heading for Leicester, and his office,' Twiggy said.

He was correct, and after Rawlings had been dropped off, Birdie turned to Twiggy. 'I'm going to call Curtis and ask him what he wants us to do with the new intel.' She hit the shortcut key on her phone for Curtis.

'DI Curtis.'

'Hello, sir. It's Birdie. Rawlings met with two men at Watford Gap services. I've taken photos of them and wanted to ask for permission to go back to Market Harborough to see if we can identify them. I think it might be a better use of our time rather than waiting here until three and the shift changes.'

'I'd rather you continue with your shift, just in case he goes out again. Email me the photos and I'll get someone else onto it. I'm in back-to-back meetings for the rest of the day, so if you have any queries, contact Sergeant Weston. I'll check in with him later.'

'Yes, sir.' She ended the call and placed her phone on the dash. 'He wants us to continue our shift. Bloody typical. We find evidence and someone else gets to investigate it, leaving us stuck here twiddling our thumbs. We should be the ones to move this case forward.'

# Chapter 17

Seb took the stairs to the second-floor flat in Aikman Avenue, New Parks, where Keith Collins lived. He walked along the external corridor and glanced over the balcony. A gang of boys had been hanging around, so he'd parked his car away from the flats, not wanting to risk it being vandalised.

When he reached the flat, he knocked on the door and waited. There was no answer, so he peered through the gap between the net curtain and the edge of the front window. A man was sitting in an easy chair, watching the television. Seb banged on the window and the man jumped. Seb then gave a sharp knock on the door again. Within a few seconds, the door was opened by a stocky, tattooed man in his late forties, about five foot eight with cropped grey hair, freckles, and a cross earring dangling from his left ear. He was a slightly older version of his brother.

'This better be good – I'm watching something,' the man said, scowling at Seb.

'Keith Collins?'

'Who wants to know?'

'My name's Sebastian Clifford and I work for Lenchester CID. I'd like a few moments of your time to ask some questions.' He showed his ID, and the man scrutinised it before returning his gaze to Seb.

'What about?'

'May I come inside?'

'I suppose so,' the man grunted, turning and heading into the living room.

Seb closed the door behind him and followed.

'Please turn the sound down,' Seb said, nodding at the TV, which was blaring out at an unacceptable level, and surely must have been annoying for his neighbours.

Collins glared in his direction and then picked up the remote and set the television to mute.

'Well?' the man said, his hand on his hips. 'Make it quick. I don't have all day.'

'I'm here to ask you about Robert Walker.'

'Never heard of him.'

'He used to be friends with your brother, Gareth. Perhaps that will jog your memory.'

'I've still never heard of him. I don't know any of my brother's friends. Not now, or in the past. Is that it?'

'Gareth and Rob went to school together, and about twenty-five years ago, when they were sixteen, they'd help you out by doing odd jobs,' Seb said, ignoring the man's comments.

'You what? How the hell am I meant to know who my brother hung out with all that time ago? Or if they worked for me? Who told you that pile of shit, anyway?'

'Your brother. He informed me that they worked for you occasionally. There was also a third young man, named Marty McNeil, who was sometimes with them.'

'If you say so.' Collins shrugged.

'Yes, I do.' Seb wasn't fooled by Collins trying to act all nonchalant. The man's eyes were darting all over the place. Seb moved so he was blocking the doorway, in case Collins decided to make a run for it, although he wouldn't get far in bare feet.

'Even if I do remember … which I don't,' Collins added quickly, 'so what?'

'Robert Walker was viciously assaulted twenty-five years ago, and the police have reopened the case.'

'And you're trying to pin it on me because I've got a record. Fucking typical of you lot.'

'I'm not here to arrest you, merely to enquire into your relationship with Walker.'

'I didn't have a *relationship* with the kid. I'll admit that Gareth used to help me sometimes, and he might have had his friends with him. I only gave him stuff to do so it kept the old woman off my back.'

'Your mother?'

'Yes, my *mother*,' Collins repeated, imitating Seb's clipped accent.

'Did they deliver drugs for you?'

Collins folded his arms and glared at Seb. 'You can't prove anything. I'm saying nothing without my solicitor.'

'For goodness' sake, I'm not here to investigate your illegal activities. I'm looking to find out what happened to this boy. Now, what sort of work did they do for you?' Seb took a step forward, closing the distance between them. It was enough to make Collins squirm.

'They didn't deliver any drugs. Just took messages to people from me, mainly to set up meetings. It helped me keep a low profile. And that's it. They did nothing else.'

Seb wasn't going to push that any further, even if Gareth and McNeil had given a slightly different version of the work they'd undertaken for the man.

'You admit that you do remember Robert Walker?'

'Maybe, now I've had time to think about it, I do.'

'Do you remember his girlfriend Charli? Her name then was Charlotte Fenton.'

Colour drained from his face. 'Nope. Never heard of her.'

He was lying. He couldn't meet Seb's gaze and was blinking furiously.

'To clarify, you definitely don't remember seeing Robert Walker with Charlotte Fenton.'

'No, I don't. It's too long ago, and I didn't keep tabs on my brother, his friends, or their girlfriends. Okay, I might remember this boy. I think he was tall with dark hair, but that's it.'

'Do you remember the attack on him?'

He shrugged. 'Why have you opened the case now, after all this time?'

'We're in possession of some new information.'

'What information?'

'I'm not able to disclose that.'

'Yeah, well, that's your problem. I know nothing, so if that's it, I'm busy.'

'Do you work?'

'What's it to you?' Collins growled.

'I just wondered.'

'Well, you can keep your wondering to yourself and piss off.'

Seb clearly wasn't going to get any further with the man, but it was interesting that he'd lied about knowing Charli. He'd definitely be investigating that.

'Thank you for your time. I might be in touch again.'

'Don't bother.'

Collins marched into the hallway and opened the front

door. He slammed it shut the moment Seb was in the corridor.

# Chapter 18

'Clifford.' Seb brought his phone to his ear. He was already at the Tea Rooms in Thorpe Langton where he'd arranged to meet with Charlotte Newton, and his voice felt conspicuously loud in the quaint café.

'It's Ellie, guv … I mean Seb. I wanted to let you know that Charlotte Fenton's dad is a Victor Rawlings, local businessman and philanthropist. According to my research, although he lived with the girl's mother, they weren't married, and Charlotte used her mum's surname. I'll text you his details.'

'That's excellent, thanks, Ellie. Would you mind doing a little more digging into him? You'll have to ask the DCI first, though.'

'I've already done some, in case you needed to know more. Rawlings owns a large company called VR Machinery, which imports and exports farm parts and machines. He's very influential in the community and is known for his charity work. He used to live in Lenchester, where he had some office premises, but fifteen years ago he moved to a village called Arthingworth, which is out your way, and his offices are now in Leicester. He's in the media all the time, and the press love him. But …' her voice fell away.

'What is it?'

'I can't validate this, which is why I wasn't sure about telling you, but when I was digging, I came across some social media posts talking about what Rawlings was like in the past. It seems he had a darker side to his character. There were rumours about people who had crossed him disappearing. Shall I continue looking into him? I might be able to dig up more?'

'What you've found so far is a great help. Don't do anything without the DCI's permission, but if she says yes, then please continue. It wouldn't be the first time a philanthropist has hidden behind their supposed good works.'

He ended his call with Ellie and kept his eyes focused on the entrance. Charlotte was already ten minutes late. He'd give her until twelve-thirty, and if she hadn't turned up by then, he'd go back to her house.

At twelve-fifteen, she walked into the café and glanced around the room. When she was looking in his direction, he raised his arm to draw her attention. She acknowledged with a nod and headed over to his table.

'Sorry, I'm late,' she said, pulling out the chair opposite and sitting. 'Have you ordered?'

'I was waiting for you.'

'Okay.' Charlotte called over one of the staff members from behind the counter and he took their order for lunch.

'Thank you for turning up to speak to me,' Seb said after the waiter had left them.

'You didn't really give me much choice, did you?' Charlotte replied through gritted teeth.

If Seb wanted to learn more about her relationship with Rob, he'd need to try a softer approach than the one he'd adopted with Keith Collins.

'Why did you choose to meet here, considering it's close to where you live?'

'Because I didn't want to be spotted in an out-of-the-way place by someone who might get the wrong idea. I told my husband I was meeting you to discuss a charity event and that you're trying to persuade me to be on the committee. That way, if we're seen together and it's reported back to him, there's a logical explanation and he can truthfully say he already knew.'

She had certainly thought it out. Almost overly. Why was she so worried about her husband finding out?

'I understand. Now, I'd like to know more about you and Rob Walker. You come from very different backgrounds in terms of your schooling and where you both lived. How was it that you became acquainted?'

'All I can tell you is that we met at a friend's party. Because we were at an all-girls school, boys had to be invited from elsewhere. I honestly can't remember exactly how, or why, Rob had an invite.'

So far, there were no indications that the woman wasn't telling the truth.

'I see. And you don't recall the two of you discussing this when you first met?'

Charlotte bit down on her bottom lip. 'I expect he knew someone from our school, or one of his friends knew someone, and that's how he ended up there. I'm not trying to fob you off. You know what these word-of-mouth parties were like. You could end up with a house full of guests and know hardly any of them. This party was no different.' She waved her hand dismissively.

'So, to clarify, you met Rob Walker at a friend's party and then began dating him?'

She shook her head. 'No, it wasn't like that. My friend, Izzy, had a thing for his friend Gareth, and one Saturday evening, when we had a weekend exeat from school, she arranged to go to the cinema with him. I tagged along for moral support, and he brought Rob. We went to see the latest James Bond film. It was fun.' Her lips turned up into a smile.

She clearly remembered Rob affectionately.

'And after the film had finished?'

'The four of us went to the local pub.'

'But you were underage.' He winced at his words. Birdie would accuse him of being out of touch, and she'd be right. Even twenty-five years ago, kids went to the pub.

'The boys looked old enough, and they were served, and no one was asked for any ID. It wasn't unusual for us to go to the pub.'

'And it was after this particular night that you began to date Rob?'

'Yes, that's correct.'

'You told me yesterday that it was a casual thing. Was that really the case because your body language is telling me otherwise?'

She sighed and glanced down at the table. 'Sorry. I played it down a bit. We were serious about each other at the time. Well, as serious as you can be at that age.'

'For how long were you a couple?'

'We went out together for six months but …' Her voice faded and a pained expression flickered in her eyes.

'But what?' Seb asked gently.

'My father found out I was seeing him after one of his Rotary friends had seen us out together. I don't know how he discovered Rob's name, but he knew exactly who he was and where he lived. Daddy forbade me to go out with Rob, and when I refused, he grounded me. He even withdrew permission for me to go into town or out with my friends while I was at school.'

'Your father being Victor Rawlings.'

'Yes. How do you know that? Rhetorical question. Of course you know, because you've been doing your research. I presume you'll also know that he's not a man to toy with.'

'Could you explain what you mean by that?'

'My father has an extremely bad temper when pushed. He does have it under control most of the time, but the threat is always there. It's the way he is.'

'Which is why your relationship with Rob ended after six months?'

'When my father found out about us, we'd only been seeing each other for four months. After that, we met in secret.'

'Despite you admitting that he wasn't a man to get on the wrong side of.'

Charlotte gave a hollow laugh. 'I was his daughter and thought I knew best.'

'How did you manage to continue meeting Rob?'

'I'd sneak out of my dorm room in the evenings, and my friends covered for me. It wasn't difficult.'

'And this went on for a further two months?'

'Yes. Until … until … the time he was attacked.' She closed her eyes and gripped the edge of the table.

'Is there anything you can tell me, however small, that might give me a better idea of what occurred that night?' Seb asked after several moments of silence.

'I don't think so. I was home for the weekend and had arranged to meet Rob outside of the cinema. My father had eased up on punishing me, and I thought he believed that it was all over. But when I told him I was going out with friends to see a film, he refused to let me go. He must have suspected that we were still together, after all. I couldn't contact Rob because he didn't have a mobile and it was too late to phone him at home because he would have already left.'

'What did you do?'

'Nothing. I assumed that Rob thought I'd stood him up. I hoped he'd realise that it was down to my father. But …' She gave a half-hearted shrug.

'How did you learn about the assault?'

'I phoned Rob's home on Sunday morning to explain, but there was no answer. I tried lots of times and still couldn't get through. I wondered if they'd all gone out for the day, then that evening, I saw the attack reported on the television news. They didn't have to say who the victim was because I knew it was Rob. Don't ask me how, I just did. And then the next day, when they gave out his name, I-I-I knew for sure.' Her voice cracked. 'It was the worst moment of my life. I wanted to go to the hospital to see him, but I couldn't, in case my father found out.' She rested her head in her hands and rocked gently back and forth.

'Why didn't you go to the police when they were asking for people who knew anything to come forward? You could've explained that you'd planned to meet, and at least they would've known where he was likely to have been beforehand.'

Charlotte glanced up at Seb. 'I couldn't. It wasn't as if I knew who carried out the attack. It was best no one knew about us.'

'Do you think your father had anything to do with the assault?'

'What?' Her eyes widened.

'If he found out you were still seeing Rob?'

'No. That's ridiculous. He might not have approved, but that doesn't mean he'd have sent his goons after Rob. He—'

'Goons?' Seb asked, interrupting.

'A figure of speech. There's no way my father would have done anything to Rob.'

'Even though you've already told me about his temper.'

'This is different. We were only sixteen at the time. We hadn't done anything wrong.'

'Are you close to your father?'

She frowned. 'Yes, why do you ask?'

'Just curious.'

He would be questioning Victor Rawlings, but he'd keep that to himself. He didn't want the man forewarned.

'Did you make any attempt to find out how Rob was afterwards? Was your friend Izzy still seeing Gareth?'

'They lasted less than a month, so no, she wasn't. I followed the case in the media and discovered that Rob was seriously injured. I realised then it would have been pointless to visit him because he probably wouldn't have even known me. And I didn't want to risk getting into trouble. I know that sounds bad, but I was only young.'

'I understand. There is something else I'd like to ask. Do you remember Keith Collins, he's Gareth's older brother?'

'No. The name doesn't ring a bell.'

'Rob, Gareth, and another young man called Marty would sometimes work for him. Did Rob ever mention that?'

'Not that I recall. Do you think he was involved in the attack?'

'I have no evidence of that. At the moment, all I'm doing is trying to get some idea of Rob's life before the assault. If you think of anything that might assist in our enquiries, then please let me know.' He pulled out a card from his pocket and passed it over to her.

'Of course. I know it's been twenty-five years, but I sincerely hope you catch the bastard who did this to Rob.'

They left the tea rooms together, and Seb waited until she'd driven out of the car park before heading in the direction of her father's house.

He had no idea whether Rawlings would be there, but he decided to risk it. If he wasn't at home, he'd visit his workplace in Leicester.

# Chapter 19

'What the …?' Birdie stared at the entrance to Rawlings' office. What was he doing there? He was supposed to be in Lenchester working on Whitney's case. But it was definitely him. No question. You couldn't mistake anyone else for him, not at that size. 'Wake up, Twig.' She shook her partner's shoulder. 'Look over there.'

'What? Eh?' He stared at her, his eyes still half closed. He stretched his arms above his head and gave a loud yawn.

'Too late, you've missed him.'

'Missed who?'

'Seb. He's just walked into Rawlings' office.'

'You mean Clifford?' He turned to her, frowning.

'How many other Sebs do we know?' She gave an exasperated sigh.

'What's he doing in there?'

'That's what I want to know. We'll ask him when he comes out, and …' She paused as her attention was diverted by the Mercedes pulling up outside. 'Crap. Rawlings' driver has arrived. That means he'll be leaving.'

'And there's Clifford, too,' Twiggy said, pointing to the other side of the road.

She kept an eye on Seb as he jogged down the steps and headed in the opposite direction to where they were parked. No wonder she hadn't noticed his car if it wasn't anywhere near them.

'We can't go after Seb now because we've got to follow Rawlings. Damn,' Birdie said.

The man came out of the front entrance, climbed into the rear of his car, and the driver pulled out into the traffic. Twiggy followed.

'Phone Clifford. He better not be interfering with our investigation, or the DI will go ballistic,' Twiggy said.

'How can he be interfering? He doesn't know what we're doing.'

'Are you sure you haven't told him?' Twiggy asked, tossing a glance in her direction. 'It would be just our luck for that stuck-up twit to be involved somehow. Maybe he's working for Rawlings.'

'Shut up, Twiggy. Of course Seb's not working for him. And stop saying mean things about him.'

'Why shouldn't I? You're my partner and he's always treated you like you're his.'

'I'm nobody's possession. I'm here to solve cases, not to be in anyone's gang. You're being ridiculous.'

'Okay, phone him and see what he's doing.'

'That's what I was about to do before you started saying stupid stuff,' she said, giving a frustrated sigh.

She pulled out her mobile and hit the shortcut key. It went straight to voicemail.

*'This is Sebastian Clifford from Clifford Investigation Services. Please leave your name and number and I'll get back to you.'*

'It's me. Phone as soon as you get this message.' She

ended the call, annoyed that she couldn't find out straight away what he was up to.

'Hmm. He didn't answer. That's suspicious.'

'No, it's not. He might be on another call. Or he might not have hands-free in his car. He'll phone me when he hears my message, and we'll find out what's going on. Where do you think Rawlings is heading?'

'I've no idea. It's not anywhere he's been before.'

Twiggy followed the car for twenty minutes across the city until they arrived outside a Victorian semi-detached property, with a Whitcliffe Accountants sign in the small front garden of the one on the right. The driver pulled up outside, and Rawlings stepped out of the car and marched up to the entrance while the car moved to park at the rear.

'He's seeing his accountant.' She glanced at the time on her phone. 'I'm guessing his appointment is at two. I wonder if he'll head back to the office after or go straight home?'

'We'll have to wait and see. I'm hungry, do you want anything from the bakery over there?' Twiggy pointed to the small shop on the opposite side of the road.

'An eclair would be lovely, thanks.'

Twiggy jumped out of the car and walked to the pedestrian crossing, waiting until the lights changed before making a beeline for the bakery. Birdie held up her phone and took a photo of him going inside. She laughed to herself, thinking of the fun she could have threatening to show Evie the evidence.

While Twiggy was in the bakery, Birdie tried calling Seb again, but it still was only picking up voicemail. Where the hell was he? Why on earth was he visiting Victor Rawlings? What could it possibly have to do with Whitney and her brother in Lenchester? It made no sense, but she wasn't going to admit that to Twiggy because he'd go on about Seb even more.

The car door opened. 'Couldn't get you an eclair, so I bought you a jam doughnut. Hope that's okay.' Twiggy eased himself into the driver's seat, holding two brown paper bags. A savoury smell permeated the air.

'It will do,' she said, taking the bag he offered and fishing out the doughnut.

Twiggy removed a large savoury pasty from his bag, which he began eating as if his life depended on it. 'Mmm. This is delicious.'

'Just so you know, I took a photo of you going to the bakery that I'm going to send to Evie,' she said, smirking at him.

'What?' he spluttered, nearly choking.

'I've got to have some ammunition.'

'I hope you're joking because I'm in no mood for the fallout at home.'

Ahh, so that was it. There were problems at home. Fingers crossed they were able to resolve them because she'd hate for them to split up. They'd been together for years.

'Rest assured your secret's safe with me.'

They finished their snack and waited a further twenty-five minutes before Rawlings came out of the accountant's.

'Right, let's see where he's going now. It's a bit early to go home,' Twiggy said.

'We'll soon find out,' Birdie said as the driver brought the car around and Rawlings hopped into the back.

They followed him all the way back to Arthingworth.

'It looks like I'm wrong. But it's very strange for him to go home this early. According to Margaret Clarke, he works until at least five most days, so what's he doing back here now?'

'Maybe he's had enough for the day. Or he's going out somewhere. He could have a charity event that he's got to get changed for. It could be any reason. He's the boss and can do what he likes. The question is are we going to stay here and watch to see if he goes out again?'

'His driver's leaving.' Twiggy nodded at the car as it returned down the drive and turned right.

'So, it looks like he's just come home early. I'll message the next team to let them know to drive here for the start of the next shift.' She pulled out her phone and sent a quick text. 'They're not going to make it here by three, but I don't suppose that matters. Shall we head back to the station and check in? They might have been able to ID the two men from this morning.'

'Sure.' Twiggy started the engine.

'Wait,' Birdie shouted, staring into the wing mirror at the car coming up behind them. 'Look.'

'At what?'

'At who's coming down the road and indicating to turn up the drive. It's Seb. He's meeting Victor Rawlings here. We can't go until we find out what's going on.'

'I always knew there was something crooked about him. I bet he's doing something he shouldn't,' Twiggy said, his top lip curled.

'For God's sake, Twiggy. Give it a rest. Of course he's not doing anything wrong. He's working for DCI Walker at Lenchester. This is something to do with the case, or it could be another job, or …' Her voice fell away. But what if Twiggy was right? Surely Seb wouldn't do anything he shouldn't.

'So you say. You've got a blind spot as far as Clifford's concerned. I can be more objective, and I'm saying there's something dodgy going on.'

'Which is why we're waiting for him so we can find out.'

# Chapter 20

Victor Rawlings' house was set in stunning, immaculately kept grounds, and to the right of the property was a large swimming pool. Seb drove to the left of the mini-round-about that had been planted with succulents and stopped on the gravel in front of a set of large garages. He left his car and made his way to the front door.

When he'd gone into Rawlings' offices and asked to speak to the man, his personal assistant had come down. Seb had explained that he was from Lenchester CID and wanted to speak to her boss but wouldn't tell her what it was about, despite her probing. After going back to speak to Rawlings, she'd returned and informed him that he should go to the house in Arthingworth at three. There had been no further explanation.

Why had Rawlings requested they speak here?

Either he knew what it was about … although how could he, unless Charlotte had warned him that Seb had been asking questions? Or he didn't want to risk speaking to the police in front of his employees. Either way, it gave Seb a chance to survey the man's habitat, and that could prove useful in the future. Despite Charlotte's protestation, Rawlings was very much on Seb's radar regarding the attack.

Using the large brass knocker, he rapped on the wooden door and waited. Footsteps approached, and the door was opened by an older woman wearing an apron. 'Good afternoon, sir. How may I help?'

'Good afternoon. I have an appointment with Mr Rawlings. The name's Clifford. If you would please inform him that I have arrived.'

'Mr Rawlings mentioned that he was expecting you. He's waiting in the drawing room. Please follow me.'

They walked through an impressive vaulted and marble-floored entrance hall, across to a room situated on the right. She knocked twice and opened the door.

'Yes, Kendra?' A voice boomed out.

'Mr Clifford's here to see you, sir.'

She stepped out of the way and Seb strode in. Rawlings stood, a newspaper in his hand. He was around five foot ten, slim build, and was wearing an open-necked shirt with a pale blue V-necked sweater and a pair of navy trousers.

'Come in, Mr Clifford, and take a seat. Would you like tea or coffee? I'm going to have one.'

'Whatever you're having is fine, thank you.'

Seb walked over to one of the deep red three-seater sofas and sat opposite Rawlings. He glanced around at the luxurious surroundings. No expense had been spared in the décor, which showed signs of having been undertaken by an interior designer. Despite this only being the drawing room, there were two huge glass chandeliers hanging from the high ceiling, and a green-and-cream striped chaise longue was situated close to a set of French doors that looked out onto the splendid garden. There was a Lowry hanging above the impressive fireplace, and large paintings adorned each of the walls. Whether or not they were prints, Seb was unable to tell from his position.

'Now, how may I help you?'

'Why did you wish to speak to me here rather than at your office?'

'I didn't have time to talk earlier because I had an appointment with my accountant, and I wasn't sure how long I'd be. I didn't wish to return to the office. There was nothing underhand by my actions. It was simply a case of logistics,' Rawlings said coolly.

'Yes, I'm sure it was. I was simply curious, that's all,' Seb said, not wanting to put the man's back up, even though he wasn't convinced by the explanation.

'So, I reiterate, why are you here?'

'I'm working with Lenchester CID on a case from twenty-five years ago, and I believe you might be able to help.'

Seb scrutinised the man's face for any signs of recognition, but there was none.

'You'll have to give me more information than that. I have no idea what you're talking about,' Rawlings said dismissively.

'Do you remember a young man called Robert Walker?'

'No. Should I?'

'He was the boyfriend of your daughter Charlotte for a few months.'

Rawlings leant forward, cupping his chin in his hand as if trying to think, but it was too forced and didn't appear genuine.

'No,' he said after a few moments. 'Sorry, I don't recall the boy. But you're talking twenty-five years ago, and that's a long time for anyone to remember. I'm sure if it was you, you'd have the same difficulty.'

'Possibly,' Seb agreed, even though, of course, it wouldn't have been an issue for him.

'If this young man only dated my daughter for a few months, then I'm unsure how I could possibly help.'

Interesting that he hadn't asked what the case was about. Was it because he already knew?

'Perhaps you could think a little harder. I have already spoken with Charlotte and—'

'You've been questioning my daughter without my knowledge?' He glared at Seb.

'Yes. Your daughter is an adult and doesn't need a parent or guardian with her when being interviewed.'

'Without a solicitor?' His eyes flashed.

'There was no need for a solicitor because it was informal.'

'I see.' Rawlings audibly drew in a breath, and his body relaxed a little.

'If you could please think back to when your daughter was sixteen. Robert Walker dated your daughter, and you forbade her to see him because you believed he wasn't suitable. He went to the local comprehensive school. A friend of yours informed you of the relationship. Do you recollect any of this?'

'Perhaps I do remember her going out with a boy who I deemed to be unsuitable. But I don't recall ever meeting him.'

'Do you remember being told about their relationship, though?'

'Yes, I believe it was someone from one of the charities I patronised. Why is it so important after all this time?'

Finally, he was asking the right questions. But it was too late. Anyone who didn't know about it would have asked straight away. Also, it had been a very high-profile media item at the time.

'Robert Walker was badly attacked and left with irreversible brain damage. The case was never solved. However, new evidence has come to light and I'm working with Lenchester CID to investigate it.'

The lines around Rawlings' mouth tightened, and his fists were clenched by his side. Did that mean he knew more about the attack than he was letting on? Everything was pointing that way.

'I'm sorry, I don't remember anything about an attack on one of Charlotte's boyfriends. Do you believe my daughter was involved?'

Maybe that was why he was so perturbed. Then again …

'We're investigating all avenues. Currently, we know that she was in a relationship with him up until the time the attack occurred. But she didn't come forward to speak to the police and inform them of what she knew. Why do you believe that was?'

'Not speaking to the police doesn't mean that she was involved. She was only sixteen and might have been worried about contacting them in case I found out.'

'Do you think that's likely?'

'I can't say, but it could be. Surely you don't think Charlotte was the person to attack this boy?'

'No, I don't believe she did. However, on the night the incident happened, Charlotte and Rob had arranged to go to the cinema, but you had refused to allow her out.'

Rawlings gave a relieved smile. 'Well, if she'd been banned from seeing him in the past and I found out she was planning to disobey me then, of course, I wouldn't have allowed her to go. At sixteen, there are more important things for children to do, like homework and studying.'

He sucked in a breath. 'And not going out with unsuitable young men. Knowing my daughter at that age, she did it to get back at me and …' His voice fell away.

Had he said more than he'd intended?

'Did you have a volatile relationship with your daughter when she was younger?'

'No different from any other parent. I could almost guarantee that if my daughter went out with this boy, it was to get back at me. And when I found out and grounded her, she would have hated me even more.'

'Did Charlotte's mother approve?'

'She was too soft with the girl and always gave in. Charlotte was the sort of child who needed discipline. My daughter and I have a good relationship now, and I have two beautiful grandchildren. Now is there anything else, because I'm busy?'

'Is there a reason for Charlotte not using your surname when growing up?'

'Her mother insisted she use the name Fenton. It was to get back at me because I'd refused to marry her. It was a tricky situation because I was still married to my first wife. Divorcing her just to marry Charlotte's mother would have cost me a fortune. So, I allowed my daughter to use the name Fenton.'

Before Seb had time to ask his next question, the door opened, and Kendra came into the room with their beverages.

He waited until she'd left the room.

'I'd like to ask you a little more about the attack on Robert Walker. Do you recall it happening?'

'No.' Rawlings shook his head.

'Are you sure your daughter didn't mention it to you? She would have been very upset at the time. Even though she didn't go to the police or visit the boy, according to her, it was a most distressing time for her. Can you remember a time when she was particularly depressed or morose?'

Rawlings stared at Seb for a while, then leant over and picked up a cup and saucer from the tray, which he passed to Seb. He then picked up one for himself and took a sip.

Delay tactics?

'I've already explained to you that I have no knowledge of the attack. I also don't remember my daughter going out with someone who was assaulted. Yes, I can vaguely remember her going out with an unsuitable boy, but that's the extent of it. And no, I don't remember a time when she was particularly distressed. I have nothing further to say on the matter.'

'If you do think of anything, then please let me know.'

'I don't want you bothering my daughter again. She clearly had nothing to do with the incident. It was unfortunate that she'd been going out with the young man at the time he was injured. I will be advising her that she is not to speak to the police without a solicitor present.'

'I have one more question, and then I'll take my leave. How long ago did you move from Lenchester to Market Harborough?'

'Why is this important?'

'I'm curious.'

'I opened new business premises in Leicester fifteen years ago, after moving here, because it was closer for me to get to work.'

'Thank you for your time. I may have further questions in the future.'

'Call before returning because, like my daughter, I will not be answering without legal representation.'

# Chapter 21

'Here he comes,' Birdie said, watching through the binoculars as Seb left Rawlings' property.

What on earth was he doing there? She trusted her gut and knew, without question, that it was legitimate, whatever Twiggy might try to imply. For some reason, Twiggy was so blinkered as far as Seb was concerned and couldn't see him for who he really was. And he said *she* had the blind spot. Fortunately, the next surveillance team had messaged to say they were caught up in a traffic hold-up and wouldn't get there for a while longer. She'd been dreading having to explain about Seb to them.

'How are we going to stop him?' Twiggy asked.

'We'll wait for him to reach the end of the drive, and you can flash your lights. He should see us then.'

'Okay.' Twiggy turned on the engine and edged the car forward slightly, so they were now in view of the road in a more prominent position opposite Rawlings' driveway.

Seb came to a halt when he reached the junction with the road, indicated to turn right, and drove straight out.

Twiggy flashed his lights several times, but without success, because Seb kept on driving.

'Damn. He didn't see us,' Birdie said, thumping her leg with a clenched fist.

'Or he's deliberately ignoring us.'

'No, he's not. Follow him, and put your foot down so we don't lose him.'

Twiggy pulled out onto the road, which was clear, accelerated, and before long, they'd caught up with Seb. Twiggy tooted on his horn and flashed the car's lights. Eventually, Seb indicated left and pulled into a lay-by. They drew up behind him, and Birdie jumped out of the car and ran over.

Seb opened the window, his engine still idling. 'Birdie? What are you doing here?' His brows furrowed.

'It's more like, what are *you* doing visiting Victor Rawlings?' She rested her arm on the roof and glared at him.

'It's in relation to the case I'm working on with Whitney. His daughter is a person of interest.'

'You have got to be kidding me.'

'No, I'm not. Why would I do that?'

'We have him under surveillance.'

'You do?' Seb's eyes widened in amazement.

'Yes. For goodness' sake. What are the odds that we'd both be investigating the same person? It's ridiculous. Especially as you're investigating a twenty-five-year-old case, and we're looking at something in the present.'

Birdie turned her head as Twiggy came marching over. 'Well?' he demanded, scowling at Seb, his hands on his hips. 'What's going on?'

'That's what we need to discuss. But we don't want to be seen together out here. Why don't we go to The Windmill pub?' Birdie suggested.

'Good idea,' Seb said.

'Do you know where it is?'

'Yes, it's on the outskirts of Market Harborough, about ten minutes from here. Would you like to drive alongside?' Seb nodded at the empty passenger seat.

'No, she doesn't. She's with me, and we're on duty,' Twiggy snapped.

Birdie's head shot to the side. 'That's enough, Twig. You don't have to go all defensive. We are on the same side, you know.' She turned back to Seb. 'But I will go with Twiggy, and we'll meet you there.'

Birdie and Twiggy returned to the car. Twiggy's face was set hard, and he was squeezing the steering wheel so tight his knuckles had turned white.

'I don't bloody well believe this,' Twiggy muttered under his breath, though loud enough for Birdie to hear.

'What are you talking about?'

'Clifford. Who do you think? How the hell does he manage to wheedle his way into whatever it is we're doing? Are you feeding him information?'

'I'll ignore that comment, Twiggy. His case is nothing to do with ours. At least, I don't think it is. It was a coincidence that he was at Rawlings' house. The main thing for us to discover is what his intentions are. We don't want our investigations colliding.'

'Collide? How's that going to happen?'

'I don't know, it's just a figure of speech. Drive to the pub and we'll find out. And while you're at it, slow down. We haven't got the siren on, and you must be way over the speed limit. Take a few breaths and calm yourself down. We'll discuss what we're all doing and see where we go from there.'

'You're not to tell Clifford about our investigation. It's confidential, remember. That's what the DI said.'

'We'll only tell him what we need to,' Birdie said to pacify him.

She trusted Seb not to divulge anything. If only Twiggy would stop being so ridiculous and see Seb for who he really was and not get so jealous.

Twiggy drummed his fingers on the steering wheel, staring at the road ahead. He knew he was being a pain, but he couldn't help it. Clifford had rubbed him up the wrong way from the moment they'd met and, now, here he was again. Turning up, like a bad smell. He took a sideways glance at Birdie, who seemed to be in a world of her own, staring out of the passenger window. Was she annoyed with him because he didn't want Clifford to be involved? She probably was, but that was too bad because this was their case, and he didn't need that man trying to take away his partner.

He didn't get why Birdie couldn't understand how the relationship between partners was sacrosanct. Partners looked out for each other. It didn't work if you had more than one, but she seemed to think it would be okay. It wasn't. He'd moaned about Clifford and Birdie to Evie the other evening, and she'd told him to stop acting like a jealous child. She didn't get it, either.

'Turn left here, Twig,' Birdie said.

'I know that,' he snapped, instantly regretting it.

'That's okay then. But with the speed you were going, I thought we were going to sail straight past.'

She was right, but he wasn't going to admit it. He'd been too busy getting annoyed about Clifford to notice how fast he'd been travelling.

'Sorry,' he muttered.

He continued along the road for a further mile and then took a sharp left into the pub car park. Clifford was already there, standing beside the entrance, looking all tall and intimidating, and … He shook his head. He should really stop being so petty. But just because they might have to work together didn't mean he had to like the man.

They followed Clifford into the pub and up to the bar.

'What would you like to drink?' Clifford asked.

'We'll both have lemonades, thanks, because we're on duty. Is that okay, Twig?' Birdie asked.

'Sure,' he said, although he'd love a beer.

'I'll find us a table,' Birdie said.

She sauntered off, leaving Twiggy standing next to Clifford.

Should he talk to him?

'It's good to see you again, DC Branch,' Clifford said.

'You can call me Twiggy.'

'I wasn't sure if you resented the familiarity,' Clifford said, raising an eyebrow.

It was like the man could see exactly what was going on in Twiggy's head. Which was a worry. Perhaps he should change his attitude, for Birdie's sake. Then again, why should he? He wasn't the one who was intruding. But … He didn't want to fall out with Birdie. He would try to be more polite.

'Everyone else calls me that, so I don't mind if you do, too,' he said, feeling extremely magnanimous.

He waited with Clifford while their drinks were poured, and then they headed over to the table where Birdie was seated. Had she deliberately engineered for them to be together?

Clifford sat next to Birdie, and Twiggy sat opposite, placing the drinks in his hands on the table.

'Right, who's going to start?' Birdie said.

'Considering the confidential nature of our case, it should be him,' Twiggy said, nodding at Clifford, who stared at him with an amused expression on his face.

'Is that okay, Seb?' Birdie asked.

'Of course. My investigation into Whitney's brother's attack led to—'

'Who's Whitney?' Twiggy asked.

'DCI Walker from Lenchester CID. She's the person who's employed me to act as a consultant on the case.'

Twiggy exchanged a glance with Birdie, who was rolling her eyes in his direction. Did he already know that? He couldn't remember.

'Is this DCI a friend of yours?' he asked.

'We have worked together in the past. I thought you knew what I was doing.' Clifford glanced at Twiggy and then Birdie.

'If we knew what you were up to, then we wouldn't be here, would we?' Twiggy snapped.

'Try letting Seb get on with explaining, Twig, and then you'll find out,' Birdie said through gritted teeth.

'Go ahead, then.'

'Whitney's brother, Rob, was dating a girl called Charli before he was attacked. I've interviewed her and don't believe she was part of the attack, but that still requires further investigation. Her father is Victor Rawlings, which makes him also a person of interest. Charli had arranged to meet Rob on the evening of the attack but wasn't allowed out because she'd been grounded by her father. I visited Rawlings at his office to discuss his daughter and the attack, but he had an appointment with his accountant and requested that I meet him at his home. Now, what's your interest in the man?'

'Not the same as yours,' Twiggy said.

'For God's sake, Twiggy, that's enough,' Birdie said.

'We're looking into Rawlings because an informant from his workplace has suggested that the man is involved in importing and exporting firearms. Because he's such a high-profile person, with connections going right to the top of the force, our inspector has insisted that the investigation is kept quiet. We're in the very early stages, and he's currently under surveillance.'

'You shouldn't have told him all that,' Twiggy muttered.

'Rest assured, I won't be repeating any of this. But we may be able to assist one another,' said Seb.

'How?' Birdie asked.

'Sharing information about Rawlings. You might have discovered something which will aid my investigation and vice versa.'

'It's not our decision to make,' Twiggy said.

'Twiggy's right. We should speak to Sarge about it. It certainly seems a waste of resources for us both to be investigating the same man. Do you believe he might be involved in the attack?'

'He hasn't been excluded from my enquiries. If he was unhappy with the relationship between his daughter and Rob Walker, that could have been grounds for having the boy beaten up. His daughter referred to him as having "goons" who he might have been instructed to assault the boy.'

'And leave him for dead?' Birdie said, her eyes wide.

'If the attack went wrong, it could have happened,' Twiggy suggested.

'Exactly.'

'We know that Rawlings has connections with some dodgy characters. I took these photos this morning at the service station.' She held out her phone.

'I interviewed the man on the left earlier. He's Keith

Collins, the older brother of Rob Walker's friend. I had no idea of a connection between him and Rawlings.'

'Do you know the other guy?'

'No, sorry.'

'Okay. Let's drink up and we'll go back to the station,' Birdie said. 'We'll explain everything to Sarge and let him make the decision about helping each other out.'

'Or should we be discussing this with Inspector Curtis, as he's in charge of the case?' Twiggy asked.

'He did say we could report to Sarge as well because he knows about the operation. What about DCI Walker, should you be speaking to her, Seb?'

'I'll phone her on my way to your station and let her know. I doubt she'll argue against us sharing information. We have a finite number of days to solve this case, so any assistance would be gratefully received.'

# Chapter 22

Seb followed Birdie and Twiggy towards Market Harborough. He'd found DC Branch's behaviour particularly childish and certainly not fitting for an officer in his position. The way he was acting certainly wasn't going to help if the overlap of their cases resulted in them assisting one another and sharing information. The man needed to understand that Seb was no threat to his partnership with Birdie … unless she decided to come and work with him at his agency. But until such time that Birdie made a decision, it was a moot point.

It may well be that the two cases had nothing to do with one another. But irrespective of that, it wasn't desirable to have two different forces investigating the same man. It made no sense from a resources standpoint for them to operate independently, and it was unlikely to remain covert for long if officers were coming at him from all sides. Certainly, if Seb was supervising the cases, he would ensure the two operations were cognisant of one another's investigation.

He'd have a word with Birdie and ask her to smooth

everything over with her partner to ensure a good working relationship. She'd be the only person who could do that because he listened to her.

'Call Whitney,' he said into his phone.

'Hi, Seb,' the officer answered after a couple of rings.

'There's been a development in Rob's case.'

'Really?' The excitement in her voice echoed around the car.

He winced, annoyed at his choice of words. It hadn't been his intention to mislead her. 'It's to do with Charlotte Newton's father, Victor Rawlings, who could possibly be linked to our case, but I'm not sure yet.'

'Oh. I thought you had a break.'

'I'm moving forward. My call is regarding the Leicestershire force, in particular Birdie and her partner at the Market Harborough station. They have Rawlings under surveillance for possible illegal activities. We discovered our mutual interest quite by chance. I was exiting Rawlings' house, after questioning him, and they spotted me. We're on our way to speak to their sergeant concerning possibly sharing our intelligence, and I wanted to seek your opinion.'

'It makes perfect sense to me. Doubling up on work is a waste of time and resources.'

'My sentiments exactly.'

'You can let the sergeant know that you have my approval, providing nothing interferes with the progression of Rob's case. Although, I can't see that being an issue. Keep in touch.'

He arrived at the station after Birdie, and they were waiting at the entrance for him.

'We'll go straight to Sarge's office,' Birdie said, her voice strained.

The tension between her and Twiggy was palpable.

Had there been words between them during the journey? He wouldn't be surprised. Birdie would always voice her opinion if she was disgruntled by something, and she hadn't looked pleased with her partner back at the pub.

'Okay, you lead the way,' he said, even though he'd been to their office several times in the past.

Unlike Lenchester, they didn't require him to have a visitor's pass, although when they walked past the reception desk, he showed his Lenchester ID to save him from having to sign in, and the person on duty nodded.

Sergeant Weston's door was open, and Birdie tapped on it. 'Do you have a minute, Sarge?'

'Come in.' The three of them walked into his office. 'What are you doing here?' Sergeant Weston asked, narrowing his eyes at Seb.

'That's what we've come to discuss with you,' Birdie said.

Seb glanced around at the office. Anyone would've been forgiven for believing it had been ransacked. He diverted his eyes back to the officer sat behind the desk with his arms folded.

'Clifford's getting in the way of our investigation,' Twiggy said.

Seb drew in a long breath and shook his head in despair. 'I—'

'That's not it at all, and you know it, Twig,' Birdie said, interrupting him. 'It turns out that Seb's case also involves investigating Victor Rawlings, and once we'd discovered that, we decided to come to you for advice. We didn't want to bother DI Curtis until we knew what you thought. We wondered if we could share information and—'

'No, that's not possible.' The sergeant banged his hand on his desk. 'We're not collaborating with a private investigator. Birdie, you and Twiggy are working on a police matter. Mr Clifford, you're going to have to step back.' The officer locked eyes with Seb.

'It's not that simple. I'm working for the police, looking into an attack that occurred twenty-five years ago and which is quite possibly linked to Victor Rawlings although, at this point, I'm not able to inform you of how exactly he's involved.'

'The police? I thought you are working for yourself as a private detective.'

'Sarge, I've already told you that he's working with DCI Walker.'

'Oh, yes … so you did. That puts a different spin on things.'

'I have been in contact with DCI Walker, and she has given her permission for me to share information with you.'

'How did you get this job with DCI Walker?'

Although it was nothing to do with the officer, Seb judged it prudent to answer the question.

'We've worked together in the past, and she asked me to take on this particular case. I have been given two weeks to complete my investigation.'

'Why have they called you in and are not working on the case themselves?'

'It's complicated,' Seb said.

'I need to hear more than "it's complicated" if sharing of our intel is to be considered. Please explain.'

'The case I'm investigating involves an attack on DCI Walker's older brother when he was a teenager. Although I'm reporting directly to her, due to the conflict of interest, her team isn't working on it themselves, and she wasn't prepared to hand it over to anyone else. She obtained authorisation from Superintendent Clyde for me to be brought in. The reason it's being investigated now is because some additional evidence has come to light,' he added, pre-empting the sergeant's next question.

'I do know DCI Walker from many years ago at a conference we both attended. I was impressed with her, even then, and certainly don't wish to stand in her way. I will contact DI Curtis and run it by him. Go and wait in the office, and I'll let you know the DI's decision.'

Birdie grinned. 'When you speak to him, ask if they've been able to identify the two men in the photo I sent in this morning. If the DI says no, tell him that Seb has already identified one of them for us. That should help make up his mind if he's wavering at all.'

'Thank you, Birdie. I'll bear that in mind. Now go.' Sergeant Weston waved them away.

They returned to the office after stopping on the way for a coffee from the machine.

'I've got some private calls to make,' Twiggy said, leaving them for the other side of the office and sitting at an empty desk.

'Ignore him, he's being silly. You know what he's like, although I've never known him to be this bad before. I'll make sure he behaves if we're going to spend some time together,' Birdie said.

'Good, because I have neither the time, nor the inclination, to be part of any petty squabbling.'

'He doesn't mean it. Oh look, here's Sarge.'

The officer strode over to where Seb and Birdie were seated.

'DI Curtis has agreed to the cooperation and has replaced you and Twiggy on the surveillance team starting Monday to enable you to do more investigative work into Rawlings.'

'That's great. Twig, over here,' Birdie called out.

'Yes?'

'Sarge said that we don't have to watch Rawlings any more after tomorrow. The DI is using someone else, and we can do some more investigating into Rawlings using information that Seb has.'

'We have to work together?' Twiggy said.

'Not as such. We're just sharing what we have, that's all,' Birdie replied.

'Remember Victor Rawlings is extremely influential, and the confidential nature of our investigation remains,' Sergeant Weston said.

'Yes, Sarge,' Birdie said.

'The DI also said that they hadn't been able to identify either of the men you saw,' Sarge said.

'I might be able to help out with discovering the name of the second man,' Seb said.

'Appreciated. I'll let the DI know. Now, keep me informed of your progress, and I don't want to hear of anything untoward happening. In other words, no arguing, Twiggy,' Sarge said, staring at the DC.

'I resent—'

'Enough, Twiggy. You know exactly what I mean.'

'Yes, Sarge.'

The sergeant left the office, and Seb glanced at his watch, it was already gone five.

'Why don't we go back to my place, and we can share what we have so far?' he suggested.

'Good idea, then I can see Elsa. Is that okay with you, Twiggy?' Birdie asked.

'You two go, I've got to get home. Evie promised the kids we'd take them bowling.'

'Are you sure?'

'Of course, I am,' he said gruffly.

'Okay.' She turned to Seb. 'Do you want to stop on the way to pick up a takeaway? I'm starving.'

'Okay. You see to Elsa, and I'll meet you back there.'

Seb drove to the local Thai restaurant and picked up a selection of meals. He'd have the leftovers tomorrow, although he doubted there would be anything, knowing Birdie.

When he arrived home, he parked behind her Mini and walked into the house. As soon as he'd opened the door, Elsa came bounding towards him.

'Hello, girl.' He crouched down and gave her a hug and a pat.

'Hurry up,' Birdie called out while standing in the doorway to the kitchen. 'I'm starving and can smell the food. It's Thai, isn't it? It's making my stomach rumble. I've taken out the plates.'

They went into the kitchen and removed the plastic containers from the bag and placed them in the centre of the table. He smiled to himself. His mother would be mortified to see them eating that way. If they ever had a takeaway at home, the staff would put it on platters and serve them.

'Pass me a bottle of beer from the fridge, please?' he asked Birdie, who hadn't yet sat down.

'Sure. I'll have a cider. I stocked up with some when I was staying here.'

'Tell me a bit more about this person who's giving you information about Rawlings,' he said once they'd started eating.

'Her name's Margaret Clarke, and she's been working at his company for two years as a management accountant. Her son, Lee, was arrested for aggravated burglary, and he gave up Rawlings based on what his mother had told him. When we spoke to her, she seemed genuine, and she definitely believes that he's dealing in firearms.'

'Could she be a plant?'

'What makes you say that?'

'It could be a ploy by one of Rawlings' competitors.'

'That's hardly likely because they wouldn't know that her son was going to be arrested.'

'I'd like to meet this woman, if I may.'

'Why?'

'To get a fuller picture of what's going on and to see if she has any information that might help my investigation. If Victor Rawlings was dealing in firearms twenty-five years ago, that could be the reason behind Rob's attack. He could have stumbled upon something while dating Charli.'

'That's a bit of a leap.'

'Yes, but considering the short space of time I have to solve this case, I need to investigate every possibility.'

'I'll give her a call. It will have to be out of work hours because we don't want to put her at risk.' Birdie took out her phone and keyed in a number. 'Hello, Margaret. It's DC Bird. I was wondering if you're available in the next day or so to speak to a colleague and myself?' She was quiet for a moment. 'Hang on a minute, I'll just find out. Seb, are you okay with Saturday morning?'

'Yes, that's fine.' He'd have liked sooner but didn't wish to jeopardise the woman's position.

'We'll be with you late morning.' Birdie ended the call placed her phone on the table.

'We?'

'I assumed you'd want me with you, seeing as I've already met the woman.'

'Do you need Sergeant Weston's permission?'

'No. It's already been agreed that we can share info. That's all this is. Anyway, it's my day off and I can do what I like.'

Seb knew better than to disagree with Birdie's logic. 'Okay. We'll go together.'

'Remember, we must tread very carefully and make sure that no one is aware of our interest in her.'

'Agreed. If Rawlings *is* engaged in dealing firearms, then he wouldn't think twice about removing her if he'd discovered she was working with the police.'

# Chapter 23

Birdie glanced at her phone. Crap. She was going to be late. Again. She ran to her bedroom window and glanced down at the street. Seb was sitting in the front seat of his car, and she could just make out his fingers strumming on the steering wheel.

She'd had a late night after going out with friends. They'd ended up going to a club in town, and she'd stayed out way longer than she'd intended. Seb knew what she was like, but that wouldn't hamper the sanctimonious look on his face when she finally made it to his car. She gave a loud sigh and went back to the mirror, where she gave her hair a quick brush, grabbed a band and pulled it back off her face, and then smeared on some lip gloss. She picked up her bag from the bed and ran downstairs.

'I don't know when I'll be back, Mum,' she called out, sticking her head around the kitchen door where her mum was baking.

'Don't forget Auntie Catherine and Uncle Pete are coming round later with Lacey. You will be here, won't you?'

Damn. It had totally gone out of her head. She hated having to miss Lacey, her aunt and uncle's foster child, who she had a special bond with, which had grown even deeper after she'd investigated the child's background with Seb over a year ago.

'I'll try to be back, but I can't promise. I'm out with Seb for work.'

'But I thought it was your day off.'

'It is, in theory. But we've got to interview someone and today was the only time.'

'At least you'll be getting some overtime, then.'

If she put in for it. She wasn't sure she would, though, because the meeting hadn't been authorised in advance.

'Yeah, maybe. If I'm not back, please tell Lacey I'll see her another time. Hopefully tomorrow I'll have time to call round to Auntie Catherine's.'

'Will do. I hope Lacey won't be too disappointed.'

Nothing like trying to make her feel guilty. Not that it was done on purpose.

'She'll be fine. Anyway, I might be here.'

'Will you be in for dinner tonight?'

'No. I'm going out with Tori. Look, I've got to go, Seb's waiting for me. I'll see you later.'

She ran out of the house and around the back of the car to the passenger side of Seb's luxury BMW.

'Where have you been? I've been out here for ten minutes,' Seb said while she slid into the seat and clicked the seatbelt in place.

'That's because you're always early. Sorry. I had a heavy night last night and got up late. It's okay, we've still got plenty of time to get over to Kilby.'

'So, how did your visit to Marie Davis go?' Seb asked as he took off down her road.'

'Confusing.'

'Would you like to talk about it?'

'Not really … but I will because it's been driving me crazy. It turns out that my mother gave me up when I was only a few weeks old. But I wasn't adopted for a further six months. On top of that, it turns out that Kim might be in the UK. Marie didn't know where. So she said.'

'Don't you believe her?'

'I don't know. She might be protecting Kim. Maybe the medium I'm seeing later will be able to tell me more.'

'You're seeing a medium? Why?' He turned to her, an incredulous expression on his face.

Damn. She hadn't intended to mention it to him. He'd no doubt have plenty to say on the matter.

'Because my friend Tori wants me to go with her.'

'You do know that there's no scientific evidence to prove there's such a phenomenon as clairvoyance?'

'I don't care. It can't do any harm, and it might help me learn about my early life.'

'Does that mean you're going to continue with your search?'

'Yes. I have to.'

'I understand, but you do need to prepare yourself for your birth mother not wishing to communicate with you.'

'I know. I've thought of every possible outcome. But if there's a chance, I have to take the risk. Because if I don't, then it's going to haunt me forever.'

'Remember, I'm always here for you.'

'Thanks.' She reached over and squeezed his arm. He looked down and frowned. A giggle escaped her lips.

'Why are you laughing?'

'No reason. Well, only you. I blame your upbringing.'

'You'll need to elaborate.'

'All I did was touch your arm in a show of affection, and your face was a picture. You can't handle it.'

'It made me start, that's all. I'm used to affection.'

'Yeah, right. You're such a liar.'

He glanced at her and shook his head. 'Have you thought any more about finding your birth *father*?'

'What do you think? Of course, I have,' she added, not giving him a chance to answer. 'But considering I was the reason they broke up, he might not want to be contacted. Anyway, my top priority is to contact my birth mother and, after that, I'll decide whether to search for him or not. If she's prepared to meet or talk then I might ask her opinion. For now, my focus is on her. I can only handle one search at a time.'

The remainder of their journey to Kilby was in companionable silence, with neither of them attempting to make conversation. It suited Birdie because her head was still tender from overindulging the night before and she leant against the window, staring at the passing scenery while they drove through the various villages.

Margaret Clarke opened the door to her cottage before Seb and Birdie had even walked up the short path. She stared at Seb, her eyes narrowed.

'You're not the officer who was here the last time,' she said to him before turning to Birdie. 'Why didn't you tell me you were bringing someone else?' Her eyes filled with panic.

'There's no need to worry, Margaret. This is my colleague Sebastian Clifford. Trust me, it will be fine.'

'You do know this is extremely confidential and I'm risking a lot talking to you?' Margaret said, turning back to Seb.

'Mrs Clarke, I'm fully aware of the sensitive nature of

your involvement. Bearing that in mind, it might be prudent if we could come inside to discuss this, rather than talking on the doorstep,' Seb said, a gentle but insistent tone to his voice.

'Of course.' They followed her into the lounge. No offer of anything to eat or drink this time, unfortunately.

'Mrs Clarke, if you don't mind, I'd like to go over what you've already told DC Bird. To make sure I fully understand. Please could you explain to me why you believe VR Machinery is a front for something else?' Seb leant forward slightly in his chair and stared directly at the woman.

Birdie had seen him use that tactic in the past. It wasn't exactly intimidating, but it emphasised the seriousness of the situation.

'Um, okay. It all started when I discovered that deliveries and exports in some instances weren't matching up.'

Hmm. She hadn't told Birdie that. Perhaps Seb had been right in going over everything again.

'Please could you be more explicit regarding these discrepancies?'

Margaret nodded. 'Many things we import are subsequently exported to a different country, but on a couple of occasions, I discovered that goods had been exported out of the country before they had time to even clear customs, let alone be delivered to us and work their way through our system.'

Birdie frowned. How come the woman hadn't told them this before? Had she been holding back, wanting to make sure her son received the treatment he was promised before divulging? Was it something they'd discussed between them?

'How did you discover this? Did you consider that the paperwork had been completed incorrectly?' Seb asked.

'My first thought was that there had been an incorrect

logging of invoice numbers, but if that had been the case, the correct numbers would have appeared elsewhere in the system, and they didn't.'

'Did you discuss this with anyone?'

'Who? I report directly to Mr Rawlings, and I didn't want to make accusations in case I'd been mistaken. Remember, I hadn't been working there long when this happened.'

'What did you do?' Birdie asked.

'I decided to dig a little deeper in case there was some human error that wasn't immediately apparent, but I couldn't find anything. In the end, I chose to ignore it, but it has always niggled at the back of my mind and, from then on, I kept my eyes and ears open. It was after that I overheard the phone conversation regarding a firearms delivery.'

'I'd like to know which members of staff have been working for Mr Rawlings over the past twenty-five years. Do you have access to that information?' Seb asked.

'It will be in the HR database, I imagine. I should be able to access it. Why are you interested in going back so far?'

Birdie glanced at Seb. Was he going to discuss the Lenchester case with the woman? It wasn't something they'd agreed on. Then again, did it matter?

'I'm working on another investigation that may involve Mr Rawlings. This case goes back twenty-five years.'

Margaret frowned. 'Look, I'm helping you because of Lee. No one said anything about another investigation.'

'If we're going to charge Mr Rawlings, and give Lee a chance, the more information we have, the better. Knowing who has worked for the company over that period will assist us on both cases. Nothing will come back on you,' Birdie said to reassure her.

'In that case, I'll obtain a list of employees. I can already tell you that his driver has been with him for at least that length of time. His name is Dennis Hunter, and from what I've observed, he's more than a driver. He has other "duties".' She made quotation marks in the air.

'Could you be more explicit?' Seb asked.

'I didn't witness this, but according to office gossip, Mr Rawlings was approached by an angry man at a fundraiser for the local hospital. It was a cycle race, and Mr Rawlings was there to present the prizes. Supposedly, Dennis intervened, marched the person away to somewhere out of sight, and then beat the man up.'

'Was there any evidence to support this?'

'Well, that's what everyone who was there assumed because this man was seen shortly afterwards with a black eye and walking with a limp.'

Supposition, and hardly going to stand up in court as evidence of Rawlings character.

'You mentioned to DC Bird that you saw Mr Rawlings with two men one evening near the office.'

'Yes, that's right. A couple of dodgy characters.'

'How many times have you seen them with Mr Rawlings?'

'Only once, but I also saw them another time in a local café just up the road from work, chatting with Dennis. The only reason I remember is because it was strange to see Dennis in a café. Normally he's in his car waiting for Victor, or he is not there at all.'

'You didn't tell me this,' Birdie said.

'I didn't think it was important. Plus, it had slipped my mind until after you'd left here.'

'Would you recognise these two men again?' Seb asked.

'Yes, I think so.'

'DC Bird, please could you show Mrs Clarke the photo you have on your phone from Thursday?'

Birdie opened it and showed the photo to Margaret. 'Have you seen these men before?'

'Yes, they're the two men. Definitely.'

'Excellent,' Seb said, smiling. 'Thank you very much for your assistance. Please let DC Bird know when you have the list of past employees.'

'It shouldn't take me long to access it. What about Lee and the witness protection?'

'Our investigation is still ongoing, as you know. Being in custody is the best place for him at present,' Birdie said.

'I suppose so. Would you like a coffee or something to drink before you leave? Sorry, I forgot to ask when you arrived.'

'We don't have time. But thanks for the offer,' Birdie said, hoping that the woman couldn't hear her stomach rumbling. She'd missed breakfast.

The woman escorted them out of the house, and once they were far enough away not to be heard, Birdie turned to Seb.

'Why did we show her the photos? We know that Rawlings has met with them.'

'I wanted to confirm whether it was a one-off meeting, or whether Rawlings had a relationship with them. It being the latter gives more weight to my theory that he was involved in Rob's attack.'

# Chapter 24

Birdie sat alone on a two-seater sofa in the front room of a semi-detached house in Morley Street, playing with the edges of her cardigan. The television was on in the background, but she couldn't concentrate enough to watch the soap that was currently showing. Why had she let Tori talk her into this? Birdie had tried to resist, but Tori hadn't wanted to go alone. She said she'd heard great things about the woman and wanted to find out whether her latest boyfriend was *the one*. He'd been interviewed for a job in Dubai but so far hadn't asked Tori to go with him. Her friend wasn't even sure if she wanted to move overseas and leave her family and friends but had decided to visit Erica anyway to get some answers.

The door opened and Tori walked into the room, smiling from ear to ear. It must have gone well. 'Your turn,' she said, dropping down onto the sofa next to Birdie.

'Where do I go?'

'Erica's in the next room and she said to walk in. No need to knock or anything. She's just normal, not all spooky or anything. Don't look so worried. It's exciting to find out what's going to happen in the future. I can't wait to tell you what she said to me. It's nothing like I'd ever imagined. You're not going to believe how accurate she is. I'm telling you, she's amazing.'

At least Tori was happy, even if Erica had made it all up. It wasn't that Birdie didn't believe in spiritual stuff because she did. But she'd never been to a fortune teller before. Not even at the fair. But she'd go in with an open mind and try not to be too sceptical, even if it was costing her sixty pounds. Which she could well do without spending because all her spare cash was going into saving for a deposit on a house. As much as she enjoyed being with her family, she was desperate to buy somewhere for herself to live in.

Birdie sucked in a breath, stood up, and headed outside into the hall. Her heart was hammering, which was ridiculous considering all the dangerous situations her job had placed her in. Then again, this was personal.

She knocked gently on the slightly open door, even though Tori had said not to, and went straight in. Because she'd been sitting in a lounge, she'd assumed this would be a dining room, but it wasn't. Instead of dining furniture, there were three chairs and a low rectangular table. There was a lit candle on the sideboard, and the smell of lavender filled the air.

'Come in, Birdie,' Erica said, smiling at her.

Erica's husband had let them into the house, and so Birdie had no idea what the woman looked like. But Tori had been right. Erica did look ordinary and nothing like Birdie had imagined. Then again, all she'd ever seen were fortune tellers in the films, always at fairgrounds, wearing elaborate scarves in dark tents, so this was quite different. Erica was wearing jeans and a jumper and looked like any other person.

'Where shall I sit?'

'Over there,' Erica said, pointing to the high-backed striped chair. 'I'm going to be quiet for a while so I can connect with you, to see where you are at the moment with your energy.'

Birdie sat on the edge of the chair, leaning forward slightly, her hands wrapped around her knees. Her eyes were drawn to Erica, who was staring up at the ceiling.

After a few minutes of somewhat awkward silence, Erica looked directly at Birdie, a gentle smile on her face. 'I'm sensing you're a very kind-hearted person and a stickler for getting things right. Even if it does mean getting in trouble.'

True, but she could have taken a guess at that. Lots of people had those traits.

'Yes, I do like to get things right,' she admitted, sensing the woman wanted an acknowledgement from her.

'Someone is coming forward. It's a man who used to be a boxer. Were there any boxers in your family?'

'Not that I know of. But then I don't know all my family. Do you mean—?'

'Ah. Yes. He's telling me he came from your birth family, on your mum's side.' Her pale grey eyes, filled with concern, locked with Birdie's.

A shiver ran down her spine. How on earth could she know about her being adopted? Unless Tori had mentioned it. But why would she? Birdie hadn't confided in her about looking for her birth mother.

Birdie drew in a calming breath. She didn't want to show how much this was disturbing her. 'Then you will know that I have no idea about the history of my birth family, so can't comment.'

Erica nodded, a smile playing at the corners of her mouth. 'He used to be a bit of a character with a great sense of humour. He said that you inherited your poor timekeeping from him. Does that mean anything to you?'

Birdie swallowed hard. 'I do have a problem with always being late.'

'He's asking me to tell you not to worry about it. It's just who you are. He said are there any questions you'd like to ask him?'

She breathed out slowly, attempting to relax her beating heart.

'Yes,' she said, her voice barely above a whisper. 'I'd like to know more about my real mother.'

'He said she's confused. She has a good life but always at the back of her mind she wonders what happened to you.'

'Then why did she tell the adoption contact agency that she didn't want me to get in touch?' Birdie blurted out.

'He's saying you should find her to put things right.'

'That's just ridiculous. How does he know that? Anyway, I can't. I don't know where she is. I don't even know her last name. Can *he* tell me what her married name is?'

Erica was quiet for several seconds. 'I'm being told that you *can* find her. You have the tools at your disposal and all you have to do is use them.'

Birdie's fists clenched by her side. She sort of believed what was happening but, if it was true, why wouldn't he give her a name? Surely that wasn't too much to ask.

'Why won't he tell me?' she demanded.

Erica shrugged. 'I don't know. Wait …' The woman nodded her head slowly. 'He's saying that you should focus on her past. Her school.'

'Why can't he just give me her name?'

'I'm sorry, Birdie, it's not my decision. I'm only here as a conduit.'

'Okay,' Birdie muttered, expelling a disgruntled sigh. Was that the end of the session? She hoped so. She wanted to get out of there. Birdie looked at Erica, who had a distant expression on her face. Had the man changed his mind and was now telling her the surname?

'I'm getting someone else who would like to be known to you.'

Birdie's heart sank. There wasn't anyone else she wanted to hear from.

'Oh,' she said.

'His name is Ronald. Does that name mean anything to you?'

Birdie sat upright. She hadn't even thought of speaking to him. 'Yes. It could be my grandad, Ronnie. But he was never known as Ronald.'

As a child, Birdie had loved her grandad and had been devastated when he'd died from pneumonia several years earlier.

'That's my fault. I interpret what I'm presented. He said, yes, it is Ronnie. He wants you to know how proud he is of you and that you're a credit to the whole family. He's saying that the time's right for you to make an important decision. Does that make sense to you? Are you aware of what he means?'

Birdie shook her head. 'Not really. Unless he's talking about finding my birth mother like the other man did.'

'No. This is something different. Have you been thinking of changing your job recently?'

Birdie stared at Erica, her eyes wide. Even if somehow the woman had found out about her wanting to find her birth mother, no way could she have known that Seb had approached her to join him as a private investigator.

'I have been offered another position. It's to go into

partnership with someone I know. What does Grandad think I should do?'

Was she really asking this question to someone who'd been dead for years? How could he possibly have an opinion?

'He's saying that it's your decision, that you'll know at the time which road to take.'

Not another person hedging his bets. This was getting seriously annoying.

'Why can't anyone give me a straight answer?' she muttered to herself more than to Erica.

'It's how it works. Your grandad has asked me to enquire if there's anything else you would like to know.'

'Yes. Can you ask him if he thinks I should continue looking for my birth mother and if I do, will it be too upsetting for my parents?'

Was he going to give her an answer? She was really buying into this now because how could it be anything other than true?

'He's saying they understand your need to search, and you shouldn't keep them in the dark.'

'I did tell them I wanted to look for my birth mother, but they seemed so upset that I haven't told them anything else since.'

'He's saying that it will be okay. Your parents know that you love them, and they understand your need to learn your true identity. You should tell them.'

'Okay. Yes, I will.'

'He's telling me you should relax and go with the flow, and everything will work out for you. Thank you, spirits, for coming forward today … Yes, I will.'

Birdie frowned. Why had she suddenly stopped talking to her grandad? 'Have we finished?'

'Yes, the spirits have left me now. It's been lovely

meeting you, and I know that whatever you decide to do, you going to make a success of it.'

'Thank you.'

Birdie pulled out her purse from her handbag, paid, and then returned to the small lounge where Tori was checking her phone. She glanced up when Birdie walked in.

'Well? Is she brilliant, or is she brilliant?' her friend asked, jumping up and heading over to her.

'I'll tell you when I've managed to digest everything,' Birdie said smiling. 'Come on, let's get to the pub.'

# Chapter 25

'DC Bird,' Birdie said, answering her phone.

'It's Margaret Clarke. I have the list of employees that you asked for from the last twenty-five years.'

'Can you email it to me?'

'I'd rather give it to you in person. I don't want a trail. I copied and pasted the details into a document and printed it straight off without saving it. I can't risk being caught. It's not information that I should have any interest in.'

'Okay. If we drive over to your office now, can you nip out to give it to us?' Birdie glanced at her watch. 'We can be with you by ten.'

'Meet me in the bakery across the road. They have a little café area. If I go in there, no one will be suspicious because most people from the company use it daily.' The woman ended the call and Birdie replaced the handset.

'What's that all about?' Twiggy asked.

'It looks like we're going to Leicester to collect a list of the firm's employees. I'll give Seb a call and ask him to meet us back here at eleven-thirty so we can go through it. If he's back from London, that is. He had a family thing yesterday that he couldn't get out of. Though, come to think of it, he must have come back the same day, or he'd have asked me to take care of his dog.' She pulled out her mobile from her pocket and keyed in his number.

'Good morning, Birdie.'

'Where are you?'

'At home.'

'How was your family event?'

'As to be expected. Fortunately, it didn't last for too long, and I was home by ten last night. Is this a social call?'

'No. I'm at work. I wanted to let you know that Margaret Clarke has the list you asked for, and she'll only hand it over face to face. Meet us here at the station at eleven-thirty and we can go through it. Unless you have something else on.'

'I'm going to Lenchester this afternoon. I wondered—'

'If I'd take care of Elsa? Of course, you know I will.'

'Much appreciated. I'll meet you later at the station.'

When Birdie and Twiggy arrived at the bakery, at ten to ten, there were several customers in there, but none of them were Margaret.

'You find us a table, and I'll get us something to eat,' Twiggy said.

'You do realise we're only here to collect an envelope?'

'We can hardly hang around not doing anything, can we? That would look very suspicious. And we don't want to be spotted outside, either. Anyway, I'm hungry. What would you like?'

'Whatever you're having, but just one.'

She found them a table and waited while Twiggy joined the queue. It didn't take long before he came over with two coffees, two doughnuts, and a Cornish pasty.

'Nice little snack you've got there, Twig,' she said laughing.

'Breakfast and mid-morning snack combined.'

At exactly ten on the dot, the door to the café opened and Margaret Clarke walked in. She scanned the room and, when they'd made eye contact, headed over to them. She handed Birdie a brown envelope.

'Everything you need is in here,' she said, her voice barely above a whisper.

She immediately turned and walked over to the counter to join the queue. When she reached the front, she placed an order, and once it was filled, she left the bakery without paying them further attention.

By the time Birdie and Twiggy had returned to the station, Seb was already waiting for them. He was seated at Birdie's desk with a mug of coffee in front of him, staring at his phone.

'I see you're making yourself at home,' she said, nodding at the steaming cup.

'Sparkle got it for me before she left to go out,' he said, referring to the DC who sat on the opposite side of the office.

'You're lucky. She never does that for me,' Twiggy said.

'That's because you know where everything is and can help yourself,' Birdie quipped.

'That's beside the point.'

'Do you have the list?' Seb asked.

'Yes.' She opened the brown envelope and pulled out several sheets of paper. 'There's got to be over a hundred names. Considering this could be useful for both of our investigations, why don't we run the names through the database and see if anything interesting comes up?'

'That will take ages,' Twiggy said.

'Not if we divide it up between the three of us. Do you have time, Seb?'

'I've got a couple of hours before I need to leave.'

'You don't have access to our system,' Twiggy said.

'I'll log you in and you can sit at Tiny's desk.' Birdie headed over to the desk and signed Seb in. She then went to the photocopier, made two further copies of the list, and split it in three with a pen. 'I'll take the first third. Twiggy, you take the second and, Seb, you do the rest.'

They sat in silence while going through their lists. Finally, an hour later, she'd finished.

'All I've found are three speeding offences and one drunk-and-disorderly. Nothing else.'

'I've found nothing useful to the case, either,' Seb said.

'Twig?'

'Nah. Nothing here either.'

'That's great,' Birdie said, sighing.

'Don't get despondent. I'll ask Whitney to instruct Ellie to delve deeper. If there's anything to learn about these people, she'll find it. But we'll need to narrow the number of names down a bit, otherwise it will take her ages and end up being non-productive.'

'Don't you trust us to do the job?' Twiggy asked, raising an eyebrow.

'DC Naylor has skills of which I've never seen comparison. The three of us could spend weeks checking these people out and discover nothing. Ellie could spend a morning and discover more than we ever could.'

'He's right, Twig. It's crazy how ridiculously good she is.'

'Okay, if you say so,' Twiggy muttered.

'So, if we're going to make up another list, who do we want Ellie to investigate first?' Birdie said.

'Dennis Hunter, Rawlings' driver, is the longest-serving employee, so let's make him top priority. If anyone is going to know what's going on, it's likely to be him,' Seb said.

'And he could be a part of it, especially if—' Birdie's

phone rang, and she reached over to the desk and picked it up. 'It's the DI.' She pressed to answer. 'DC Bird.'

'It's Curtis.'

'Yes, sir.'

'I want you and DC Branch back on surveillance tomorrow at seven. DS Mattas has broken his leg and will be off work for several weeks. I'm having to restructure the operation.'

'Sorry to hear that, sir. How long are we to continue with the surveillance?'

'Until I tell you to stop. Remember to report in after each shift.'

'Yes, sir.' She ended the call. 'Okay, Twig, Curtis wants us back watching Rawlings, starting tomorrow. DS Mattas is on sick leave.'

'Great. I thought we'd got out of the boring stuff.'

'Take no notice of him. He's been in a funny mood all week,' Birdie said, looking over at Seb and rolling her eyes.

'No, I haven't.'

'If you say so. Come on, let's look again at the names and decide the ones Seb should take to Ellie. Any ideas?' Birdie asked.

'The longer-serving employees, definitely, because that could be linked to Rob's case. Also, we should consider anyone working in the warehouses. If he is smuggling firearms, they have to be housed and moved on,' Seb said.

'Are you sure the DCI won't mind Ellie working on people who could be involved in our investigation as well as yours?' Birdie asked.

'There may be an overlap. The driver, for example.'

'True. Right, Twig, you call out names. Seb, you give an opinion on whether they need to be checked, and I'll type up a new list. We'll get it done in no time.'

'No need,' Seb said. 'I already know everyone on the list. I'll do it.'

'Don't be ridiculous,' Twiggy said. 'It—'

'Susan Wilson joined the company on the tenth of October 2003 in the accounts department. Stuart Brent joined the company on the second of March 1999 and works in the warehouse. Harry O'Brien joined the company in—'

'Okay. You've made your point,' Birdie said, laughing. 'Don't tell me you'd forgotten about Seb's superpower, Twig.'

'I'd hardly call it a superpower. More like a freak of nature,' Twiggy snapped back at her.

'Stop it, or I'll tell Sarge you're not playing nice.'

'Whatever.' He turned and stormed off.

'Sorry about that. I don't know what's got into him. One day, he'll get used to you.'

'I wouldn't bet on it.'

'We're a week into the case, and I'd like a debrief on where we are and how you're going to proceed,' Whitney said to Seb when he walked into the incident room at Lenchester for their meeting that afternoon.

The smile on her face didn't hide the tension, which was accentuated by the tight lines around her eyes. The importance of the case for the DCI was clear, and he'd become as invested as she was in a successful outcome, which would give closure for the family.

He walked over to the board, picked up a marker, and wrote Rob's name at the top in the middle. 'Currently, Victor Rawlings is my prime suspect. I'm not suggesting that he was the person to carry out the attack, but all the intelligence is pointing towards him being involved in some way.' He wrote Rawlings' name at the bottom of the board under Rob's. 'There are several threads to my enquiry, which together put me on alert. First, we know that before the incident Rob was dating Rawlings' daughter, Charlotte, aka Charli, and he was extremely displeased when he found out.' He wrote *Charli* on the board with one arrow going up to Rob's name and one to Rawlings'.

'But having Rob beaten up and left for dead is crazy, even if he was acting like a possessive father,' Whitney said, standing next to him and staring at the board.

'Which brings me to my second point. On the evening of the attack, Charli had arranged to go to the cinema with Rob, but Rawlings grounded her, thereby ensuring that she wasn't able to meet him. Coincidence?'

'Not even a question to ask,' Whitney said, a wry smile on her face.

'Third, Keith Collins, the elder brother of Rob's friend Gareth, has been seen in the company of Rawlings by his employee Margaret Clarke and, more recently, by DC Bird.' He wrote *Keith Collins* on the board. 'That in itself isn't a link, if it wasn't for the fact that Gareth, Marty, and Rob would do odd jobs for this brother around the time of the attack.' He wrote the boys' names and drew connecting arrows.

'What sort of "odd jobs"?'

'Delivering packages and taking messages to arrange meetings. I've no idea if they were related to anything the older brother was doing for Rawlings at the time. But we can't leave this link uninvestigated.'

'I agree, there's certainly a connection between Rob and Rawlings, which is worth looking into further, but I'm not convinced on the motive for the attack being dating his daughter. Could it be to do with these "odd jobs"?'

'It's a possibility. The most I was able to get from the Collins brothers was they delivered messages and packages.'

'I vaguely remember Rob being a bit wayward but learning what type of work he'd been doing with his friends doesn't feel good. Mum and Dad would've been beside themselves if they'd known.' Whitney ran a hand through her hair, a pained expression on her face.

'It's in the past. Don't dwell on it. I'd like Ellie to research into Dennis Hunter, Rawlings' driver. He's been with him for at least twenty-five years, probably longer. It also might help the Market Harborough team with their investigation.'

'Okay, we can do that. I'll ask her to prioritise it.'

'If she has time, there are other people who have worked for Rawlings over the years. I'll email you a list of names.' He pulled out his mobile and within a few seconds the phone in Whitney's hand pinged.

'Let's go over to see Ellie,' Whitney said, making a beeline for the officer's desk.

'Hi, guv, do you want me?' Ellie asked, looking up from frowning at her computer screen.

'I'd like you to stop what you're doing and research the names on the list I'm about to email to you. Start with Dennis Hunter, who's a driver for Victor Rawlings of VR Machinery and has worked for him for many years.'

'He also acts in an unofficial capacity as security and is not averse to using his fists, according to one of our sources,' Seb added.

'No problem, guv. I'll close this document and start.'

'Thanks. Inform me immediately if you turn up anything of interest.'

'Will do,' Ellie said, turning back to face her screen.

'Let's go downstairs and grab a coffee. I'm in need of a

caffeine fix after the day I've had,' Whitney said after forwarding the list of names to her officer.

'What's happened?' Seb asked, frowning.

'Just the usual internal stuff. I bet you're glad to be away from it.'

When they reached the cafeteria, the queue was almost out of the door, and it took ten minutes before they were finally seated. Seb sat opposite Whitney, his legs so long they wouldn't go under the table, so he had to stretch them out between the tables.

'I wanted to ask—'

Whitney's mobile rang, interrupting him from broaching the subject about showing her brother some photos. They'd got to the point in the investigation that they needed Rob's input, if it was at all possible.

'Walker.' She paused. 'Already? That's fantastic. We're on our way back now.' She ended the call. 'Bring your coffee, we've got something on Hunter.'

'Impressive.'

'Well, this is Ellie we're talking about,' Whitney said, pride in her voice.

They returned to the incident room and headed straight over to the officer's desk.

'Hi, guv. The first thing I discovered was that Dennis Hunter isn't his real name. He changed it by deed poll twenty-eight years ago. His previous name was Donald Hunt, and he has a record for several offences under that name, including three counts of assault.'

'Has he ever been inside?' Whitney asked.

'Once, when he was in his early twenties, thirty-five years ago, for aggravated burglary.'

'Does he have a record since the name change?'

'No, guv.'

'Nothing? Are you telling me he's kept clean since

then? I find that very hard to believe, considering his prior history.'

'I agree, it seems unlikely,' Seb said.

'This is where it gets interesting,' Ellie said, a smile crossing her face. 'Hunter has been charged with offences, but every time, he hasn't been convicted.'

'I'm assuming there's a reason for that,' Seb said.

'Ever since the name change, any time he was arrested, he had representation from a major London firm of solicitors who got him off.'

'That would have cost an arm and a leg. How could he afford it?' Whitney asked.

'His whole financial situation is interesting, guv. He has no mortgage and lives in a large, detached property in Desborough with his wife. The money he earns working for Victor Rawlings, according to the income tax he pays, certainly doesn't match his lifestyle. He goes on holidays overseas at least three times a year, is a member of an exclusive golf club in Leicestershire, and his credit card is always paid off monthly. There's no evidence of any inheritances for him or his wife, so my guess is he's being subsidised by someone on the side.'

'And that someone is most likely Rawlings. Confirmation that he is more than a driver to him,' Seb said.

'But why would he allow Hunter to openly live a lifestyle like that? One that could be traced. Didn't he envisage being investigated at all?' Whitney asked.

'You'd be surprised how even the most careful person can be blind to the obvious,' Seb said.

'True. Ellie, I want you to continue looking into Victor Rawlings. Go deeper than you have done so far. I know the other CIDs are looking at him, but if we want results, then we should too.'

'Agreed,' Seb said, refraining to add that he doubted

the teams would find anything, considering they hadn't even been able to identify Keith Collins. Which reminded him, he hadn't yet asked for Ellie to identify the man with Collins in Birdie's photo. Then again, he didn't want to push his luck by overloading Ellie. He'd leave it until tomorrow.

'What about the other people on the list you forwarded to me?' Ellie asked.

'Keep going with Hunter and Rawlings initially. They're the ones who are most interesting to us. Oh, also Margaret Clarke, the person providing inside information regarding Rawlings. I'd like to check her reliability. She could be feeding us information simply to ensure her son is freed from custody,' Seb said.

'Will do,' Ellie said.

Whitney and Seb returned to her office.

'I have a question for you,' Seb said. 'How would you feel about us showing Rob photos of Rawlings, Hunter, the Collins brothers, and Charli?'

Whitney chewed on her bottom lip. 'I don't want to cause him any distress, but he's probably our best chance of finding out their involvement, especially if it jogs his memory a little more. Before we decide, we'll ask George's professional opinion. If she approves, I'll ask her to come with us. We'll go later if that works for you?'

'That's an excellent idea. It would be good to catch up with her again. While you're speaking to George, I'll contact Birdie and ask her to focus their surveillance on Hunter as well as Rawlings.'

# Chapter 26

'Hi, how's it going?' Birdie mouthed, 'It's Seb,' to Twiggy, who was looking in her direction. Twiggy rolled his eyes and then turned back to his computer screen. She really needed to sit him down and discuss his whole "anti-Seb" attitude because not only was it ridiculous, but it was also putting a strain on their relationship, and that wasn't a good situation for partners to be in.

'Good, thanks. A couple of things. If I stay in Lenchester for longer than tonight, are you still okay to—?'

'Take care of Elsa? No problem. I'll stay over for as long as you need me. You know how much I love her. What else did you want?'

'In conjunction with your surveillance on Rawlings, I'd like you to start watching the driver, Dennis Hunter, aka Donald Hunt. He's got a record under the latter name and nothing since working with Rawlings. We also know he lives way beyond his means.'

'Okay. But we'll need to clear it with Sarge or Curtis. Did you discover whether Hunter had any dealings with firearms in his past?'

'Nothing has come up so far. Ellie is also going deeper into Rawlings. I'll let you know if she turns up anything that will assist your investigation.'

'Thanks. I'll speak to Sarge regarding the additional surveillance and let you know what he says.'

'When will you get a chance to speak to him?'

'He's out at the moment, but I'll see him once he's returned. I don't see why we can't combine watching the two men, considering Rawlings doesn't go anywhere without Hunter.'

'I agree, it could dovetail nicely.'

'So, what have you got planned tonight? Taking Lenchester by storm?' Birdie teased, knowing full well that he was bound to be working.

'Whitney and I are meeting up with George, and we're planning to visit Whitney's brother to show him some photos.'

'George? Who's he, and why is he going with you?'

'Dr Georgina Cavendish. She's a forensic psychologist. I'm sure I've mentioned her to you before.'

'Oh … yes. I think you might have.'

'Okay. I'll let you know whether I'm returning tomorrow and—' He paused.

'And what?'

'Sorry, I've just had a text from Whitney. George can't meet with us until Wednesday, so don't expect me back for a couple of days.'

'Whenever. And don't worry about Elsa, we'll be fine.'

'Thanks. Keep in touch.'

She ended the call and then turned to Twiggy. 'As soon as Sarge is back, we need to speak to him about putting Rawlings' driver under surveillance.'

'I take it from your conversation that Clifford's not coming back to Market Harborough any time soon.'

'He's not sure when he'll be back.'

'He's welcome to stay away for as long as he likes, as far as I'm concerned, because he's a massive pain in the arse.'

She tensed. 'For God's sake, Twiggy. Give it a rest.'

'No. You give it a rest,' he snapped, glaring at her. 'All the time you stick up for him and don't care about me. You—'

'What are you talking about? I'm not taking sides between the two of you. That's so childish for you to even think that,' she interrupted, unable to hide the incredulity in her voice.

'Oh yeah. That's right. Call me childish now. I suppose Mr High-And-Mighty Viscount is very grown-up and wouldn't dream of moaning about someone as inconsequential as me. I'm surprised he even bothers to acknowledge my existence …' His voice cracked, and he coughed as if trying to hide it.

But he wasn't quick enough.

'Twiggy … what is it?'

'Nothing,' he said, quickly. Too quickly.

'Look, Twig, we've worked together a long time now, and I know when things aren't right. You've been acting weird all week. Please tell me what's wrong,' she begged.

He stared at her, uncertainty in his eyes. 'Um—'

'I won't say anything. Whatever it is. Promise.'

He stared at her for what seemed like an eternity until, finally, he spoke.

'You know you laugh about how much I eat, well—'

'It's only done in fun. It's not like I mean anything by it.'

'I know. Well, Evie made me go to the doctor's for a check-up. She thought I must be developing diabetes or something. But it's not that.' A pained expression crossed his face, and she reached over and took hold of his hand.

'What is it?'

'The doctors have given me a full examination, and it turns out they think I might have the start of FTD. Frontotemporal dementia.'

Birdie's breath caught in the back of her throat. 'Dementia. B-b-but isn't that what old people get? You're not even fifty.'

'Not this sort. Younger people can get it.'

'Why didn't you tell me that you were sick?'

'Because I didn't know. Okay, my mood has been going up and down like a bloody yo-yo recently, but that happens to everyone sometimes. The same as having trouble sleeping. I must admit I got a bit worried when my balance was affected the other day and it made me feel really seasick, but then I decided it was because I was tired.'

'And this FTD causes you to eat more?'

'They put my increased appetite down to psychological factors linked to my emotional state. It was comfort eating. So, all those diets Evie has been putting me on were a total waste of time. I was never going to stick to them.' He shrugged and gave a shallow laugh.

'Oh my God, Twiggy. I'm so sorry. What's going to happen to you?'

Tears filled her eyes, and she blinked them away. She couldn't bear the thought of him becoming so ill he could no longer do anything. She knew nothing about this particular form of dementia. She'd have to look it up. She'd do whatever she could to help him and the family.

'The doctors don't know. It could take years to get worse, or it can happen sooner. They told me there's medication I can take when necessary, like antidepressants for my mood swings, and sleeping pills. It depends on my symptoms.'

'How's Evie taking it?'

'You know her, determined to soldier on whatever.'

Birdie grinned. That was exactly what Evie was like.

'Do the kids know?'

'No. There's no point in worrying them while my symptoms aren't severe.'

'What about work?'

'I don't know. I haven't told anyone else yet. All this only happened last week.'

'No wonder you've been gunning for Seb the whole time. You were taking out your shock on him.'

'Yeah. And I'm sorry. Although I still don't like him.' He gave a weak smile.

'When are you going to tell Sarge?'

'Not yet. I'll wait until the Rawlings case is over.'

'I won't say anything to anyone. Promise,' she told him again to make sure he understood that she was on his side.

'Thanks. And that includes Clifford.'

'For goodness' sake, I do know how to keep a secret.' She gave him a playful punch on the arm.

His admission had explained so much. Her heart went out to him. The force was his whole life. He'd never known anything else. If he had to leave, how would he cope?

'No harm in checking.' Twiggy smiled.

'Fingers crossed your FTD takes years to progress, and everything stays the same.' She paused a moment. 'Apart from you being all sensitive and moody. We can all do without that.'

'Ha. Ha. Very funny.'

Birdie returned to her desk, but she was unable to do any work. She just stared at her screen, trying to come to terms with Twiggy's revelation. She kept glancing over at her partner and he, too, seemed deep in thought.

'Anything happen in my absence?' Sarge said behind her, causing Birdie to jump. She hadn't noticed him come in.

'Yes, Sarge. I've been in touch with Clifford, who's currently in Lenchester, and it seems they've discovered Dennis Hunter, Rawlings' driver, has a record from when he used another name. They believe he's probably more than just a driver, and Clifford has asked that we put surveillance on him as well as Rawlings. Considering he drives Rawlings all the time, we could combine the two, if that's okay with you. Obviously, when we're not on our surveillance shift, we can concentrate solely on Hunter.'

'I'll run it by the DI. From my point of view, it's fine. Especially if it moves the Rawlings investigation on.'

# Chapter 27

Seb's phone pinged, and he glanced up from the desk he was sitting at in the Lenchester incident room. It was one he'd used when he'd worked there before with Whitney. It was the furthest away from the rest of the team and gave him an element of privacy. He pulled out his phone and saw it was from Birdie, confirming that they would be tailing Hunter and asking if he'd had any luck identifying the man who'd been with Keith Collins. He'd planned on asking Whitney later, but he'd do it now, as the officer had just walked into the room. He hurried over to her.

'I have a photo of two men Victor Rawlings met with at the Watford Gap service station. One of them is known to us, and the other we need to identify. Is Ellie able to do that?'

'You're lucky because we're currently trialling some new software which should help. This way.' He followed Whitney over to Ellie's desk. 'Ellie, we're looking to identify someone from a photo that Seb has.'

'It's the man on the left,' Seb said, showing her his phone. 'I'll email it to you.'

'We've got some new retrospective facial recognition software, and this would be an ideal time to try it. It means we can match him up with anyone already in our system,' Ellie said.

'Who's the other man?' Whitney asked.

'Keith Collins.'

'The brother of Rob's friend Gareth?'

'The very same.'

Whitney and Seb stood beside Ellie while she entered the image into the new software. Within seconds, she had a result.

'I've got him. He's Bernie Simpson, aged fifty-five. He has a record for several offences, including dealing drugs, burglary, and assault. He's been inside on three separate occasions, one of them for fifteen years, commencing three years before Rob's attack. These offences are from when he lived in Lenchester. He's now living in Hinckley.'

'Thanks, Ellie. We can assume that he wasn't involved in Rob's assault, but he's still a person of interest in respect to Rawlings' current activities, which I'll pass onto DC Bird. He hangs around with Keith Collins. Can we find out how long they've known each other? Simpson is a fair bit older than Collins,' Seb said.

'Give me a few minutes, and I'll see what else I can find,' Ellie said.

'We should get Simpson in for questioning. He might know something about the attack on Rob, even if he was inside at the time,' Whitney said.

'I'm not convinced that's the right thing to do. Questioning the older Collins was fine because it ties directly into Rob's case. Gareth, Marty, and Rob worked for him. What we don't want to do is put Rawlings on alert because he might do a runner if he discovers he's being investigated by us *and* the other force,' Seb said.

'Simpson was in prison with Dennis Hunter when he was younger. They shared a cell for twelve months,' Ellie said, looking up from her computer screen.

'Interesting. One could assume, therefore, that Simpson was brought into the Rawlings fold by Hunter. Have you turned up anything on Margaret Clarke?' Seb asked.

'I've looked into her employment history and finances, and there's nothing out of the ordinary.'

'Thanks. I didn't imagine there would be, but it's good to know. I'll let Birdie know we've identified Simpson. In my judgement, our two cases are linked, and it might be advantageous if we worked together, rather than simply sharing information. What's your opinion, Whitney?'

'I agree, but we must ensure that it's not to the detriment of Rob's case, especially as we only have five days of funding left.'

# Chapter 28

'Seb has suggested that we join forces from now on because of the overlap between our two cases, and the DCI agrees. Supposedly she's going to inform Curtis, but I don't know if she has yet,' Birdie explained to Twiggy while they were watching the house in Arthingworth the following morning.

She'd received the message from Seb the previous day after Twiggy had finished early for a doctor's appointment. She hadn't thought it important enough to disturb him. Now she knew about his illness, she was determined to keep the pressure off, whenever possible, but without him realising what she was doing. Last night, she'd spent time researching the disease and what to expect in the future, and already, she could identify other aspects of Twiggy's behaviour that could be attributed to the FTD diagnosis, in particular the way he was far less inhibited than he had been previously. She'd also read several case studies from people who knew someone with FTD, including a celebrity. But whatever happened, whether Twiggy's condition worsened quickly or slowly, she'd be there for him, in one way or another.

'I suppose it was bound to happen,' Twiggy muttered. 'Here's Rawlings. Let's see where he goes today.' He turned on the engine, letting it idle.

'It's got to be a good thing. They were able to identify Bernie Simpson as the other guy who met with Rawlings at Watford Gap, and none of our guys could.' She glanced at Twiggy, whose eyes were focused on the drive.

'I'll take your word for it,' Twiggy mumbled.

She was under no illusion that one day Twiggy might say something positive about Seb, even now he'd confided in her about his illness, but he also needed to understand that it was good for them to work together and maybe solve two cases.

'I'm glad that you agree with me.' She smirked when he tossed a glance in her direction.

'Rawlings isn't heading to Leicester. I wonder if he's going to Watford Gap to meet with Collins and Simpson.'

'Again? How likely is that?' She frowned. 'Then again, we should be prepared in case he does. I'll ask Sarge to stand by because we need him to send backup. That way, we can ensure both Rawlings and the people he's meeting are followed. I'll call him.' She pulled out her phone, keyed the number for their boss and then put the phone on speaker, resting it on the dashboard.

'Weston,' their boss answered after a couple of rings.

'It's Birdie, Sarge. We're currently following Rawlings and he's not heading for the office. We thought that if he went to Watford Gap again, it would be useful to have the people he's meeting followed. Can you send a team out to do that?'

'Where are you?'

'On the A508, driving towards Northampton.'

'We should wait until you know for certain that's where he's heading. Although if Rawlings doesn't stay long, the team might not make it in time. I'll send them out now.'

Birdie exchanged a glance with Twiggy, who was frowning and no doubt thinking the same as she was. It would be a total waste of resources if Rawlings didn't end up attending a meeting. Then again, because it was Sarge who'd authorised it, they wouldn't be held accountable.

'Are you going to ask Sparkle and Tiny?' she asked, referring to two other officers in the Market Harborough team.

'Sparkle's in court today,' Twiggy said.

'The case finished early, so she's available. I'll check where Tiny is and let you know once it's all set up. If Tiny isn't free, then I'll track down one of the Wigston team to meet Sparkle at the service station, assuming that's where you end up,' Sarge said.

'Okay. We'll wait to hear from you. We've just reached Northampton and we're on the road to the motorway, so it's still looking like we may be correct.'

'Right. I'll be in touch.'

Sarge ended the call and Birdie replaced her phone back in her pocket. 'Okay, that went well.'

'What were you expecting?' Twiggy asked.

'You never know with Sarge, so I'm not sure. One thing's for certain, I'm glad he made the decision to send out the others, so if it all goes pear-shaped, we don't get it in the neck.'

While they followed Rawlings up the motorway, Birdie allowed herself some time to dwell on what the medium had said about her birth mother and changing job. Should she still consider working with Seb now she knew about Twiggy? Then again, she couldn't put her future on hold for him when they had no idea how the disease was going to progress. The other thing to consider was that she loved her career in the police. But working with Seb, especially if they were selective about which cases to take, would also be enjoyable.

There were so many options to consider that, in a way, she wanted to bury her head in the sand and forget about it until they'd got this case sorted. Except that her head had different ideas and the thoughts poked their way through at every available opportunity. Of course, if she did make the decision to go with Seb, then her career in the police force would be over for good. Although they might be asked to act as consultants from time to time, there would be no guarantee.

It would be good to work with Seb and be in control of what she did and not have to answer to the likes of Sarge all the time. As much as she liked her boss, she often ended up treading on eggshells as far as he was concerned. But would Seb have a go at her instead, especially regarding her timekeeping? So, she'd still end up being answerable to someone …

'They're indicating to go into Watford Gap services,' Twiggy said, interrupting the myriad thoughts careering crazily around her head.

'I'll call Sarge.'

He answered straight away.

'It's me, Sarge. We were right. Rawlings has come to the service station.'

'Sparkle and Tiny are ten minutes away.'

'Okay, we'll wait for them.'

'You follow to see who he's meeting, and I'll stay in the car and wait for the other two,' Twiggy said once Rawlings had got out of his car and was walking towards the café.

'Okay. I won't stay long. I'll just peep through and check. It's not like we'll be able to hear what's being said.'

'Can you grab me something to eat? A pie or pasty would be great.'

'What? And risk the wrath of Evie? By the way, does she know that you've told me?'

'Yes. So now you know it's fine to buy me something to eat.'

'But surely you still need to watch your weight. It can't be good for you to keep stacking it on.'

'Will you give me a break?' Twiggy snapped.

She stiffened at the sharpness in his response, then immediately relaxed, realising that he couldn't help it.

'I'll bring you something back, but seriously, Twig, you still have to be careful. Even more so now. I'm sure Evie isn't going to stop putting you on diets, even with this.'

'Okay, clever clogs, you're right. She's still nagging me. Now, clear off and check on Rawlings. Look, there's Sparkle's car.'

When Birdie reached the café, Rawlings was seated at a table with Collins and Simpson. She grabbed a pie from out of one of the hot units and took it to the counter, where she ordered two coffees to go. She hurried back to the car.

'Yep, it was the same men. Here's a pie and coffee. Have you spoken to the others?'

'Yes. I'll send them a photo of Collins and Simpson, so they know who they're to be following.'

'Great. Now we wait.'

Twiggy stared at Birdie, who was, once again, looking out of the car window. Rawlings had been in the service station café for forty-five minutes already. Longer than the last time. What was he plotting? Usually Birdie was quite chatty, but today she'd seemed a very subdued, thoughtful person. Was it because he'd told her about his illness, and she couldn't handle it? Or was it something else?

To be honest, she'd been a little quiet before then, but he'd just dismissed it because he had too much else to think about. Should he ask her what was wrong? She'd probably deny there was anything, especially now. But they were still partners, whatever the future was going to hold.

Maybe she'd spoken to Clifford instead. She was totally different in his company. She was relaxed, cracked jokes, and didn't seem to be concerned about anything. Did that mean that whatever was on her mind was something to do with Clifford, or was Twiggy just imagining it?

Maybe Clifford had asked her to leave the force and work with him again. Twiggy couldn't imagine Birdie being a private investigator, though. Never in a million years. She was a police officer through and through, and a good one, with a bright future ahead of her. That was where she should be and not following people to find out whether they were cheating on their spouses or other such boring work.

Except Clifford didn't seem to be doing that. He'd got work from the Met and now from Lenchester, so he must have serious clout. Did that mean that if Birdie decided to work with Clifford, she'd still carry on doing police work but without the ties of a small team like Market Harborough? Without having Sarge breathing down her neck. He could sort of understand the appeal. Assuming she was thinking of leaving, he was only guessing at the moment. But now that he'd confided about his illness, would that factor in her decision? He hoped not. He didn't want to stand in her way if she really did want to go. It was all so …

'Twig.' He felt an elbow in his upper arm.

'Ouch. What did you do that for?' He rubbed the place where she'd hurt him.

'Because you were miles away – probably dreaming about food, knowing you. Rawlings has left the café and is heading back to his car. Start the engine so we're ready to follow.'

'Yes, boss.'

'I'm glad you realise who's in charge. I'll let the others know we're leaving.'

Twiggy turned on the engine and waited until Hunter had driven past and was going towards the exit. He kept his distance while at the same time making sure the man didn't veer off and leave him unable to follow.

'He's not going back to Leicester because he's gone in the other direction.'

Birdie's phone rang. 'It's Sparkle.' She put it on speaker. 'Hello.'

'Collins and Simpson have left the café, returned to their car, and driven off. They're going in the same direction as Rawlings.'

'Thanks, Sparkle, keep in touch.'

They continued for a few miles when suddenly Hunter took the exit off the motorway, with less than twenty yards to spare and no use of his indicator. Twiggy only just managed to follow.

'What the hell was that about?' he said.

'He's either clocked that he's being tailed and is trying to lose us. Or he's doing it as a precaution *in case* someone's on his tail. What do you think?'

'I doubt that he's seen us. I was careful about being far enough behind for him not to. We'll soon find out if they try to lose us.'

'I think he might be heading for Lenchester. I'll text Sparkle.'

A few minutes later, Birdie's phone pinged.

'Is that her?' he asked.

'Yes. It looks like they're also heading in the same direction. Perhaps I should phone Seb and let him know where we are.'

'Why does he need to know? We're the ones in pursuit.'

'If we end up in Lenchester, he might want to join us.'

'We can't all follow because it will be too obvious. This is meant to be on the down-low, remember?'

'Okay, but Seb should still be informed, especially as both Collins and Simpson are heading that way, too.'

'Do what you want, then,' he muttered, sounding like a child, even to himself.

'Don't be daft, Twiggy. We're now all working together, so he should know we're heading towards him. Okay?'

Twiggy sighed. He really had to stop this. 'Yes, you're right. Give him a call and let him know what we're doing.'

'I've just texted him. He—' Her phone pinged, and she held it up, staring at the screen. 'It's from Seb. He's asked that we keep him informed of Rawlings' whereabouts. He's out with DCI Walker, on their way to meet up with the forensic psychologist, Dr Cavendish, so it's not possible for him to join us. Happy now?'

'It's got nothing to do with being *happy*. Forget I mentioned it.'

They drove in silence while following Rawlings' Mercedes. Twiggy made sure to keep his distance, always keeping one or two cars between them. When they got to the edge of Lenchester, they turned into Greymills Industrial Estate.

'This is a bit run-down,' Birdie said as he drove through the estate, passing warehouses of varying sizes on either side of the road.

'It's certainly seen better days, although the units all

look to be occupied, judging by the cars parked outside of them.'

They followed Rawlings until they arrived at a large warehouse in a small cul-de-sac. Twiggy parked on the corner of the adjacent street, ensuring that they were out of sight. Rawlings and Hunter got out of the car and went into the warehouse through the open door in the centre.

Birdie's phone rang.

'Hello.' She paused for a moment. 'Hang on, I'll put you on speaker so Twiggy can hear.' She changed the setting on her phone and placed it on the dashboard. 'Go ahead, Tiny.'

'We just saw you drive into the estate. We've parked across the road and up a bit. You can probably see us in your rear-view mirror, Twiggy.' He glanced in the mirror and caught sight of them.

'I've spotted you. But how did you get here before us?'

'Our guys must have taken a shortcut that your driver didn't know about. One of them had a key and he unlocked the warehouse and went inside. I see your guys have now followed. What's the plan?' Tiny asked.

'If they've all come to the same place, we can assume that they've got some business here. Do you think it's the firearms?' Twiggy asked.

'What firearms?' Sparkle said.

'Crap. You didn't hear that from me. This operation is meant to be on a need-to-know basis.'

'Our lips are sealed,' Tiny said.

'Thanks.'

He could trust them both; they'd all worked together for years and would always have each other's back.

'What I want to know is why they didn't meet here straightway and instead met at the service station first?' Birdie said.

'Maybe only one of the parties knew about this place, and the other person instructed them how to get here?' Tiny said.

'No, I don't buy it. I'm sure they've got satnavs.'

'We need to find out what this place is used for,' Twiggy said.

'We can look at that when we get back to the station or …' Birdie paused.

'Or what?' Twiggy asked, frowning.

'We get in touch with Lenchester CID and ask who owns the warehouse and what they can tell us about them.'

'Why can't we investigate?'

'What do you suggest? That we wait until Rawlings has left and break in without a warrant? If we do anything illegal, their barrister will get them off on a technicality quicker than you can say *firearms*. And I doubt looking around the outside is going to tell us anything because there aren't any windows. I'm telling you, Lenchester CID is the way to go. For a start, we're on their patch. Also, they've got people who'll be able to assist, especially as Seb's working their case. Surely you're not bothered about that, Twig?'

Twiggy sighed. 'No, I'm not. Look, Rawlings is leaving and the other two are behind him,' Birdie said.

'Shall we follow them?' Twiggy glanced at Birdie for her response.

'No. I think we all should go back to Market Harborough and report to Sarge what we've witnessed. Rawlings is planning something. This is a breakthrough, I'm sure of it.'

# Chapter 29

Dr Georgina Cavendish was already standing by the entrance to the home where Rob lived when Seb and Whitney arrived.

'Hello, George, it's good to see you again,' Seb said when they reached the forensic psychologist. He'd met her when he was working with Whitney previously. George assisted Lenchester CID on their more serious cases and was an extremely useful asset. He wished he'd had someone of her calibre to work with when he was in the force.

'You, too,' George said, holding out her hand to shake his.

'Oh my God. Look at you two. I always feel like I'm in *Land of the Giants* when we're together. Why is it I'm surrounded by such tall people? I know, don't say it, everyone's tall compared with me,' Whitney added. 'I phoned ahead and they're expecting us, and they've also told Rob that we're coming. Before we go in, let's decide our plan of action.'

'It's important to ensure that Rob doesn't feel intimidated with the three of us being there,' George said.

'He enjoys mixing with people, and he's used to being in the company of several people at the same time. I'm sure it will be fine,' Whitney said.

'You know him best, but remember we're going to be discussing things he may find difficult.' George turned to Seb. 'Have you already met Rob?'

'No, I haven't.'

'In that case, I advise that Whitney and I do most of the talking, as he knows both of us, and Seb should observe, looking for any triggers or tells on Rob's face that might aid the investigation. Even if Rob believes he has no recollection of an event or a person, he may inadvertently give something away through his body language that might assist.'

'As long as it doesn't traumatise him at all. Do you think it might?' Whitney asked.

'I understand your concern and want you to be aware that even if Rob does have some latent memories triggered, it's highly unlikely that they'll make any notable difference to the brain damage he received because that's irreversible.'

'Yes, I know that's not going to change. I wish it could, but …' Whitney sighed. 'My worry is that we might upset him. Do you think if any memories are triggered, it would hurt him emotionally?'

'It's hard to know. Forensic psychology isn't an exact science. What I suggest is that we show Rob the photos, and if from his reactions we can see that it's painful, then we'll know not to probe further.'

'If we don't get an adverse reaction from him, then how should we follow up?' Whitney asked.

'We'll keep the conversation light, so he doesn't understand how important it is because that could alarm him and inhibit him from answering. You lead and start with a general conversation about the attack. We'll keep before and after the attack separate, so he's not confused. Stick to specifics, if you can, to keep the conversation focused.'

'I understand. And after that?'

'Find out if he remembers being in hospital. Again, keep it relaxed, so he doesn't feel under pressure to give you an answer. We really need to play it by ear and assess his reactions. Remember, I'm there for support, and will guide you.'

'Thanks. Seb, do you have anything further to add before we go inside?' Whitney asked.

'No. I'll hold back, as planned, and observe.'

'Let's go.' Whitney rang the bell, and after a couple of minutes, the door was answered by one of the care assistants.

'Hello, Ethan.'

'Hi, Whitney, good to see you. Rob's waiting for you in the lounge.'

'Thanks. This is Sebastian Clifford, and Dr Cavendish, who you've already met. Is there anyone else in there because we'd like to speak to Rob alone?'

'You won't be interrupted. The others are at a local day centre. I'm in the middle of some admin, if you don't mind going in on your own.'

'No problem.'

Ethan left them, and after signing in, Seb followed Whitney and George down the hallway.

'He seems a nice guy.'

'Yes. He'd started working at the home the day Rob moved in, and the two of them have formed a tight bond. Fingers crossed, he's here for the long haul.'

The lounge was light and spacious, with a set of French

doors leading out to the garden. The TV was on, and a man was staring directly at it. It was most definitely Rob because, again, there was the distinctive family likeness. It was uncanny how closely Whitney and her family resembled each other. Very different from Seb's own family.

'Hello, Rob.'

Whitney's brother jumped up from his seat and rushed over to them. He was a lot taller than Whitney, and he leant down and gave her a hug and a kiss on the cheek.

'Hello, Whitney,' he said after releasing her. 'Hello, George,' he said, turning to the psychologist and giving her a coy smile.

'Good to see you again, Rob,' George said.

'I've brought my friend Seb to see you,' Whitney said.

Rob bit down on his bottom lip and looked at Seb from under his eyelashes. 'Hello, Seb,' he said in a low voice.

'Hello, Rob. It's nice to meet you.' Seb debated whether to hold out his hand for Whitney's brother to shake, but before he could do so, Rob took a step backwards until standing behind Whitney, peering over the top of her head.

'We'd like to have a chat with you, so shall we turn off the telly?' Whitney suggested.

Rob picked up the remote and pointed it at the TV. 'I've done it. What do you want to talk about?'

'Let's sit down, so we're all nice and comfortable.'

'Okay. That's my chair.' Rob pointed to the one he'd been in when they'd arrived. 'I want you next to me, Whitney, and George can sit next to you. Seb can sit on the black leather chair over there.' He pointed a few feet away.

Seb didn't mind being relegated because it was easier to scrutinise Rob's reactions from that distance.

'Rob, do you remember any of your friends at school?' Whitney asked.

'Umm. I'm not sure.'

'You were friends with Gareth Collins. Does his name ring a bell?'

'Did he take my lunch box one time when we were in the playground and then tell the teacher that I gave it to him? Which was a lie. And we don't tell lies, do we?'

'No, we don't, that's right. Do you remember him?'

Rob shook his head. 'No.'

'What about Marty McNeil?'

Rob giggled. 'Marty sounds like *farty*. Farty Marty. Farty Marty.'

Whitney laughed. 'Yes, it does sound like *farty*. Was he at your school?'

'Nope. But his name's funny.'

'Yes, it is. What about Charli?'

'Is this my girlfriend, the one you asked me about when we were with Mum?'

'That's right. Here's her photo.' Whitney pulled out her phone and showed it to Rob. 'Does Charli look familiar?'

Rob stared at the phone, chewing on his bottom lip and frowning. 'She has nice hair, and she's very pretty.'

'Definitely very pretty. Do you know her?'

'I don't know, Whitney. Why are you asking me? Am I in trouble?'

'Of course you're not. Don't worry about Charli. It doesn't matter, I just wondered, that's all.'

'Don't tell Mum that I can't remember, will you? She might get worried. And you mustn't either, George.'

'I promise not to mention it to your mother, Rob. And not remembering doesn't matter at all. I forget lots of things,' George said.

'Like what?'

'Last week I was meant to meet Ross to go for a drink

and I forgot all about it. He was left on his own in the pub for ages.'

'Oh. Did he shout at you and get cross?' Rob took hold of the neck of his T-shirt and scrunched it up in his hand.

'No, because he knew I didn't mean it. It's the same as you not remembering things.'

'So, I won't get into trouble?'

'Of course not,' Whitney said. 'Rob, I want you to think about being in hospital after your accident. What can you tell me about that time?'

'Do you mean when there were nurses looking after me, and I was in bed?'

'Yes, that's right. I came with Mum and Dad to visit you while you were there.'

'Did you?'

'Yes. Did anyone else visit?'

'I don't remember. But that doesn't matter, does it, because George forgets things, too?'

'No, it doesn't matter at all. I'm going to show you some more photos. Tell me if you recognise any of the people in them.' Whitney held out her phone. 'What about him?'

Seb moved to the side to view the screen. Whitney was showing her brother a photo of Victor Rawlings.

'No.'

'And this man?' Whitney showed a photo of Dennis Hunter.

Rob's eyes widened, and he immediately looked away. 'N-n-no.'

Seb tried to catch Whitney's attention, but she wasn't looking in his direction. Rob was clearly affected by seeing the photo of Hunter. He glanced at George, whose expression indicated that she'd spotted the same reaction.

'Rob, take another look at the photo Whitney showed you,' George said.

'Do I have to? He didn't look nice.'

'No, you don't have to,' George said.

'What about either of these two?' Whitney held out her phone again and showed Rob two photos. One of Collins and the other of McNeil.

Rob put his hands over his eyes and shook his head. 'Nope.'

'Is this anything to do with the secret you told me about?' Whitney asked gently.

'There isn't a secret. Stop asking me these questions, Whitney. I don't want to play with you anymore.'

Whitney put her arm around his shoulders. 'I'm sorry, Rob, I didn't mean to upset you. No more questions, I promise. I've brought you one of your favourite chocolate bars. Would you like it now?' She opened her bag and pulled it out.

'Yes, please.' The troubled expression on his face vanished and was replaced by an eager smile. He reached out and grabbed it from her, ripping off the wrapper.

Whitney had obviously touched a nerve, but he seemed to have got over it. They weren't going to get any more from him, and it wouldn't be good for him if they tried to push further.

'It's been lovely seeing you, Rob, but I must get back to work. This was a quick visit to make sure you're okay. I'll come back soon, and we'll visit Mum together. Are you going to be making your own lunch today?'

'Yes. I'm having beans on toast, and this afternoon I'm going to do some painting.'

'That sounds lovely. I'll see you soon.' She bent down and kissed him on the cheek and gave him a hug.

They left him eating the chocolate and watching the

TV, which he'd switched on before they'd even left the room.

Seb followed Whitney and George down the hall, and once they were out of earshot, he turned to her.

'The photos and your questions definitely triggered something, particularly when you showed him Hunter,' he said.

'I know. But I couldn't push him. It wouldn't be fair.'

They'd almost reached the front door when an older woman came out of an office along the corridor.

'Hello, Whitney, I've been looking out for you. I wanted to have a word before you left.'

'What is it, Jan?'

'It's probably nothing, but Rob had a visitor the other day, and I wondered if you knew about it. Did Rob mention it to you?'

'No, he didn't tell me. Who was it? I didn't think anyone visited other than me.'

'That's why I wanted to let you know. The guy said he was an old school friend. He did appear to be about the same age as Rob. He told me his name was Mark.'

'Can you describe him?'

'He was average height, had a shaved head, and a bit overweight.'

'Did he have tattoos on both arms and a gold stud in one ear?' Seb asked, immediately recognising the man she described.

'Yes, he did.'

'How long did he stay for?' Whitney asked.

'Not for very long. Maybe ten minutes, if that.'

'Did Rob recognise him?'

'At the time, I assumed he did because the man went over to him smiling and being friendly and Rob appeared to respond. I didn't wait while they were talking because the guy seemed genuine enough, but after he left Rob was most definitely distracted.'

'In what way?' Whitney asked.

'He wasn't his usual smiling, chatty self. He spent the rest of the afternoon sitting quietly, not even watching his favourite telly programme. But by the next day, he was fine.'

'When did this visit take place?'

'It was one day last week – Wednesday, I believe. It will be in the visitors' book with the exact time.'

Jan walked over to the book on the hall table.

'Here it is. Wednesday at two-thirty. His name is Mark McNeil. I should've called you at the time, but it didn't seem important.'

'No need to apologise. There was no harm done. If he does turn up to see Rob again, please notify me immediately.' Whitney exchanged a glance with Seb, her eyebrow raised.

They left the building and returned to the cars. 'I think he was visited by Marty McNeil. The description matches. Obviously, something about my visit prompted him to do that,' Seb said.

'Did you tell him that Rob lived here?'

'No. He must have found out from someone else or did a little research. It wouldn't be too hard to find out.'

'True. Let's grab something to eat at the pub at the end of the road and continue our discussion there.'

'I have to get back for a meeting, so I'll leave you both to discuss it further,' George said.

'Why do you think Marty McNeil visited Rob after all this time?' Whitney asked once they'd ordered food and were outside into the garden. It had been a lovely June day, and Seb was glad to have time outside in the sunshine.

'It would have been my visit. We discussed the attack, and he denied all knowledge of it. He was also cagey about his relationship with Gareth. He informed me that they weren't in contact, but I found proof that they were on social media. His recollection of the work they did for Keith Collins was limited, and he insisted he didn't work as often as Rob and Gareth because of family commitments.' He picked up his beer and took a sip.

'And if both Marty and Gareth know more about the attack than they're letting on, the visit to Rob might have been to find out if he'd revealed anything,' Whitney said, nodding.

'That's possible. All the people who've been interviewed are aware that the case has been reopened because of new evidence. It stands to reason that the evidence might have come from Rob himself.'

'I think we should bring McNeil in for questioning. Let's make it more formal and see what we can get out of him. We'll question him about Dennis Hunter, especially after Rob's reaction to the photo. I'll contact Brian and ask him to arrange it for after lunch.' She pulled out her phone and made the call. 'Done.'

Seb enjoyed being with Whitney because she got things done straight away without deliberating for too long. It was what made her such a good detective. She was decisive and insightful, and that made her an excellent colleague.

'Thank you.'

'What's your take on Rob not mentioning the visit?' Whitney asked Seb.

'He might have forgotten because of the questions you were asking him. Is that likely?'

'He does struggle to concentrate on more than one

thing at a time, so it's entirely possible. I don't want to ask him now, though, because today was upsetting enough.'

'I agree. I believe it might be prudent for me to interview Charlotte Newton again. I'll ask Birdie if she'd like to accompany me to provide the female perspective.'

Whitney stared at him over the top of her glass. 'The two of you work very well together, don't you? Has she given you an answer yet?'

'No. It's a big step for her to take, especially at her age, when she's got a career mapped out in the police.'

'She could still have a career as a PI. I'd have thought it was perfect timing, considering she doesn't have any responsibilities. She doesn't, does she?'

'She's saving up for a deposit to buy a house but, other than that, none that I'm aware of. I don't want to twist her arm, though. If she decides to join me, that's great. But if she refuses, then there's not a lot I can do about it.'

'It's not like you to give up so easily. Do you have another reason?' Whitney said. Her voice suggested she wasn't convinced by his answer.

He sighed. 'She's already found herself in trouble after working with me. It would've damaged her career if not for Sergeant Weston's support. My concern is if she decides to leave the force, what happens if it turns out that we're unable to work well together? Or we're unable to obtain sufficient work and the company folds. Where would that leave her?'

It was the first time he'd admitted out loud his reservations regarding a possible partnership with Birdie.

'Seb, you can't hold yourself responsible for any of those things happening. Birdie is an adult and must look out for herself. You're usually so clear-sighted. What's got into you?'

'Spending too much time with you and Birdie, I expect. You're both similar in many ways.'

'You mean, all that heart-on-the-sleeve emotional stuff, and rushing into a situation without thinking.' Whitney laughed.

'No. I mean being prepared to put yourself on the line for the good of the job. Prioritising solving a case first without thinking of how it affects you. Need I go on?' He arched a brow.

'Stop it, you're making me blush,' she said, grinning. 'I'm even more convinced now that you'll make a good team.'

'It's still got to be her decision, without any pressure from me. I'll contact her and arrange for us to visit Charlotte Newton. If Hunter had anything to do with the attack, she might be prepared to give him up if she thinks we'll leave her father alone.'

'We should bring Hunter in for an interview.'

'We'll make that decision after questioning Charlotte again. At the moment, all research into Rawlings is being done on the quiet. As far as we are aware, he has no idea of our interest in him other than as Charlotte's father and in connection to Rob's attack. If we involve Hunter at this stage, Rawlings might suspect we know more about his illegal activities.'

'Yes, that makes sense.'

'I'll give Birdie a call.' Seb picked up his phone from the table at the same time as it started ringing. He stared at the screen. 'It's her. Hello, Birdie. I was about to call you.'

'I'll go first. Rawlings, Collins, and Simpson all visited the Greymills Industrial Estate in Lenchester. Please could you ask Ellie to find out who owns the warehouse in Dorset Close? It's the only one in that street.'

'I will. We're reinterviewing McNeil later because he's

been to visit Whitney's brother. After that, I'll return to Market Harborough. Tomorrow morning, I'm planning to interview Rawlings' daughter Charlotte again, focusing on Hunter. Are you able to come with me?'

'Yeah, sure.'

'Good. Text me a time, and I'll pick you up. I'll see to Elsa this evening, so no need for you to go back there.' He ended the call.

'I take it Birdie needs some help?' Whitney said.

'Yes. They'd like to find out who owns the warehouse in Dorset Close, Greymills.'

'I can do that for her as soon as we're back at the station.'

# Chapter 30

Seb drummed his fingers on his leg in frustration. They'd returned to Whitney's office over half an hour ago, and Marty McNeil still hadn't been brought in. He'd wanted to be away from Lenchester by four, but that was looking less likely by the minute.

Whitney had spent the last twenty minutes on the phone discussing administrative matters, and he hadn't yet run past her how he intended to conduct the interview.

'Sorry about that,' Whitney said, replacing the handset on the phone on her desk.

'No problem. I wonder what the hold-up is with McNeil.'

'I'll find out.' She reached for the handset at the same time as there was a tap on the door and it opened. It was her sergeant, Brian.

'Guv, Martin McNeil has arrived. He's in interview room three.'

'Finally. What was the hold-up?'

'No idea. I contacted uniform to bring him the moment you asked. Am I required for the interview?'

'No, I'm going to question him with Seb. We'll go down shortly. Please let the front desk know.'

The officer left the room, closing the door behind him.

Seb frowned. Whitney hadn't mentioned wanting to be part of the interview.

'Are you sure it's okay for you to question McNeil with me? I don't want you to get in trouble with Chief Superintendent Douglas. You could watch from the observation room, instead?'

Ultimately, it would be her decision, but he had to point it out to her.

'I hear what you're saying, but I want to be in the room with him. I'll let you lead and will only ask a question if necessary. If the super, or Douglas, challenges me being there, I'll justify it by saying that I was keeping an eye on proceedings because I have the background information on my brother. Anyway, they won't find out because I'm not going to mention it, nor will any of the team. Not to mention that nobody else is aware of why we're interested in him.'

'As you wish,' he said, not convinced that Whitney's approach was correct.

They headed down to the interview room in silence and when they were outside Whitney turned to him.

'If he turns out to be responsible for what happened to Rob in any way, this is going to be hard.'

Finally, she was admitting what he'd already assumed to be the case.

'You must push those emotions to one side and act objectively. I understand that it's not easy, but we have no idea of his involvement or otherwise. Our main aim is to find out why he went to see Rob, what he said, and how Rob responded.'

'Thanks, Seb. I'll be fine. I'm going to put into practice

what George is always telling me to do: compartmentalising. I'll view him as nothing more than a suspect in a criminal investigation.'

'Excellent,' he said, hoping that she would be successful.

He opened the door to the interview room. McNeil was seated behind the desk, his hands tightly balled and resting on the table.

Seb started the recording and introduced everyone in the room.

'Why am I here?' McNeil asked.

'Because we wish to question you further regarding Rob Walker.'

'I could lose my job over this. You can't just send officers into the supermarket and escort me out. It made me look like I was under arrest. I'm not, am I?'

'You're here to assist us with our enquiries. We were told by a member of staff at the home Rob Walker resides that he had a visitor, and after eliciting a description and looking at the visitors' book, it wasn't hard to work out who it was. "Mark McNeil". Hardly different from your real name.'

'Okay, so I went to visit Rob. What did he say about it?' McNeil's eyes narrowed.

'We didn't ask him, and that's why we're asking you.'

The man let out a sigh. Was it one of relief?

'After you came to see me, it got me thinking about Rob. I wanted to see how he was getting on. I hadn't seen him for twenty-five years, and it seemed like a good idea at the time.'

'But you left a false name. Why?'

McNeil averted his eyes. 'I don't know.'

The man was clearly lying and wasn't good at it either.

Seb was confident that they'd soon be able to extract the truth from him.

'How did you know where Rob lived?'

'I'm not sure. You must have mentioned it to me. Yeah, that's it.'

'No, I didn't,' Seb said, leaning forward slightly and locking eyes with him.

McNeil squirmed. 'Um … You must have forgotten.'

'I can assure you I did not. I repeat. How did you know where Rob Walker lived?'

McNeil clenched his fist and started banging it on his mouth. He was blinking hard. 'Someone must've told me, all right? Why does it matter? I went to see him, we had a chat, and then I left. That's it. He's not in a prison. He's allowed to have visitors, and that's all I was doing. Visiting. That's the truth.'

'Who told you?'

'I don't remember.'

'Then let me have a guess. Was it Gareth Collins? The man you informed me you are no longer in contact with, and yet I was able to trace a connection on your social media account.'

Silence hung in the air while Seb stared directly at McNeil, waiting for a response.

'Look. If I tell you everything, you've got to promise to keep me out of it? I was only doing a favour for a friend. I can't afford to lose my job or be caught up in anything bad. My family needs me,' McNeil finally said.

Seb glanced at Whitney, whose face remained impassive.

'We'll try our best. That's all I can offer,' he said.

'Okay. I don't have much choice if I want to get out of here.' McNeil sucked in a breath. 'You're right about Gareth Collins. He came round to my house and asked me to visit Rob to find out why the police were looking into his attack. He said he didn't want to go himself because it could get him in trouble. And before you ask, no, I don't know what "trouble" he meant.'

'Do you believe that he might have been involved in the assault?' Seb asked.

'Yeah, well, that's what I thought. But … we were only sixteen, and Rob was way bigger than both of us, so how could he have done it? And *why* would he? Rob and Gareth were good mates. Better than I was with either of them. I was like the third wheel.'

'Did you ask Gareth why he wanted to know?'

'Yeah, but he wouldn't give me a straight answer. He said it was for someone else. I told him I didn't want to, but he told me that if I didn't, my kids might not be safe. So, I had to do it. He met me after in the Block and Tackle pub, and I told him that Rob didn't know anything about it. Which he didn't.'

'Did Rob remember you?' Seb asked.

'Not at first. But after about ten minutes, when I said Gareth's name, he acted a bit strange. Like he was scared.'

'Scared, how?' Whitney asked.

Seb turned to the DCI. Her face was set hard. This was what he was afraid would happen. Whitney was finding it difficult to remain detached.

'Please describe Rob's reaction,' he said, drawing the attention back to himself.

'He sort of screwed up his face and rocked backwards and forwards. After that, he wouldn't look at me. I didn't stay much longer.'

'Did you inform Collins of his reaction?'

'No. All I said was that Rob knew nothing about the attack or why the police were looking into it. Maybe I should have, but after seeing Rob like that and remembering how he used to be when we were kids … I couldn't do it.'

'Interview suspended,' Seb said, leaning past Whitney and stopping the recording. 'You're free to go, Mr McNeil. But if you are contacted again by Gareth Collins, please let me know. Here's my card.'

Seb and Whitney remained in the interview room as a uniformed officer escorted McNeil off the premises.

'Sorry, I meant to stay quiet. But the thought of him upsetting Rob … It just …' Whitney said once they were alone.

'I understand. It was hard for me, too, having now been introduced to Rob. Before I leave, we need to bring in Gareth Collins for questioning.'

'Yeah, absolutely. I'll instruct uniform to pick him up ASAP.'

# Chapter 31

'What the fuck am I doing in here?' Gareth Collins growled.

'I have some more questions for you.' Seb pulled out the chair opposite and sat. He gestured for Collins to do the same, and Collins dropped back down onto his seat.

'Why didn't you come round to my house like you did last time? I didn't need you lot knocking on my door and escorting me out my own home for the whole street to see. How do you think that made me look?'

'What do you know about Martin McNeil visiting Rob Walker on Wednesday, the sixteenth of June, at the home where he now lives?' Seb asked, ignoring the question.

'Nothing. Who said I did?' Collins said, turning up his nose.

'You were seen with McNeil in the Block and Tackle pub shortly after he left the home.'

'So what? Just because I met with Marty doesn't mean that I know where he'd been beforehand.'

'Why did you meet?'

'We're mates. Have been since school. Why don't you

ask him? He'll tell you the same. We often meet for a catch-up.'

Collins leant back in his chair with his arms folded, looking smug.

'That's very different from what you told me when we last spoke. You said you hadn't seen or heard from him since he left school.'

'It had slipped my mind. No crime in that.'

'And when you met last week, are you sure that McNeil didn't mention Rob at all? Considering you were all friends at school, it seems unlikely. Even more so since the investigation into his assault has recently resumed.'

'I've told you what I know, and that's it.' Collins folded his arms across his chest and began looking around the room, acting like he didn't care about being there. Was it an act? Seb would soon find out.

'Was it your brother, Keith, who instructed you to order McNeil to visit?'

A startled expression fleetingly crossed Gareth's face before he pulled himself together, but it wasn't soon enough to hide it from Seb.

'No. Why would he do that?'

'You tell me.'

'You're talking shit. I had nothing to do with a visit to Rob Walker, and nor did my brother.'

'If you say so. Let's talk a little bit more about your brother. You used to work for him when you were at school, is that correct?'

'You already know it is.'

'This is for the recording,' Seb said, nodding at the equipment.

Collins sighed. 'Yes, I helped him out sometimes.'

'What sort of jobs would you do for him?'

'Delivering stuff. It wasn't a big deal. It was to save him the bother. It was easy money.'

'And Rob and Marty would assist you?'

'If we were together, Rob would. Marty wasn't with us much. He was a bit of a wuss, anyway. Got scared sometimes if we had to visit dodgy areas. If we were together, we'd split the money Keith gave me.'

Seb wasn't learning anything new. He'd have to up the ante.

'Did you also do jobs for Victor Rawlings?'

Collins froze. 'No. Never.'

Just the reaction Seb had been hoping for. Now he could push forward.

'I find that hard to believe, considering we know your brother currently works for Victor Rawlings and that most likely their relationship goes back many years.'

Seb had no idea whether that was accurate, but Collins was unaware of that.

'I haven't a clue what you're talking about. I never did anything for Rawlings. And you can't prove that I did.'

'But you knew of him all those years ago.'

'Yeah. Everyone did.' He slammed his hands on the table. 'I'm saying nothing more without a solicitor present. Are you going to arrest me? Because if you are, go ahead. I haven't done anything. I don't know anything about what my brother does. He's nothing to do with me.' The words tumbled out of his mouth in panic.

'One more question, and you can go.'

'What?'

'Dennis Hunter.'

'What about him?'

'When did you last see him?'

'I don't remember …' His voice fell away.

'So you admit to knowing him.'

'Maybe. No. I don't know. That's really it. I'm saying no more.'

'Interview suspended.' Seb stopped the recording.

'Can I go now?' Gareth asked.

'For now.'

'Nice work. He's definitely hiding something,' Whitney said after Collins had left.

'Yes, and I suspect it's to do with his brother and Rawlings. He was clearly scared when I talked of them working together. I'll ask Charlotte about him when I question her tomorrow. I'm still reluctant to bring in Keith just yet, considering I've already spoken to him. It would put everyone, including Rawlings, on alert. The question is, will Gareth inform Keith?'

'There's not a lot we can do about that,' Whitney said as her phone pinged. 'It's a text from Ellie. She's identified the owner of the warehouses and has found something else. Come on, let's go and see what it is.'

When they reached the incident room, the room went quiet.

'You're back,' Frank said.

'Nothing like stating the obvious,' Whitney replied, frowning. 'What's going on?'

'This is big. Go and see Ellie.'

Whitney exchanged a glance with Seb.

'We're here, what have you got?' Whitney said as Ellie glanced up from her screen.

'First, Rawlings owns the warehouse in Greymills. He bought it in 1990 via an offshore company, and it was also diverted through several other businesses. It wasn't easy, and it took me all over the world, but eventually I tracked it back to him. Well, to his company, VR Machinery.'

'That's excellent work, Ellie. Thank you,' Seb said.

'You said "first". What's second?' Whitney asked.

'I've been doing a thorough investigation into Rawlings, in particular those negative stories about him when he was in Lenchester. I didn't find anything to corroborate them, but I came across this photograph taken at an MG car rally in Bedford a month before your brother's assault.' She loaded the photo on her screen and pointed to a group of men. 'Rob, McNeil, Gareth and Keith Collins, Hunter, and to the left, almost out of shot, is Rawlings.'

# Chapter 32

Birdie ran out of the station, her bag slung over her shoulder. She grabbed hold of her hair and pulled it off her face and into a band. She'd been late for work and rushed getting ready this morning. She'd intended to look more presentable for the interview with Rawlings' daughter, but it wasn't to be. She scanned the car park. Of course, Seb was already there. She ran over to the car and jumped into the passenger seat.

'Sorry I'm—'

'I thought we were over you apologising every time you're late. Perhaps you should have a sign made up that you can hold up instead,' Seb quipped.

'Look at you, making a joke. It must be hanging around with the DCI that's done it. She's bringing out the flippant side of you.'

'Very funny.' He started the engine and drove out of the car park.

'What time did you get home yesterday? I popped back in the afternoon to collect some things I'd left and took Elsa out for a quick walk when I saw you weren't there. I also gave her a few treats because I didn't know what time she was going to be fed.'

Birdie was pleased he hadn't asked her to stay there last night because she'd arranged to go out with her friends, and it was much easier for her to go home than have to traipse all the way back out to Seb's place, especially by taxi, which would have cost loads.

'I wasn't too late. I think Elsa was disappointed when the door opened and it was me. She definitely loves you.'

'True. But I'm sure she did miss you.' Birdie grinned in his direction. 'A little.'

'I'll take your word for that.'

'Tell me about the interviews yesterday.'

'Marty McNeil visited Rob, but he was sent there by Gareth Collins. Collins knows more than he's letting on. He didn't give us anything concrete, but as soon as Rawlings' name was mentioned, he clammed up. I suspect he was ordered to send McNeil to visit Rob to find out what he knew.'

'And to make sure he stays silent?'

'It's impossible to know. Rob didn't give any information to Marty, and he didn't mention the visit to us when we were there. Rob was upset by Whitney's questions regarding what happened around the time of the assault, which means we must solve this without his help. We do now have evidence of Rob being in the company of Rawlings, Hunter, and the two Collins brothers a few weeks before the assault, however.'

'Do you think this Charli will help, even after all this time?'

'She goes by Charlotte now. If she believes that Collins or Hunter have something to do with Rob's attack, she might be more forthcoming. If we keep her father out of it, that should help, because she certainly wouldn't want to incriminate him.'

'That makes sense.'

'I'm only going to focus on Rob's attack and twenty-five years ago. Again, if she's not alerted to the current interest in him, it might persuade her to be more helpful.'

When they reached Charlotte's house, Birdie let out a low whistle. 'It looks like they're not short of money. Is that her Merc?' she asked as they pulled up alongside a flashy car.

'Yes, I believe it is.'

Before they'd even reached the front door, it was opened by a well-dressed woman in an expensive-looking navy trouser suit and full make-up.

She stared directly at Seb. 'Why are you here? I'm on my way out.'

'This won't take long. This is DC Bird. We'd like to ask you a few more questions regarding Robert Walker.'

'My father told me not to speak to you without a solicitor present.'

'This can always be done at the station if you'd rather. You may call your solicitor from there,' Birdie didn't mind playing bad cop if it helped.

Charlotte glanced over her shoulder. 'Okay, I'll talk to you, but you're not coming inside. Be quick and keep your voices down. My husband's here. We have an appointment shortly to see our accountant.'

'Rob's friend, Gareth Collins, has a brother called Keith. What can you tell me about him?'

'Nothing. I don't recall ever meeting him.'

'Are you sure, because we know that Rob was seen in the company of both of them?'

She folded her arms and leant against the door frame. 'What do you want from me? We're talking twenty-five years ago. I have enough trouble remembering things from last week. So, when I tell you I don't recollect Gareth's brother, I mean it. Is there anything else?'

'A few weeks before Rob was attacked, he attended a car rally in Bedford. Did you go with him?' Seb asked.

'I doubt it.'

'How can you be sure if your memory is so suspect?' Birdie asked.

'Because I went to boarding school and I most likely would have been there. I've never been to a car rally in my life. I couldn't think of anything worse.'

'So you didn't accompany your father to a rally?' Seb asked.

'No. I doubt he's ever been to one either. He's not into cars. He buys the best to be driven about in, but that's it. He wouldn't know an exhaust from a … I don't know … a tyre. You know what I mean.'

This made no sense. Was the woman deliberately acting dumb?

'He imports and exports farm machinery, surely he must have some knowledge of engines?' Birdie said.

'I don't know. But I don't ever remember him going to a car rally. Now, is that all?'

'Not quite. When we last spoke, you referred to your father as having "goons". Could Keith Collins have been one of them?' Seb asked.

'It was a figure of speech. I never took much notice of the people who worked for Daddy when I was younger. Nor do I now, for that matter.'

'What about Dennis Hunter, your father's driver?' Seb asked.

'What about him?' Charlotte stiffened. There was definitely something about Hunter that bothered her.

'Would you be surprised to learn that we think he may have been connected to Rob's attack?'

Charlotte paled. 'Are you sure? He's worked for my father since … forever. I can't remember him not being there. But …'

'But what?' Birdie asked.

'I've never liked him. And I've always wondered why my father kept him on. I asked once and was told it was because he knows everything about the business and he's reliable. Daddy said that Hunter doesn't have to be like-able. Do you believe he might have been connected to the attack?'

'That's what we're currently investigating. Do you know anything about Hunter that might help?' Seb asked.

'Nothing. And I can't get involved, or my father will be angry. All I will say is that I don't particularly like him. I'm sorry, but you really must leave.'

'Thank you for your assistance. If you do think of anything else, please let me know. You have my card,' Seb said.

The detectives left the house and drove away.

'Thoughts?' Birdie said. 'Was it a wasted journey?'

'I don't think so. From her verbal and non-verbal reactions, I suspect she has no idea how her father operates his business, nor whether he had any part in the attack on Rob. I've held off until now, but it's time to question Hunter. Can you find out where Rawlings is at the moment? If he's at the office, we may well find Hunter at home. We'll only focus on Rob's case when we speak to him.'

# Chapter 33

'Wow, look at this,' Birdie said as they walked up the circular drive belonging to the large stone bungalow in Stoke Albany Road, Desborough, where Dennis Hunter lived.

'It looks like he's in,' Seb said, pointing at Rawlings' Mercedes, which was parked beside some outbuildings.

'Who knew that being a driver was such a well-paid job? Maybe I should consider it.'

'According to Ellie's research, he lives way beyond his pay cheque, including being mortgage-free here. And, before you ask, no, he hasn't inherited any money.'

'What you're saying is that it's most likely Rawlings who's paid for all this.'

'It's certainly a consideration. I'll lead the questioning, and we'll focus on him working for Rawlings at the time of the attack on Rob. In particular, we want to discover what he knows about the relationship between Charlotte Newton and Rob. Rawlings may have informed him of our interest, so he could plan his responses.'

'Assuming he was told. Rawlings might not have seen the investigation as important.'

Birdie rang the bell, and the door was opened by Hunter, a tall, well-toned man who looked to be in his mid-sixties. His white hair was cropped close to his head, and he had a goatee beard.

'Yes?'

'Mr Hunter, I'm Sebastian Clifford from Lenchester CID, and this is DC Bird from Market Harborough. We would like to ask you a few questions.' Birdie and Seb both held out their IDs, and Hunter gave them a cursory glance.

'What about?'

'We'd rather talk inside, if we may, and not on the doorstep,' Seb said.

Hunter looked over his shoulder into the long hall and then back at them. 'Okay, come in. We'll go into the sitting room.' He ushered them inside and took them into the first room on the left. It was a bright room, lit by the large bay window that overlooked the front of the house, and was tastefully furnished with a black leather three-piece sofa and a mahogany coffee table. There were floor-to-ceiling curtains which were held back by ties, and also an onyx feature fireplace in the middle of the wall opposite.

Hunter gestured for them to sit down.

'We're investigating a case from twenty-five years ago. Do you remember a young man called Robert Walker who lived in Lenchester?' Seb asked once they were all seated, and he had Hunter's full attention.

The man's body language gave nothing away, and it was impossible to detect whether or not he'd been fore-warned that he might be a person of interest.

'No.'

'He was the boyfriend of Charlotte, Victor Rawlings' daughter, for a while. She went by the name Charli then.'

'Why would I know anything about her boyfriends?' He focused his attention on Seb, maintaining what appeared to be a calm exterior.

'Because she'd been forbidden to see him by her father, and she disobeyed him. Mr Rawlings might have mentioned it to you.'

'Well, he didn't. So, if that's all you want to know, then please could you leave. I'm due out shortly.'

Neither Seb nor Birdie made any attempt to move.

'Rob Walker was viciously attacked twenty-five years ago and left with irreversible brain damage. We have reopened the case as further evidence has come to light,' Seb said.

'And you think I might have something to do with it?'

'That's not what I'm saying. We're looking at all possible connections, including that Victor Rawlings was against their relationship, and you worked for him. It wouldn't be beyond the realm of possibility for you to have been asked to warn the young man off.'

'I'm Mr Rawlings' driver, not his security. It's not my job to "warn off" people for him.'

Hunter outwardly appeared relaxed in the way he was seated, but he couldn't hide the telltale tightness around his eyes.

'Even at charity events?' Birdie asked.

Seb winced. He didn't want to push the man into a corner.

'I have no idea what you're referring to,' Hunter said. 'Wh—'

'How well do you know Keith and Gareth Collins?' Seb asked, cutting across Birdie.

'The names don't mean anything to me.'

'They should do because Keith Collins has known Mr Rawlings for many years, so I'm sure you've come across him. We also know that Gareth and Rob worked for Keith sometimes.'

Hunter gave a loud sigh. 'Okay, I might know Keith Collins. But that doesn't mean that I know anything about the attack.'

'Did Gareth Collins and Rob Walker do any work for Mr Rawlings?'

'I can't answer that.'

'So, they might have done?' Seb pushed.

'Look, I have no knowledge of an attack on Rob Walker. Whatever happened, it was many years ago. Maybe I do remember Charli seeing someone that Mr Rawlings didn't approve of, but that's all. It wasn't important at the time. If you have no more questions, then that's it. Mr Rawlings is expecting me to pick him up from work.'

Seb glanced at Birdie and nodded for them to leave. As he stood, he reached in his pocket for a card. 'If you do think of anything, please let me know. Here's my card.'

Hunter showed them out of the house, and they returned to Seb's car.

'He clearly knew more than he was letting on. What do you want to do now?' Birdie asked.

'He said he's going to pick up Rawlings, so let's see if he's telling the truth. We'll follow him and see where he goes.'

'Drive to the end of the street and wait around the corner, it will give us a view of his house.'

After five minutes, Hunter drove off, and Seb followed, keeping his distance. The man turned right towards Market Harborough town centre.

'Interesting. He's not going to Leicester to collect Rawlings, so where is he going?'

They followed as he took the A508 out of Market Harborough and then onto the Lenchester Road. A mile out of the city, he turned left into an industrial estate, pulling into the car park of a self-storage company and parking in a vacant space.

Seb stopped on the other side of the road, and they watched Hunter head towards a block of units, coming to a halt at one overlooking the front entrance.

'So, he's got a storage unit, and he came straight to it immediately after our visit. Why?' Birdie said.

'That's what we need to find out.'

They waited a further ten minutes, watching the unit, until Hunter left empty-handed.

'It's weird that he hasn't brought anything with him. In which case, what was he doing in there? Unless he's carrying something so small it would fit in his pocket.'

'We need a search warrant, and then we'll find out more.' Seb pulled out his binoculars and focused on the door belonging to the unit Hunter accessed. 'It's unit D34 of Stockton Self-Storage.'

'Do you want to ask the DCI, or shall I ask Sarge?'

It wouldn't matter who obtained the warrant, though if it went through Whitney, then it might get back to Douglas, which she wouldn't want.

'You get it.'

'I'll ask Twiggy to speak to Sarge, and he can ask DI Curtis for a warrant. I'll say it's urgent and it should come through today.'

# Chapter 34

After collecting the search warrant, Birdie, Seb, and Twiggy went to Stockton Self-Storage. They'd parked on the road and walked through the entrance towards the reception. When Birdie had suggested at the station that they drove here in one car, Twiggy had refused, saying he had somewhere else to go after. She wasn't sure if that was true or not, but she hadn't challenged him. In the end, she'd driven there with Seb, and Twiggy had followed separately. She'd been expecting Seb to comment on Twiggy's behaviour but, fortunately, he hadn't. She had no intention of breaking Twiggy's confidence, but equally, she didn't want to lie to Seb either.

'You two stay here, and I'll speak to the manager,' Birdie said once they were outside the office.

She pushed open the door and stood waiting for the woman behind the desk to finish on the phone.

'May I help you?' the woman said after replacing the phone in its cradle.

'I'm DC Bird with the Market Harborough station of

the Leicestershire police force. Is the manager here?' She held out her ID.

'That would be me. I'm Glenda York.'

'I have a warrant to search unit D34. Please could you open it?' Birdie passed over the warrant and the manager scrutinised it.

'Why are you searching this particular unit?'

'It's part of an ongoing investigation. What can you tell me about the person who rents it?'

Glenda stared at the computer screen and clicked her mouse. 'The storage unit belongs to a Mr Hunter, and he's been renting it for thirty years. Ever since this depot opened, in fact. He pays six-monthly in cash.'

'Has there ever been an issue regarding payment or any other matter?'

'I've been managing here for twelve years, and there's been nothing that I recall. I can't speak for before then.'

'Does your system record how often he accesses the unit?'

'It does now. Eight years ago, we changed to electronic keypads, and all access is recorded. According to our records, Mr Hunter goes into his unit once a month.'

'On the same day each month?'

'The days vary, but it looks like it's always in the last two weeks, in the evening, after the office is closed, except … he was here earlier today. That is unusual.'

Birdie suppressed a smile, not wanting the manager to realise that she'd unwittingly given them some vital infor-mation. 'Thank you. If you can take us there now, we'll take a look.'

'I can give you a code to get in if you would prefer.'

'You have Mr Hunter's access code?' That had surprised her.

'No. But I do have one that overrides the codes of all units. This master code is changed daily for security.'

'Thank you, that would be most helpful.'

After being given the code, Birdie went back outside to Seb and Twiggy.

'Where's the manager?' Twiggy asked.

'She gave me the code to get in, so we don't need her. She also looked up Hunter's use of the unit. He visits monthly, during the last two weeks, and always in the evening.'

'Except earlier today,' Seb said.

'We must have spooked him. Let's get to the unit, quick.'

When they reached the building containing Hunter's unit, Birdie keyed in the number and Seb lifted the roller door. The unit was small, about twelve feet by twelve feet, and lining the left wall was a stack of boxes, each of them with removal company labels on them.

'I'll take these,' Twiggy said, heading over to the boxes, pulling one down from the top row and opening it. 'A lot of this looks like items from when he's moved house.'

'I'm going to look over there,' Birdie said, pointing to a filing cabinet situated in the far-right corner. 'It stands at my height, so I should be able to see inside. You can check over there, Seb, as it's piled high with what looks like sports equipment and tools and you're the only person who can reach it all.'

Birdie pulled open the top drawer of the cabinet. It was very neat, unlike everything else in the unit, and each divider was labelled by year going back for thirty years, when he first rented the place. She pulled out a wad of documents from two years ago and flicked through them. She returned them to their folder and then took documents from another two years. Each year contained the same information.

'You guys need to see this,' she called out, holding up some of the papers. 'This filing cabinet contains details relating to all imports and exports for VR Machinery going back years.'

'What's Hunter doing with them?' Twiggy asked.

'Do you mind if I take a look?' Seb said, stepping towards the cabinet.

'Be my guest. You'll be much quicker than me.'

Birdie moved out of the way and watched while Seb started at the back, pulling out and scanning documents from every year. He returned each set of papers to the divider in which he found them. After ten minutes, he was finished.

'Well? What has your *super brain* found?' Twiggy said.

Birdie gave him a warning look. 'It's his memory, as you well know. But what did you find out, Seb?'

'I suspect that Hunter has all these documents to use as security if required. The information relates to all transactions made by the company. And if, as has been reported, Rawlings is dealing in firearms, then they're worth a great deal in the right hands.'

'You're right, and not just monetarily. He could trade the information with the police in exchange for not being prosecuted. Or he could turn Queen's evidence.'

'But how would Hunter have access to all this?' Twiggy asked.

'We already know that his duties go beyond that of simply being a driver. Let's consider the possibility that Hunter is heavily involved in the firearms dealing and Rawlings distances himself from it,' Seb said.

'Yes, that would make sense because Rawlings can't be seen anywhere dodgy or to be engaging in the actual transactions. Except, he has been seen with Collins and Simpson,' Birdie said.

'But in faraway places, like the service station, or at night,' Seb said.

'If we could intercept a deal, that would be a slam dunk. We could nail him. Are there any firearms due to be imported or exported soon, or is nothing recorded about that?' Birdie asked.

'According to what I've read, there's been a pattern over the years. On the twenty-fifth of the month, goods come into the country, and on the twenty-seventh, they're exported out.'

'That's perfect. Tomorrow's the twenty-fifth. We just need to find out where the firearms are going to be stored and raid the place. My bet's on Greymills Industrial Estate, here in Lenchester because there's nowhere else that we know of,' Birdie said.

'What about the place in Oadby that we followed him to?' Twiggy said.

'What place is this?' Seb asked.

'It was small and didn't seem large enough to house farm machinery. Margaret Clarke thought Rawlings was looking for some additional warehousing about twelve months ago and we wondered if this was it, but when we looked into it, the owner was an offshore company. We went back there later and didn't see anything, apart from a scarf I found outside, which I took back to the station. It's waiting to go to forensics. I can't see it being relevant because no way would they be able to store the amount of machinery and equipment that's imported each month, according to these records,' Bridie said.

'In that case, we'll assume Greymills is the place. Any operation needs to be coordinated between DCI Walker and DI Curtis,' Seb said.

'I'll phone Sarge, and he can sort it out. We better get back to the station straight away. Is that okay with you, Twiggy?' She glanced in his direction.

'Why wouldn't it be?'

'I thought you had an appointment.'

He averted his eyes. 'Yeah, well. It's not important.'

'Good. Let's go.'

# Chapter 35

'Sarge wants you in the meeting room, now,' Tiny said the moment Seb, Birdie, and Twiggy walked into the CID office. 'He's with Curtis and several others from Wigston. What's going on?'

'We'll fill you in later. We'd better not keep them waiting,' Birdie said.

The three of them hurried to the meeting room. At one end of the large, rectangular table, Sergeant Weston was engaged in an intense conversation with another man, who Seb assumed was DI Curtis. Seated further around the table were three other officers. Out the corner of his eye, Seb observed Birdie nodding at them.

'Come in and sit down,' Curtis said, gesturing to them, before looking directly at Seb. 'You must be Clifford.'

'That's correct. I'm working with Lenchester CID on a separate case, which has overlapped with yours.'

'Yes, I am aware of this. Didn't you used to be with the Met?'

Seb resisted the urge to roll his eyes. Either he was going to be questioned about his family background or the fact that he'd been part of a team that was disbanded because one of its members had been working with the overseas gang under investigation. It never ceased to amaze him that people thought one bad apple meant the whole team was on the take.

He could pre-empt the DI, but then he wasn't sure which aspect he was going to focus on, and Seb had no desire to let everyone in on his past if it was avoidable.

'Yes, that's correct.'

He followed Twiggy and Birdie and sat opposite the other officers.

'And I'm given to believe that you're still working for them?'

He'd clearly done his homework.

'Yes, I'm working with DI Lawson as a consultant.'

Was there a purpose to his questions? Surely it wasn't relevant to the task in hand.

'Good. We're glad to have your expertise on board, Clifford.'

Birdie nudged his leg, and he quickly glanced in her direction. She winked, no doubt finding it funny.

'Thank you.'

'Right, DC Bird. Please update everyone on the events of today.'

'Yes, sir. We obtained a search warrant for a storage unit belonging to Dennis Hunter, who is Rawlings' driver, and discovered a filing cabinet full of documents relating to the import and export of goods. From assessing these, we believe there's going to be a shipment of firearms brought into the country tomorrow, with a view to moving them on two days later. We believe the delivery site will be the warehouse owned by Rawlings on Greymills Industrial Estate in Lenchester. This would be an ideal time to close in on the operation.'

'I already have measures in place. The one sticking point is that we're after Rawlings, who's allegedly the king-pin. According to our research, the warehouse can't be traced back to him. It's owned by an offshore company,' Curtis said.

'DC Naylor from Lenchester CID was able to link the offshore company to Rawlings,' Seb said.

'Are you sure? Because my people couldn't determine ownership,' Curtis said.

'One hundred per cent.'

'I see. Then that settles it.' The inspector leant forward and rested his chin in his hand.

'Do you have a plan in mind, sir?' Sergeant Weston asked after a few minutes of silence.

'I do. We're going to raid the warehouse tomorrow when the shipment comes in and arrest any people working there. The testimony from Margaret Clarke, the documentation you obtained, and the fact that Rawlings owns the building is certainly enough to bring him in for questioning. It goes without saying that he'll have top-notch lawyers, so if we could find someone who will give him up, that will go a long way towards nailing him.'

'We could try Keith or Gareth Collins. If we offer them a deal, they might turn on him. Or there's Simpson, who works with Keith Collins. It's quite possible that they will be at the warehouse when we raid it,' Birdie said.

Seb wasn't convinced that the Collins brothers would cooperate.

'Rather than the brothers, it's my opinion that the ideal person to turn is Dennis Hunter because he's been with Rawlings for a very long time. I'm convinced that he kept this information to give him some leverage, should he need it. He's clearly been prepared for something like this, and I believe we can use it to our advantage,' Seb said.

'I agree,' Curtis said. 'We'll raid the warehouse at the same time as Hunter is brought in for questioning. That will ensure he's not forewarned. Clifford, you and DC Bird can pick him up. Wigston and Braunstone teams, I want surveillance on Rawlings' home and offices at all times to ensure he doesn't escape. DC Branch, you can join me at Lenchester for the raid on the warehouse.'

'Why do you need Twiggy to go?' Birdie asked.

Seb frowned. Why had she asked that question? Surely she didn't want Twiggy with the two of them. Three people interviewing Hunter would be overkill, in his opinion.

'He can identify any of the people from your surveillance.'

'Yes, I can,' Twiggy said, shooting daggers in Birdie's direction.

There was definitely something going on. But he wasn't going to ask. If it wasn't to do with the case, then it was none of his business. If they wanted him to know, they'd tell him.

'I assume DCI Walker is aware of our plans?' Seb said.

'Yes, I've spoken to the DCI, and she'll be arranging for an armed squad to meet us at the industrial estate. It's going to be a joint operation.'

'Excellent,' Seb said, nodding.

'If everyone knows what they're doing, we'll meet back here tomorrow after the raid and the driver has been arrested,' Curtis said.

'Who's going to interview Hunter?' Birdie asked.

'You and Clifford. You've been in contact with him before and know him better than the rest of us. Good luck, everyone. Let's nail Rawlings and get him off the streets for good.'

# Chapter 36

Twiggy had left home early to ensure he reached Lenchester with plenty of time to spare. Getting caught in roadworks wouldn't have gone down well with his superior officers. He was both anxious and excited at the day's prospects, having never been on an armed raid before. Hardly surprising, having worked most of his policing career in Market Harborough. He'd have much preferred Birdie to be by his side. Visiting another force always put him out of his comfort zone. He had no idea what DCI Walker would be like, even though Birdie had said she was okay.

Lenchester police station was jaw-dropping. He'd known it was brand new and purpose-built but seeing it in real life was another matter. When he walked up to the reception, he caught sight of a cafeteria. He felt more than a pang of envy. It would be tempting to ask for a transfer. Except, of course, he couldn't. Not now. He'd known exactly why Birdie had questioned the decision to have him here, and it had confirmed that he had to keep it secret for as long as possible. Once his condition was public knowledge, he'd end up being excluded from almost everything, and he couldn't work like that.

'I'm DC Branch from Market Harborough. I'm here to meet with DCI Walker and DI Curtis,' he said to the civilian on the front desk.

'They're in conference room five, which is straight down there, through the double doors, and you'll see it on the left. The number's on the door.'

He followed instructions and found it easily enough. The door was open and when he walked in there were already four people seated around the table.

'Ah. The last member to arrive. Come on in, Twiggy,' Curtis said. 'This is DC Branch from Market Harborough. He's been part of the surveillance team on Rawlings, and I've asked him to join us because he may have information that will assist us.'

Twiggy swallowed. How come they were already at the meeting? He hadn't been late. They'd said nine o'clock and it wasn't even a quarter to.

'Good to meet you, Twiggy,' DCI Walker said.

'Thank you, ma'am.' He sat on the closest empty chair.

'It's *guv*, the DCI isn't royalty,' an officer next to Walker said. Twiggy didn't like him straight away, with his expensive suit and condescending attitude. Especially as he hardly looked out of his twenties.

'Thank you, Brian. He's right. Just call me guv,' Walker said, offering a friendly smile.

'Will do, *guv*.'

'Let me introduce the others. DS Brian Chapman, and DC Meena Singh. Both are members of my team.'

Twiggy nodded to them both, much preferring the older DC from the DS. Her smile, at least, was genuine. Not that it mattered; he wasn't there for a party.

'DCI Walker's going to explain how the operation will proceed,' Curtis said.

'Thanks, Alan. We're going to have a squad of twenty armed officers, who will meet us in an hour's time at an adjacent section of the industrial estate, where there are only two warehouses, both empty. There have been two officers keeping surveillance on the warehouse we're raiding since last night. Once they've notified us of the delivery, the armed squad, followed by us, will drive there. Remember, we keep out of the way and let them do their work. Our job is to go in when the place is secure, identify those people we can, and bring in everyone for questioning. There will be several uniformed officers in vehicles waiting nearby to take the suspects. Any questions?'

Twiggy glanced around the table; they were all staring intently at the DCI.

'No, I believe that's all straightforward, thank you,' Curtis said.

'Good. In that case, I'm heading to the cafeteria. I'm in need of a caffeine fix. I get extremely grumpy if I don't have coffee at very regular intervals, as my team will attest.' DCI Walker grinned at both Curtis and him.

Twiggy smiled to himself. Birdie was right, she was okay. He'd definitely be going to the cafeteria, too. Obviously not to join her, but it was as good a place as any to wait until they were ready to leave. He certainly didn't want to spend too much time with DS Chapman, that was for sure.

Forty-five minutes later, Twiggy accompanied the DI to his car, and they followed the DCI, who was being driven by her sergeant, to the warehouse meeting point. When they arrived, there were three police vans, which he assumed contained the armed officers. He was as twitchy as hell from the adrenaline pumping through his body and was already regretting the coffee and cake he'd consumed before leaving.

'Wait here while I speak to the DCI,' Curtis said.

'Yes, sir.'

The DI went over to Walker and then they both headed to one of the vans. They chatted to the driver for a short while before Curtis returned.

'According to the surveillance team, a delivery arrived thirty minutes ago, and they've just finished unloading. The driver has left and will be stopped by uniform once he's well away from the vicinity. They'll ensure he won't be able to contact anyone inside the warehouse.'

'Does that mean we're going in now?'

'Yes. It will all be coordinated.'

The radio crackled. '*Commencing in three. Three. Two. One. Go.*'

Excitement surged through Twiggy as he tried to steady his breathing. He couldn't lose his shit. Not now.

The vans pulled out, followed by DCI Walker's car and then theirs.

Tyres squealed as they turned into the warehouse, and the vans separated, ensuring there was only one way in and one way out.

No way could anyone escape.

The back doors of each van swung open and armed officers jumped out.

Twiggy looked at over Curtis. His fists were clenched and his knuckles white.

'Quick, get out of the car and shelter behind it. There could be stray bullets,' Curtis said.

They crouched down, out of sight, and waited.

'*Go! Go! Go!*' came the voice over the radio.

The armed officers ran to the warehouse, making sure each entrance was covered. In unison, they kicked in the doors and entered.

Twiggy held his breath, waiting for shots to be fired.

There were none.

'*All clear*,' the radio crackled.

Twiggy exhaled and, together with Curtis, ran around the side of the car until meeting up with DCI Walker.

'Let's go,' Walker said.

Inside, armed officers had their guns trained on five men, all handcuffed.

'Everywhere is clear, guv,' one of the officers said to the DCI.

'Thanks. Keep everyone here while we split up and check the warehouse.'

Twiggy wasn't sure what he should be looking for, so he kept close to DC Singh. The building was full of farm machinery, and on the workbenches were a variety of tools.

'Over here, guv,' the DS called out after they'd been searching for several minutes.

The officer was beside several wooden crates, a crowbar in his hand and a pile of engine parts on the floor beside him. Everyone made a beeline for him.

'What have you found?' Walker asked.

'Take a look. They were underneath the engine parts.'

They all peered into the open crate, and there were at least a dozen handguns nestled in a protective sponge cover.

'Good work, Brian. Let's open the rest and see what turns up.'

Twiggy was about to approach one of the crates when he heard a thud. He looked in the direction from where the sound came but saw nothing. That was weird. He was about to turn back when he heard the noise again.

He marched over to the back of the warehouse and looked around. It couldn't be someone hiding because there was nowhere to go. This part of the warehouse was empty. He stood still and listened again.

Silence.

He'd imagined it. Perhaps the sound was being reflected from a surface somewhere else in the warehouse and he'd been mistaken.

He turned to return to the crates when there was a loud bang. This time, he knew it was for real. He strode over to the rear wall where the sound came from.

Was there another room? He couldn't see a door.

'Guv,' he shouted. 'I've got something.'

Walker jogged over, closely followed by Curtis.

'What is it?' the DCI asked.

'There's some banging coming from this end of the warehouse, like it's coming from another room. But there isn't a door.'

'Have you tried listening at the wall?'

Crap. He'd been so busy looking for an entrance that he hadn't done that. What an idiot she must think he was.

'Not yet. I called you over first.'

Walker put her ear to the wall. 'I can definitely hear something,' she said after a few seconds.

She walked over to one of the men who was being held in handcuffs. 'What's in there?' she demanded, pointing to the back of the warehouse.

The man's shrugged. 'Nothing.'

'Don't give me that. What's in there, and where's the entrance?'

Twiggy shuffled along beside the wall, tapping with his knuckles to see if there was a change in sound that might indicate a door. He'd almost got to the end when he heard it.

'Guv. I think I've found the door, but there's no handle.'

Walker ran over and he tapped again, so she could hear.

'Right, we need to break it down. Yates, over here and bring the battering ram.'

Two officers ran over. They stood by the place Twiggy had found, and together swung the ram backwards and then into the wall. With a loud crash, a hole appeared, revealing where a metal door had been, which was now on the floor. It opened a small six-foot square room.

Huddled together in the far corner, Twiggy counted ten women who looked barely older than his youngest daughter, Jade. Nausea washed over him. No explanation was needed.

'It's okay, we're the police,' Walker called out in a gentle voice as she stepped towards them, stopping in front of the nearest one. 'Who are you?'

Several of the women spoke, but Twiggy didn't recognise the language.

'Does anyone speak English?' Whitney asked.

'I do. A little,' said one of the women who stepped out from behind the front row. She had straight brown hair and a pretty face with freckles. If she was fourteen, that was pushing it.

'I'm Whitney. What's your name?'

'Kasia.'

'Have you been kept here against your will?'

'Yes,' Kasia nodded, tears filling her eyes. 'They said we had job, but when we arrived, they locked us up and took our passports.'

'Everything's going to be okay now. We're going to take

you somewhere safe. Please could you explain to the others?'

'Guv, ask them if this was the only place they were kept?' Twiggy said.

Walker frowned. 'Why?'

'DC Bird and I were checking out a place in Oadby that Rawlings visited on Wednesday. We found a scarf outside. I just wondered if it belonged to one of them. It could be proof that Rawlings knows all about this if he tries to deny it.'

'I'll ask once Kasia has finished explaining to the others who we are and what's going to happen.'

'Thanks, guv. Thank God we found them.'

'That's down to you, Twiggy. And only you. It's unlikely we'd have discovered them otherwise. I can't begin to think about what might have happened to them. Well done. You're a credit to the force.'

Twiggy leant against the side of the room to stop his legs from giving way, the enormity of what he'd been a part of finally hitting him. He wasn't normally so pathetic. It had to be the FTD that was making him like that.

He watched while the DCI and DC Singh escorted the young women out of the room.

When he got home, he was going to give both of his daughters a big hug.

# Chapter 37

'We were right. He's come back home,' Birdie said as they drove up to Hunter's house and saw Rawlings' car in the drive.

The surveillance team had kept them informed of Rawlings' movements and, once he'd been dropped off at the head office, they'd headed straight to Hunter's house, bringing with them uniformed officers in a patrol car to escort him to the station if necessary.

Seb rung the bell and the door opened almost immediately. Hunter glared at them.

'What do you want? I've told you everything I know.'

'Mr Hunter, you're to accompany us to the station in Market Harborough,' Birdie said.

'Why?'

'We'll explain when we're there.'

'I can't go anywhere,' he said, panic marching across his face. He turned and looked over his shoulder.

'It's not up for negotiation. You're coming with us, or we'll arrest you.'

'I can't leave my wife because she has MS. She had a

fall earlier and I'm just replacing her dressings. I don't want to leave her on her own while she's still in shock.'

'Who is it, Denny?' a woman's voice called out from the sitting room.

'It's to do with work, love,' Hunter replied.

'But you said you didn't have to go back there until later.'

'Is there someone who can sit with her?' Birdie asked.

'I can try, but it depends if they're available.'

'May we come inside while you sort something out?' Birdie asked.

He ushered them inside and took them into the sitting room, where his wife was sitting in a wheelchair.

'Hello, Mrs Hunter. I'm DC Bird, and this is Sebastian Clifford. We're sorry, but we need to talk to Dennis at the station.'

'What's it about?'

Did she have any idea what her husband did for a living? Surely she must suspect something if they could afford to live in such a lovely home and go on all those luxury holidays.

'I'm sorry, we're not allowed to discuss ongoing investigations.'

'But—'

'There's nothing to worry about, Lizzie. Let me finish your dressings, and I'll ask Felicity if she can stay with you until you feel better.' He turned to Birdie and Seb. 'She's our neighbour.'

'We'll wait in the hall for you to finish,' Seb said.

'She'll need more than the neighbour taking care of her because there's no guarantee Hunter will make bail if he's charged for his part in all this,' Birdie said once they were on their own and couldn't be overheard.

'We'll keep that between ourselves for now. It's important for him to cooperate. I think it is best for him to be taken to the station in the police car and not with us, in case he tries to abscond.'

After several minutes, Hunter joined them in the hall.

'Is this to do with Victor?'

'We'll discuss everything at the station, as we've already explained,' Birdie said.

'I can't go to prison and leave Lizzie on her own. We have no children, and her sister is in no position to look after her. Going into a care home isn't an option either. It would destroy her. If I tell you everything I know, can I avoid prosecution?'

Birdie and Seb exchanged a glance. She hadn't expected him to crumble so quickly.

'That's not a decision we can make, but it can be discussed when we get to the station,' she said.

'Thank you. I'll go next door for Felicity.'

'I'll come with you,' Seb said.

After Seb and Hunter had left the house, Birdie returned to the sitting room. 'How are you feeling, Mrs Hunter?'

'Okay, thanks. And a bit foolish. My legs had improved recently, and I was in the kitchen earlier, standing by the sink, when one of them gave way. I tried to grab hold of the kitchen table, but I missed and fell. I cut my leg on the side of a chair and grazed my arms. Luckily, Denny was here because he'd come back from driving Mr Rawlings to work. Not many jobs would allow him to take care of me at the same time as work.'

'How well do you know Mr Rawlings?'

'I've met him many times over the years. Sometimes he calls in to say hello. He's a good boss, and he does a lot of charity work.'

'Does Dennis ever talk about his work for Mr Rawlings?'

'Not really, and I don't ask. All I know is he's a good man and values Dennis's loyalty. That's why he pays Dennis well and gives him bonuses so we can go on lovely holidays.'

'Don't you think it's strange that your husband is so well rewarded for being a driver?'

'Mr Rawlings is very rich. A thousand pounds for us is only like five pounds for him. All I know is you don't look a gift horse in the mouth. If he wants to help us, then that's fine by me.'

Was she really so naïve?

The front door banged. 'They must be back,' Birdie said.

Hunter and Seb walked into the sitting room, followed by an older woman.

'Felicity will stay with you for now. I'll call and let you know when to expect me back.'

They left the house and escorted Hunter to the police car waiting on the opposite side of the road.

'Why am I not going with you?' Hunter asked.

'It's standard procedure. We'll see you back at the station.'

# Chapter 38

Seb's phone rang while he was on the way to the interview room with Birdie to question Hunter, who had declined his right to have a solicitor present.

'I should take this, it's DCI Walker.'

'I'm assuming you're aware of what's happened here regarding the trafficking and firearms?' Whitney said.

'Yes, I've just been given a briefing by DI Curtis. Excellent work. Birdie and I are about to interview Dennis Hunter, who's asked for immunity in return for providing evidence against Rawlings.'

Whitney snorted. 'If I had a pound for every time someone offered to do that, I'd be a very rich woman. It looks like we've got Rawlings over a barrel, but you know how slippery guys like him can be, so anything Hunter gives us will help. I also want you to question Hunter about Rob's attack, but not until I'm with you. I'm on my way to Market Harborough and should be there in half an hour.'

'But …' Seb paused. He understood Whitney's need to be part of the operation, but after her inability to keep her distance with McNeil, for her to be interviewing Hunter with him wasn't advisable.

'I know what you're thinking, but all I want to do is observe from behind a two-way mirror. I'm not going to take part, that's down to you.'

Was that a good idea? He wasn't convinced, but he didn't have time to dwell on it.

'We'll carry out an initial interview with him and only focus on the current case.'

'Thanks, Seb. I'm praying that Hunter will know something. If he doesn't, I don't know what we'll do because the funding runs out in two days.'

'Whatever happens, I'll investigate Rob's case for you. Funding or no funding. We'll continue until all avenues have been exhausted. I promise.'

He couldn't leave the case unsolved, even if he did pay for it himself. Whitney was a friend, and she needed him. He wouldn't let her down.

'Oh, Seb ...' Her voice broke and she sniffed loudly. 'Now look what you've made me do. I can't cry while I'm driving, it will blur my vision.'

'Sorry. It wasn't my intention to upset you.'

'You haven't. This is me being happy. Thanks so much for your generous offer. Hopefully, we won't need it.' She gave a watery laugh and then ended the call.

'DCI Walker is going to observe the interview with Hunter when we question him about the attack on her brother, which we'll carry out separately,' Seb said to Birdie.

'Yes, I got the gist of your conversation. I also heard you offer your services for free. You'd better not do that too often, or you'll be out of business within a few months.'

'It's a one-off.'

'Make sure it is.'

Did that mean she was seriously considering working with him? If she wasn't, then whether he charged his clients or not wasn't her concern. Should he have hope …?

'I promise.'

'Good. Right, let's see what Hunter's got for us. We're so going to nail Rawlings. The disgusting bastard.'

Seb and Birdie walked into the interview room and faced Hunter, who was seated with his arms folded, staring straight ahead.

'Interview on the twenty-fifth of June. Those present: DC Bird, Sebastian Clifford, and, please state your name,' Birdie said, looking directly at him.

'Dennis Hunter.'

'Mr Hunter, I would like to confirm that you're here to discuss Victor Rawlings' business. You're here voluntarily, but if you do try to leave, you will be arrested and cautioned. Do you understand?'

'Stop with all the legal crap. I know, okay? Let's get on with it. I want to go home to my wife.'

Birdie audibly drew in a breath. Seb hoped she wouldn't allow herself to become rattled. They required Hunter to be relaxed and willing to talk. Although Seb doubted he'd change his mind about giving up Rawlings because of his family situation. But the more cooperative he was, the better the quality of information.

'For the recording, please confirm you told us earlier that you have information regarding VR Machinery and Victor Rawlings,' Birdie said, her voice low and calm.

'I'm only going to do that if I'm not prosecuted for my part in the activities,' Hunter said.

'You have already been informed that's not a decision we are able to make. Once you've provided us with the information, we will contact the CPS and they will decide whether or not you'll be charged and, if you are, what those charges will be,' Seb said.

'Before I speak, I need your assurance that my wife and I will be put into witness protection. What I'm going to tell you will have far-reaching consequences, and our lives will be in danger.'

For the first time, Seb witnessed tension emanating from the man's body. Was the enormity of what he was about to do hitting him?

'We are very much aware of this and will make the necessary arrangements. I'd like to start with your storage unit, in which we found documents going back thirty years regarding the import and export of what we now believe to be firearms.'

'What?' Hunter spluttered, his eyes wide. 'But … How did you know that place even existed?'

'We followed you to the unit after our first interview, obtained a warrant, and searched it.'

Hunter shook his head. 'I don't believe it. How could I have been so stupid to have led you there? You're right, I kept a log of every time firearms were shipped in and out of the country. It was my insurance, as you've rightly guessed.'

'From where did the firearms originate?' Seb asked.

'Victor has links in Europe. In the past, he dabbled in importing drugs, but over the last few years, he's moved away from that because the competition is fierce and the returns not so good. He also had issues with his supply chain, which made him jittery and not prepared to take the risk.'

'Is that when he started trafficking young women?' Birdie asked.

'Don't tell me you know about that, too. How? There's no evidence in my storage unit because it wasn't part of the firearms operation. They're two separate businesses, overseen by Rawlings.'

'Why did he keep these two businesses apart?' Birdie asked.

'Mainly because I refused to have anything to do with the trafficking. You can say what you like about me, but I have principles. And trading young women goes against them. Rawlings didn't like me saying no, but he soon got used to it. He had no choice because I knew too much and had made myself indispensable by then.'

'He could have just "got rid of you",' Birdie said, making quote marks with her fingers.

'Do I look stupid? I made sure he knew that if anything did happen to me, I'd be bringing him down. Even if it was posthumously. He understood and said that he'd do the same in my situation. We only ever discussed it once, and it's never been mentioned again.'

Seb admired the man in a perverse sort of way. He hadn't left anything to chance and made sure that his back was covered, making no bones about where his loyalties lay. Which, when it came to the wire, wasn't with his boss.

'Until now,' Birdie said.

'That's correct. How did you find out about the girls?'

'Our officers raided the Greymills warehouse and discovered them in a secret room.'

'You know about the warehouse, too? You have been busy.' He leant back in his chair and placed his hands behind his head, with his elbows spread. A typical pose of someone trying to assert control over the situation. But it didn't work. He might be controlling his boss's destiny, but that would be as far as it went.

'Rawlings has been on our radar for some time. What else can you tell us about the trafficking?' Seb asked.

'Like I said, it's only been going on for a few years. He

has a partner overseas who arranges it and people over here to take delivery and move the women on. Victor doesn't like to get his hands dirty.'

'Although he was observed at the unit in Oadby, where the girls are initially taken. You were with him.'

'Victor went to do a spot check to make sure he got what he'd paid for. I stayed in the car and wasn't involved.'

'We already have the files from your storage unit. What other evidence do you have that we can pass onto the CPS for assessment?' Seb asked.

Hunter leant forward and rested both hands on the table. 'That's it until I have some firm assurances. The documents you have in your possession show transactions going back over thirty years. That should be enough. It can all be tied back to Victor. I've been the one who has driven him everywhere and listened to conversations he's had. You must know how much he pays me if you've done your research. Which doesn't quite match up to our lifestyle. Victor has always paid me on the side. That's all you're getting from me for now. I've done my bit. You go to the CPS and do yours.'

Seb's phone pinged, and he picked it up from the table and stared at the screen. 'Interview suspended.'

Birdie followed him out of the interview room and into the corridor.

'What's happened? Why did we end the interview so abruptly?'

'He's given us enough to enable the CPS to make a decision, and Whitney has messaged to say she's arrived. It's now time to move onto Rob.'

They headed to the front desk, where Whitney was waiting for them.

'How's the interview going?'

'Hunter's prepared to testify against Rawlings, and

together with thirty years of evidence, it's looking good. We've left him in the interview room believing he's done his bit for now. He has no idea we'll be returning to question him about Rob,' Seb said.

'How sure are you that he knows anything about the attack?' Birdie asked.

'He's already informed us he knows everything there is to know about Rawlings going back thirty years, which means if Rob was caught up with them in some way, because of dating Charli, or for another reason, then Hunter will know about it. It's our best shot of finding out the truth, I'm convinced of it.'

'I hope you're right,' Whitney said.

Seb turned to Birdie. 'Before we return, do you mind giving us a couple of minutes?'

'Um … yeah … If you like. I need the loo before we go back, anyway.'

Seb waited until Birdie was out of earshot. 'I'd like a quick word in private.'

'I gathered that. I'm not sure Birdie appreciated it, though.'

'She'll be fine. I don't think you should be observing the interview. I'd rather you left us to speak to Hunter and we'll relay what he said afterwards.'

'You've got to be kidding me. I didn't drive all this way, knowing that we might actually discover what happened to Rob for you to fob me off. I am your superior officer, you know … Well, I'm not because you're not in the force, but you know what I mean. This is my investigation, and I want to witness the interview.'

Having Whitney watching had bothered him ever since she'd told him. He had no idea what they might uncover, and it could be extremely painful for someone so close to the victim to hear. It wasn't like the detachment she felt when interviewing suspects, whether they were serial killers, arsonists, or other criminals. This was personal.

'I'm serious, Whitney. You should leave this to us.'

'Well, I'm not going to. As soon as you begin your interview, I'll go into the observation area. So, you might as well tell me where it is to save me the bother of having to find it.'

'Is it okay for me to come back?' Birdie called out from along the corridor.

'Yes, Birdie. We were discussing me being in the observation area to watch the interview,' Whitney said.

'I'll show you where it is, and you can watch from there, ma'am,' Birdie said.

'It's guv,' Whitney said.

'Oh, right. This way then, *guv*,' Birdie said with a smile.

Seb watched while Whitney positioned herself in front of the two-way mirror, facing Dennis Hunter. The lines were tight around her eyes, and her fists were balled. Seb wasn't happy with her being on her own, but it was too late to find someone to sit with her.

'If Hunter knows anything, we'll find out,' Seb said, resting a comforting arm on her shoulder.

'I know you will. My heart's hammering so hard it feels like it's going to explode out of my chest at any moment.'

'Take some deep breaths and sit on one of the stools. You don't have to stand the entire time.'

'I'm too fidgety to sit. You go, I'll be okay.'

They left Whitney and returned to the interview room.

'You were quick. I take it that's a good sign. The CPS didn't need to think too long about what I've got for them.' Hunter asked.

'We haven't yet contacted the CPS because there's another matter we wish to discuss with you first,' Seb said in a controlled voice, not wanting to betray how important the following questions were going to be.

'I've already told you that I'm saying nothing else until you've spoken to the CPS, and I've got immunity.' He thumped the table with the flat of his hand.

'Then we've reached an impasse. We won't be contacting the CPS until this other issue has been discussed. Take it or leave it.' Seb locked eyes with Hunter, who squirmed under the scrutiny. 'But if you do decide on the latter, you'll be arrested and taken into custody with the recommendation that bail is refused because of you being a flight risk. And we both know what that means.'

'We had a deal, and now you're trying to back out of it. What sort of game are you playing?' Hunter said, his eyes flashing.

'This most certainly isn't a *game*. We'll uphold our end of the agreement after we've had this further discussion. Do you understand?'

'Just ask your questions and let's get on with it,' Hunter said with a loud sigh.

'The attack on Robert Walker twenty-five years ago.'

The colour drained from Hunter's face and his whole body tensed.

Now they were getting somewhere. Had Whitney been able to see Hunter's reaction from that distance? Was she finally going to find out what had happened to Rob? Why hadn't he taken the time to find someone to be with her?

'I assume from your reaction that you know more about this incident than you told me when you were first questioned?'

Hunter twisted the watch on his wrist, his eyes darting from Seb to Birdie and back again.

'Look, if I tell you what you want to know, it can't go

against me with the CPS. Because if it does, then I'll refuse to cooperate with all the other stuff.'

Hunter was less sure of himself now than he'd been the entire time he'd been interviewed. This put them at an advantage, and Seb was determined to make good use of it.

'The CPS will be presented with all the evidence you have given us. What happens will be up to them but, at this stage, it's pointless for you to backtrack. You've already explained how difficult it might be should Rawlings discover you're implicating him,' Seb said, keeping his voice low.

'Okay. Okay. Ask your fucking questions.' Hunter muttered.

'Did you know that Rawlings' daughter had been forbidden to see Robert Walker but had ignored her father's instructions?'

'Yeah, I knew because Victor had her tailed. He knew everything she did. He's always been very protective of her. Even now he keeps an eye on her.'

'Was Rob Walker assaulted to warn him off Charli?'

'No. Of course that wasn't the reason,' Hunter said, looking horrified. 'What do you take us for? It was because the boy witnessed Victor shoot someone. Walker and his friend Gareth had been sent by Keith Collins to collect a package. But instead of staying with his friend like he should have done, Walker decided to look around, and that's when he saw the shooting. He was spotted by one of Victor's men. We couldn't leave it in case he decided to blab.'

'So, Rawlings was responsible for the assault on Rob Walker, though I'm guessing that he didn't carry it out himself?' Birdie said.

Hunter gave a hollow laugh and glanced over at her.

'What do you think? He'd never get his hands dirty. Victor wanted it done, but it was me who made it happen.'

Seb forced the expression on his face to remain neutral. He glanced over his shoulder to the spot where he knew Whitney was standing, staring at the man who'd ruined her family's life. He desperately wanted to be with her, but before that could happen, they needed the exact details regarding that night.

'Why was Walker beaten up and his friend wasn't?'

'Walker told his friend what he'd seen and that he wanted to go to the police. Gareth then told his brother, who told Victor. I was instructed to deal with it. My plan was to pick him up in the car, drive him to the warehouse in Greymills Industrial Estate and have him beaten up.'

'If he hadn't been found in Anderson Park by a passer-by, he would have died. Was that the intention?' Seb asked.

'It was a warning that went a little far.'

'You think?' Birdie said. 'Why didn't you stop it if you could see what was happening?'

'I was in the car and didn't realise. It all happened very quickly. Look, I regret what happened to the boy. But what could I do once the damage was done? I certainly wasn't going to own up to being a part of it. These things happen.'

'*These things happen!*' Birdie exploded.

Seb rested his hand on her arm to stop her from continuing. As abhorrent as what the man was saying, they still didn't have all the information they needed to make an arrest.

'Who was the person who carried out the attack?' Seb asked.

'There were two of them. Keith Collins and Reg Parks, who died a couple of years ago. The boy ran, and we had to drive after him. Once he'd been beaten, we put him in the boot of the car and then drove to the park and left him there.'

Nausea bubbled in the pit of Seb's stomach. He could usually remain objective when faced with abhorrent crimes, but this was getting to him.

'How did Gareth Collins figure in all this?'

'He was at the warehouse when I brought Walker and was in the car when we drove after him. He didn't take part in the attack, though.'

'But he still knew exactly what had happened. How could you be sure that he wouldn't come forward to the police?'

'Because his brother warned him not to. Blood is thicker than water.'

'Did you visit Walker in hospital after the attack to warn him not to say anything? Did you tell him it was a secret and, if he said anything, his family would be hurt?'

'I sent Keith Collins to do it because Walker knew him. Nothing has been said for twenty-five years, so why is it being investigated now?'

'Rob Walker spoke about having a secret, and we went from there.'

'Someone here must have a lot of clout to get a case reopened after something a *retard* said,' Hunter said, rolling his eyes.

Seb leant over the table and grabbed the man by his shirt. 'Don't you *ever* speak like that again, or you'll regret it for the rest of your life.'

'Seb. Stop!' Birdie shouted, grabbing at his arm.

He released his grip and dropped back down in his chair. What had happened? He'd never lost his cool before.

'Dennis Hunter, I'm arresting you on suspicion of orchestrating the attack on Robert Walker. You do not have to say anything, but it may harm your defence if you do not mention when questioned something which you later rely on in court. Anything you do say may be given in evidence. Do you understand?' Birdie said.

'But what about my immunity?'

'Everything will go to the CPS as we've already explained to you. You'll now be taken into custody and processed.'

'What about bail? I need to get home to my wife.'

'We'll sort something out for her.'

Seb stayed in the interview room while Hunter was escorted to the cells. They'd solved the case, but he'd crossed a line.

The door opened, and Whitney walked in.

'We've done it,' she said, taking the chair from the opposite side of the table and sitting next to him. 'Thank you.'

'I'm sorry,' he said.

'For what?'

'Losing my cool with Hunter. If he says anything, it could jeopardise the whole case against him. I can't believe I acted so rashly.'

'You did what anyone would have under the circumstances. Don't worry about it. So you grabbed hold of him … I've done a lot worse, I can assure you.'

'But I haven't. With my height and build, I can't afford to lose my temper.'

'Seb, look at me.' He did as she requested. Her eyes were bright. 'It's taken twenty-five years, but it's finally over. And before you say anything about me handling it so well, rest assured that when my adrenaline levels drop, I'm going to be a snivelling wreck. Come on, we'd better go to the office. I expect Sergeant Weston will be wanting an update.'

# Chapter 39

Birdie glanced up from her desk when Seb and the DCI walked into the office. She'd left them alone downstairs, knowing they'd need to discuss the case. It was weird because while the DCI had a spring in her step, Seb appeared deflated.

She left her desk and headed over to them. 'Are you okay, Seb? Considering we've just solved your case you're not looking too happy about it.'

'He's annoyed with himself for getting angry at Hunter. I was very impressed with the way you diffused the situation, Birdie. You two make a good team.' The DCI gave a knowing wink in Seb's direction.

What was that all about? Surely, he hadn't told her about his job offer. What if she blabbed to Sarge? Or to anyone else, for that matter. How could he do that to her? Just because Whitney was his friend, to Birdie, she was simply a superior officer.

'Yeah, something like that,' Birdie said, forcing a smile.

Her attention was diverted when the door opened and Twiggy walked into the office. He headed over to her, pulled out a chair from behind one of the desks, and dropped down into it, giving a weary sigh. His face was ashen and there were bags under his eyes. Had it all been too much for him?

'The traffic from Lenchester was awful. I thought I'd never make it back here,' Twiggy said.

'You look knackered. How was it?' Birdie asked, pleased to have him to talk to and not have to worry about what Seb had told the DCI.

'You should've seen those poor young girls, Birdie. Honestly, they were no older than my Alex and Jade by the looks of them. Thank God we found them when we did. It's all being wrapped up. Victor Rawlings should have been arrested by now. He's being taken to Leicester for interrogation by the DI.'

'So the inspector didn't offer you the chance of being part of the interrogation then?' Birdie asked.

'No. Our part in the operation is over. But it's been enough for me, to be honest. Did you hear about that place in Oadby we checked out? The girls were taken there first before being moved. So, that scarf—'

'I know. It's on the way to forensics.'

'How did you get on with Hunter?' He frowned, looked past Birdie, and stood. 'Sorry, guv, I didn't see you there.'

'No problem,' the DCI said.

'He's provided information, which will go to the CPS. He's also admitted to being the one who orchestrated the attack on DCI Walker's brother,' Seb said.

'I'm sorry about that, guv, but glad that you know who did it.'

'Yes. It's taken twenty-five years, but at least now we have some resolution. And—'

'DCI Walker, good to see you. I understand that we've

managed to solve both cases,' Sergeant Weston said, marching up to them, a full smile on his face.

Birdie did a double take. It was rare to see Sarge ingratiate himself. Had Twiggy noticed? She glanced at him and made a subtle nod in the direction of their boss. Twiggy winked to show he'd witnessed it, too.

'Yes, we have, and I'm very grateful for the use of your team to help with this. In particular, DC Branch's assistance was invaluable. Without his input, those young women might not have been discovered. I will be recommending him for a commendation.'

'It was nothing, ma'am— guv,' Twiggy muttered.

'Don't play it down, Twig. You've never had a commendation before. Me neither, come to think about it. It's a big deal, isn't it, Sarge?' Birdie said, thrilled that her partner was being recognised. It would show him that he could still do his job and do it well. At least for now.

'It most certainly is. Well done to the pair of you. Right, Twiggy and Birdie, I expect your reports on my desk shortly. I believe Inspector Curtis has already contacted the CPS, and they are prepared to do a deal for Hunter.'

'As long as that doesn't mean he's going to get away with what he did to the DCI's brother,' Birdie said.

'They are two separate cases, so no, he won't. But for the time being, witness protection has been arranged for his wife and for him if he's granted bail, which I suspect he will be, considering the offence took place so long ago,' Sarge said.

'Keith Collins has also been brought in for questioning and will be charged with grievous bodily harm against my brother,' DCI Walker said.

'What about Gareth?' Birdie asked.

'He'll be questioned again, but considering he only

witnessed the crime and didn't take part then it's not likely he'll be charged,' the DCI said.

'Let's hope Rawlings doesn't use his legal team to get them both off.' Birdie shuddered at the thought.

'Rawlings' assets will most likely be frozen, and he won't have time to worry about Hunter or Collins. Especially as the former will be testifying against him. I'm convinced that justice will be done.'

# Chapter 40

Birdie sauntered across the open fields, enjoying the warmth of the sun on the back of her neck. Elsa was running all over the place, stopping every couple of minutes for a sniff. She loved being in the fields because there was so much for her to investigate.

When Seb had asked Birdie to look after Elsa for the night because he had to go to Lenchester to meet with DCI Walker, she'd jumped at the chance. It was the one place where she could think without there being any distractions. She'd kept Seb hanging on for long enough and had decided that when he came back, she'd give him an answer one way or another. The only problem was, she still hadn't made up her mind. At least, every time she thought she had, niggling doubts crept in and started her off again.

One thing she did know for certain was that she enjoyed working with him. They complemented one another and had a 100 per cent success rate. He was the pragmatic, objective person, and she tended to let her heart run away with her. That was why they made such a good pair. They balanced each other out.

Apart from when he'd gone for Dennis Hunter. Wow. That had come way out of left field. And yet, she'd stepped up and calmed the situation down. They were a perfect combination.

In which case, why was the decision to join him at CIS so difficult?

Was she scared that it might not work out? Yes, they'd worked together, but there had been gaps between cases. Or was it leaving the force, the place where she thought she'd work forever?

And then there was Twiggy to consider. How was she going to support him at work if she wasn't there? But no way would he want to hold her back. If only it was possible to know how much longer he'd be working.

Suddenly, Elsa ran over, wagging her tail.

'What is it, girl?'

She glanced back at the house and noticed Seb's car parked on the drive. 'Ah-ha. Now I know why you're so excited. Come on, let's go and see him.'

Birdie broke out into a jog, and they ran across the field to the house, circling around the back so they could go in through the rear door and into the kitchen and not bring too much dirt inside.

'Hey, Seb. You're back.' She glanced over to the sink where he was filling the kettle.

'I wondered where you were. Coffee?'

'Yes, please. We've been out for a walk, haven't we, girl?' She bent down and gave Elsa a pat.

The dog then wandered over nonchalantly to see Seb, acting like she wasn't at all bothered by him being there.

'Okay. I get it. You much prefer to be with Birdie than me.'

He didn't mean it. Seb and Elsa were inseparable.

'She's letting you know that you shouldn't go away and leave her. Although we do always have a good time together. How was your evening with DCI Walker? Has she offered you any more work?'

'It was good for us to talk through what had happened to her brother and how the family finally had closure. She doesn't have another case but intimated there may be something in the future if I was interested. She did mention how impressed she was with you. So, if you ever want to move to Lenchester, there could well be a position for you.'

'What? She said she was going to offer me a job?'

*Wow.*

'Not in so many words. She was more interested in whether you were going to join my company. I said you hadn't yet decided.' Seb filled the two mugs and handed one to her. 'It's only instant because I couldn't be bothered to wait for the machine to warm up.'

'Fine by me.'

They sat at the table, and he opened a packet of biscuits and offered her one. The only sound to be heard was their crunching, as both seemed absorbed in their own thoughts.

'Suppose I did agree to join your company, how's it going to work exactly?'

Seb glanced across at her, his eyes wide. 'Does that mean you've made a decision? I thought you were still thinking about it.'

'I am. There are some areas that we need to discuss first. Like, deciding which cases to take. You've always said you wanted to be selective. But what if we can't do that? If we have no cases on the books, we'll have to take the more boring cases, like matrimonial issues. Or background checking.'

'I agree. I was being a little idealistic in my aims. However, we can also do police consultancy if we find ourselves scratching around for work.'

'That's good. Because what I don't want is to find myself with no income. Especially as I know you might offer our services for free,' she said with a smirk on her face.

'That won't happen again. It was different with Whitney. And my cousin Sarah, before you bring that up.'

She'd forgotten that the first case they'd worked on together, looking into the suicide of his cousin's husband, he'd also done for no money.

'Good. I also want to ask whether I'm to be a partner or an employee.'

'That would be entirely your decision. If you recall, we've already discussed this and I suggested a payment plan, to buy your way in, which would mean you won't have to break into your savings. We could do a five-year plan if you would be happy to make that commitment.'

She bit down on her bottom lip. Five years. That would mean she'd be in her thirties. She couldn't be in his debt for that long.

'That wouldn't work for me. If I'm coming in, then I want to pay straight away, or we'd always be on an unequal footing. If we make a go of it, then I'll soon be able to save up for a house deposit, even if it does mean living at home a while longer.'

The doorbell rang and Seb groaned. 'Perfect timing.'

'I'll go, you stay here.'

Birdie left the kitchen, glad of the reprieve, and headed for the front door.

Seb looked down at Elsa, who was sitting under the table. 'Well, what do you think? Is she going to say yes? You'd love it if she did because this is where our office is based.' Elsa wagged her tail in agreement. 'And we'd certainly have fun. It won't be boring.' Elsa moved out from under the table, heading towards the hall. 'And yes, you're right. It was rude of me to let Birdie go to the door. I'll go check who's there.'

Seb left the kitchen and headed to the front of the house. As he got closer, he heard voices.

'Are you a member of staff?' a woman asked.

He recognised that condescending tone. But surely not … He carried on walking until the front door was in sight. Standing on the stone steps, staring down at Birdie, was a very tall, elegant, and extremely attractive woman with short dark hair cut into a sleek bob. It was Annabelle, his ex.

'I'm his partner,' Birdie said.

'You and Sebastian are *together* as in …' The woman cleared her throat.

'Yes, that's right. Do come in, and I'll let Seb know you're here. We were in the kitchen having a coffee.'

Seb chuckled to himself and then stepped forward. 'Annabelle. What a surprise.'

Birdie visibly jumped when he spoke, and she looked over her shoulder, guilt written all over her face.

'I came to see you about a matter, and your … *girlfriend* was about to inform you of my arrival.'

'My girlfriend?'

'I didn't say that,' Birdie said, her face turning pink.

'You said you were his partner. What else could that mean?' Annabelle said, glaring at Birdie.

'I think that means that Birdie and I have now officially gone into business together. Am I correct?'

'It sure looks like it,' Birdie said.

He turned his attention back to Annabelle, who was staring at them, a puzzled expression on her face. 'What are you doing here?'

'I have a case for you.'

**Book 4** - Seb returns in ***Hidden From Sight*** when, with the help of Birdie, he investigates the whereabouts of his ex-girlfriend's fiancé, who's disappeared along with some valuable pieces of art.

Tap here to buy

GET ANOTHER BOOK FOR FREE!

To instantly receive **Nowhere to Hide,** a free novella from the Detective Sebastian Clifford series, featuring DC Lucinda Bird when she first joined CID, sign up here for Sally Rigby's free author newsletter.

# Read more about Sebastian Clifford

**WEB OF LIES: A Midlands Crime Thriller (Detective Sebastian Clifford - Book 1)**

**A trail of secrets. A dangerous discovery. A deadly turn.**

Police officer Sebastian Clifford never planned on becoming a private investigator. But when a scandal leads to the disbandment of his London based special squad, he finds himself out of a job. That is, until his cousin calls on him to investigate her husband's high-profile death, and prove that it wasn't a suicide.

Clifford's reluctant to get involved, but the more he digs, the more evidence he finds. With his ability to remember everything he's ever seen, he's the perfect person to untangle the layers of deceit.

He meets Detective Constable Bird, an underutilised detective at Market Harborough's police force, who refuses to give him access to the records he's requested unless he allows her to help with the investigation. Clifford isn't thrilled. The last time he worked as part of a team it ended his career.

But with time running out, Clifford is out of options. Together they must wade through the web of lies in the hope that they'll find the truth before it kills them.

Web of Lies is the first in the new Detective Sebastian Clifford series. Perfect for readers of Joy Ellis, Robert Galbraith and Mark Dawson.

**SPEAK NO EVIL: A Midlands Crime Thriller (Detective Sebastian Clifford - Book 2)**

**What happens when someone's too scared to speak?**

Ex-police officer Sebastian Clifford had decided to limit his work as a private investigator, until Detective Constable Bird, aka Birdie, asks for his help.

Twelve months ago a young girl was abandoned on the streets of Market Harborough in shocking circumstances. Since then the child has barely spoken and with the police unable to trace her identity, they've given up.

The social services team in charge of the case worry that the child has an intellectual disability but Birdie and her aunt, who's fostering the little girl, disagree and believe she's gifted and intelligent, but something bad happened and she's living in constant fear.

Clifford trusts Birdie's instinct and together they work to find out who the girl is, so she can be freed from the past. But as secrets are uncovered, the pair realise it's not just the child who's in danger.

Speak No Evil is the second in the Detective Sebastian Clifford series. Perfect for readers of Faith Martin, Matt Brolly and Joy Ellis.

**NEVER TOO LATE: A Midlands Crime Thriller (Detective Sebastian Clifford - Book 3)**

**A vicious attack. A dirty secret. And a chance for justice**

Ex-police officer Sebastian Clifford is quickly finding that life as a private investigator is never quiet. His doors have only been open a few weeks when DCI Whitney Walker approaches him to investigate the brutal attack that left her older brother, Rob, with irreversible brain damage.

For nearly twenty-five years Rob had no memory of that night, but lately things are coming back to him, and Whitney's worried that her brother might, once again, be in danger.

Clifford knows only too well what it's like be haunted by the past, and so he agrees to help. But the deeper he digs, the more secrets he uncovers, and soon he discovers that Rob's not the only one in danger.

***Never Too Late*** is the third in the Detective Sebastian Clifford series, perfect for readers who love gripping crime fiction.

**HIDDEN FROM SIGHT: A Midlands Crime Thriller (Detective Sebastian Clifford - Book 4)**

**A million pound heist. A man on the run. And a gang hellbent on seeking revenge.**

When private investigator Detective Sebastian Clifford is asked by his former society girlfriend to locate her fiancé, who's disappeared along with some valuable pieces of art, he's reluctant to help. He'd left the aristocratic world behind, for good reason. But when his ex starts receiving threatening letters Clifford is left with no choice.

With the help of his partner Lucinda Bird, aka Birdie, they start digging and find themselves drawn into London's underworld. But it's hard to see the truth between the shadows and lies. Until a clue leads them in the direction of Clifford's nemesis and he realises they're all in more danger than he thought. The race is on to find the missing man and the art before lives are lost.

A perfect mix of mystery, intrigue and danger that will delight fans of detective stories. '***Hidden from Sight***' is the fourth in the bestselling, fast-paced, Midland Crime Thriller series, featuring Clifford and Birdie, and the most gripping yet. Grab your copy, and see if you can solve the crime.

# Also by Sally Rigby

**THE CAVENDISH & WALKER SERIES**

**DEADLY GAMES - Cavendish & Walker Book 1**

**A killer is playing cat and mouse……. and winning.**

DCI Whitney Walker wants to save her career. Forensic psychologist, Dr Georgina Cavendish, wants to avenge the death of her student.

Sparks fly when real world policing meets academic theory, and it's not a pretty sight.

When two more bodies are discovered, Walker and Cavendish form an uneasy alliance. But are they in time to save the next victim?

*Deadly Games* is the first book in the Cavendish and Walker crime fiction series. If you like serial killer thrillers and psychological intrigue, then you'll love Sally Rigby's page-turning book.

Pick up *Deadly Games* today to read Cavendish & Walker's first case.

**FATAL JUSTICE - Cavendish & Walker Book 2**

**A vigilante's on the loose, dishing out their kind of justice…**

A string of mutilated bodies sees Detective Chief Inspector

Whitney Walker back in action. But when she discovers the victims have all been grooming young girls, she fears a vigilante is on the loose. And while she understands the motive, no one is above the law.

Once again, she turns to forensic psychologist, Dr Georgina Cavendish, to unravel the cryptic clues. But will they be able to save the next victim from a gruesome death?

*Fatal Justice* is the second book in the Cavendish & Walker crime fiction series. If you like your mysteries dark, and with a twist, pick up a copy of Sally Rigby's book today.

**DEATH TRACK - Cavendish & Walker Book 3**

**Catch the train if you dare...**

After a teenage boy is found dead on a Lenchester train, Detective Chief Inspector Whitney Walker believes they're being targeted by the notorious Carriage Killer, who chooses a local rail network, commits four murders, and moves on.

Against her wishes, Walker's boss brings in officers from another force to help the investigation and prevent more deaths, but she's forced to defend her team against this outside interference.

Forensic psychologist, Dr Georgina Cavendish, is by her side in an attempt to bring to an end this killing spree. But how can they get into the mind of a killer who has already killed twelve times in two years without leaving a single clue behind?

For fans of Rachel Abbott, L J Ross and Angela Marsons, *Death*

*Track* is the third in the Cavendish & Walker series. A gripping serial killer thriller that will have you hooked.

~

## LETHAL SECRET - Cavendish & Walker Book 4

### Someone has a secret. A secret worth killing for....

When a series of suicides, linked to the Wellness Spirit Centre, turn out to be murder, it brings together DCI Whitney Walker and forensic psychologist Dr Georgina Cavendish for another investigation. But as they delve deeper, they come across a tangle of secrets and the very real risk that the killer will strike again.

As the clock ticks down, the only way forward is to infiltrate the centre. But the outcome is disastrous, in more ways than one.

For fans of Angela Marsons, Rachel Abbott and M A Comley, *Lethal Secret* is the fourth book in the Cavendish & Walker crime fiction series.

~

## LAST BREATH - Cavendish & Walker Book 5

### Has the Lenchester Strangler returned?

When a murderer leaves a familiar pink scarf as his calling card, Detective Chief Inspector Whitney Walker is forced to dig into a cold case, not sure if she's looking for a killer or a copycat.

With a growing pile of bodies, and no clues, she turns to forensic psychologist, Dr Georgina Cavendish, despite their relationship being at an all-time low.

Can they overcome the bad blood between them to solve the unsolvable?

For fans of Rachel Abbott, Angela Marsons and M A Comley, *Last Breath* is the fifth book in the Cavendish & Walker crime fiction series.

**FINAL VERDICT - Cavendish & Walker Book 6**

**The judge has spoken……everyone must die.**

When a killer starts murdering lawyers in a prestigious law firm, and every lead takes them to a dead end, DCI Whitney Walker finds herself grappling for a motive.

What links these deaths, and why use a lethal injection?

Alongside forensic psychologist, Dr Georgina Cavendish, they close in on the killer, while all the time trying to not let their personal lives get in the way of the investigation.

For fans of Rachel Abbott, Mark Dawson and M A Comley, Final Verdict is the sixth in the Cavendish & Walker series. A fast paced murder mystery which will keep you guessing.

**RITUAL DEMISE - Cavendish & Walker Book 7**

**Someone is watching…. No one is safe**

The once tranquil woods in a picturesque part of Lenchester have become the bloody stage to a series of ritualistic murders. With no suspects, Detective Chief Inspector Whitney Walker is once again forced to call on the services of forensic psychologist Dr Georgina Cavendish.

But this murderer isn't like any they've faced before. The murders are highly elaborate, but different in their own way and, with the clock ticking, they need to get inside the killer's head before it's too late.

For fans of Angela Marsons, Rachel Abbott and L J Ross. Ritual Demise is the seventh book in the Cavendish & Walker crime fiction series.

**MORTAL REMAINS - Cavendish & Walker Book 8**

**Someone's playing with fire…. There's no escape.**

A serial arsonist is on the loose and as the death toll continues to mount DCI Whitney Walker calls on forensic psychologist Dr Georgina Cavendish for help.

But Lenchester isn't the only thing burning. There are monumental changes taking place within the police force and there's a chance Whitney might lose the job she loves. She has to find the killer before that happens. Before any more lives are lost.

Mortal Remains is the eighth book in the acclaimed Cavendish & Walker series. Perfect for fans of Angela Marsons, Rachel Abbott and L J Ross.

**SILENT GRAVES - Cavendish & Walker Book 9**

**Nothing remains buried forever…**

When the bodies of two teenage girls are discovered on a building site, DCI Whitney Walker knows she's on the hunt for a killer. The problem is the murders happened in 1980 and this is her first case with the new team. What makes it even tougher is that with budgetary restrictions in place, she only has two weeks to solve it.

Once again, she enlists the help of forensic psychologist Dr Georgina Cavendish, but as she digs deeper into the past, she uncovers hidden truths that reverberate through the decades and into the present.

Silent Graves is the ninth book in the acclaimed Cavendish & Walker series. Perfect for fans of L J Ross, J M Dalgleish and Rachel Abbott.

**KILL SHOT - Cavendish & Walker Book 10**

**The game is over…..there's nowhere to hide.**

When Lenchester's most famous sportsman is shot dead, DCI Whitney Walker and her team are thrown into the world of snooker.

She calls on forensic psychologist Dr Georgina Cavendish to assist, but the investigation takes them in a direction which has far-reaching, international ramifications.

Much to Whitney's annoyance, an officer from one of the Met's special squads is sent to assist.

But as everyone knows…three's a crowd.

Kill Shot is the tenth book in the acclaimed Cavendish & Walker series. Perfect for fans of Simon McCleave, J M Dalgleish, J R Ellis and Faith Martin.

## DARK SECRETS - Cavendish & Walker Book 11

### An uninvited guest…a deadly secret….and a terrible crime.

When a well-loved family of five are found dead sitting around their dining table with an untouched meal in front of them, it sends shockwaves throughout the community.

Was it a murder suicide, or was someone else involved?

It's one of DCI Whitney Walker's most baffling cases, and even with the help of forensic psychologist Dr Georgina Cavendish, they struggle to find any clues or motives to help them catch the killer.

But with a community in mourning and growing pressure to get answers, Cavendish and Walker are forced to go deeper into a murderer's mind than they've ever gone before.

Dark Secrets is the eleventh book in the Cavendish & Walker series. Perfect for fans of Angela Marsons, Joy Ellis and Rachel McLean.

## BROKEN SCREAMS - Cavendish & Walker Book 12

### Scream all you want, no one can hear you….

When an attempted murder is linked to a string of unsolved sexual attacks, Detective Chief Inspector Whitney Walker is incensed. All those women who still have sleepless nights because the man who terrorises their dreams is still on the loose.

Calling on forensic psychologist Dr Georgina Cavendish to help, they follow the clues and are alarmed to discover the victims all had one thing in common. Their birthdays were on the 29th February. The same date as a female officer on Whitney's team.

As the clock ticks down and they're no nearer to finding the truth, can they stop the villain before he makes sure his next victim will never scream again.

Broken Screams is the twelfth book in the acclaimed Cavendish & Walker series and is perfect for fans of Angela Marsons, Helen H Durrant and Rachel McClean.

# Writing as Amanda Rigby

Sally also writes psychological thrillers as **Amanda Rigby**, in collaboration with another author.

**REMEMBER ME?: A brand new addictive psychological thriller that you won't be able to put down in 2021**

**A perfect life…**

Paul Henderson leads a normal life. A deputy headteacher at a good school, a loving relationship with girlfriend Jenna, and a baby on the way. Everything *seems* perfect.

**A shocking message…**

Until Paul receives a message from his ex-fiance Nicole. Beautiful, ambitious and fierce, Nicole is everything Jenna is not. And now it seems Nicole is back, and she has a score to settle with Paul…

**A deadly secret.**

But Paul can't understand how Nicole is back. Because he's pretty sure he killed her with his own bare hands….

Which means, someone else knows the truth about what happened that night. And they'll stop at nothing to make Paul pay…

**A brand new psychological thriller that will keep you guessing till the end! Perfect for fans of Sue Watson, Nina Manning, Shalini Boland**

≈

**I WILL FIND YOU: An addictive psychological crime thriller to keep you gripped in 2022**

**Three sisters…One terrible secret**

**Ashleigh:** A creative, free spirit and loyal. But Ash is tormented by her demons and a past that refuses to be laid to rest.

**Jessica:** Perfect wife and loving mother. But although Jessica might seem to have it all, she lives a secret life built on lies.

**Grace:** An outsider, always looking in, Grace has never known the love of her sisters and her resentment can make her do bad things.

When Ashleigh goes missing, Jessica and Grace do all they can to find their eldest sister. But the longer Ashleigh is missing, the more secrets and lies these women are hiding threaten to tear this family apart.

Can they find Ashleigh before it's too late or is it sometimes safer to stay hidden?

## Acknowledgments

Bringing together two of my series in this one book wasn't an easy task and I couldn't have done it without the insightfulness, brilliance, and support of my editor, the fabulous Rebecca Millar.

Thanks also goes to Kate Noble and my Advanced Reader Team, who between them have hopefully caught all of my many errors.

Thanks to Stuart Bache for yet another brilliant cover.

Congratulations to Len Mattas for winning one of my contests and having a character named after him.

Finally, thanks to all my family for your continued support.

# About the Author

Sally Rigby was born in Northampton, UK. After leaving university she worked in magazines and radio, before finally embarking on a career lecturing in both further and higher education.

Sally has always had the travel bug and after living in Manchester and London moved overseas. From 2001 she has lived with her family in New Zealand (apart from five years in Australia), which she considers to be the most beautiful place in the world.

Sally is the author of the acclaimed Cavendish and Walker series, and the more recent Detective Sebastian Clifford series. In collaboration with another author, she also writes psychological thrillers for Boldwood Books under the pen-name Amanda Rigby.

Sally has always loved crime fiction books, films and TV programmes. She has a particular fascination with the psychology of serial killers.

Sally loves to hear from her readers, so do feel free to get in touch via her website www.sallyrigby.com